WRONG TURN

ROAD TRIPPING SERIES

SAMANTHA CHASE

WRONG *Turn*

Editor: Jillian Rivera

Cover Design: Uplifting Designs/Alyssa Garcia

PRAISE FOR SAMANTHA CHASE

"If you can't get enough of stories that get inside your heart and soul and stay there long after you've read the last page, then Samantha Chase is for you!"

-*NY Times & USA Today Bestselling Author* ***Melanie Shawn***

"A fun, flirty, sweet romance filled with romance and character growth and a perfect happily ever after."

-*NY Times & USA Today Bestselling Author* ***Carly Phillips***

"Samantha Chase writes my kind of happily ever after!"

-*NY Times & USA Today Bestselling Author* ***Erin Nicholas***

"The openness between the lovers is refreshing, and their interactions are a balanced blend of sweet and spice. The planets may not have aligned, but the elements of this winning romance are definitely in sync."

- ***Publishers Weekly, STARRED review***

"A true romantic delight, *A Sky Full of Stars* is one of the top gems of romance this year."

- ***Night Owl Reviews, TOP PICK***

"Great writing, a winsome ensemble, and the perfect blend of heart and sass."

- ***Publishers Weekly***

"Recommend Chase to fans of Susan Elizabeth Phillips. Well-written and uniquely appealing."

- ***Booklist***

1

"So...WHAT's new in the history world?"

Chelsea Cooper fought the urge to roll her eyes.

Hard.

Taking a sip of her wine, she glanced over at the person responsible for quite possibly the dumbest question ever.

Drew Russo.

Sadly, *his* best friend and *her* best friend were dating. This meant that Chelsea and Drew were forced to hang out together–a lot.

As in...far more frequently than Chelsea would like.

She had meant to turn to the right after she got her wine and head toward the dartboards, but instead, she'd gone the wrong way and ended up here.

With Drew.

He gave her an easy smile before taking a sip of his beer.

"There's nothing *new* in history," she replied primly. "History is history. As in it's in the past."

Nodding, Drew moved in closer. "Depends on how you look at it, doesn't it?"

Is he insane or just plain clueless?

"Actually, no. That's not the case at all. History is the study of *past* events, Drew. And last I checked, there haven't been any new findings in...the history world."

Now she fought the urge to shudder.

Leaning even closer–like seriously infringing on her personal space–he said, "Well, the past could be anything that happened before right this minute. Me walking over and asking you that question is technically in the past, right?"

For a moment, all Chelsea could do was sputter and try to come up with a witty comeback.

Or at least an intelligent one.

Instead, all she could say was, "Why are you like this?"

"Like what?" His grin never faltered.

Glancing around, she prayed someone would catch her eye and come save her from another pointless conversation. They ended up in this position most weekends. It was almost as if Drew sought her out with the sole purpose of aggravating her.

And every weekend, he succeeded.

"Isn't there someone else you'd rather talk to? One of the guys, maybe?"

Bumping her shoulder gently, he replied, "I can talk to them anytime. But you? You and I only get to catch up on Fridays. Besides, I was just curious about what you do. You're always talking about these books you narrate, so I just thought I'd ask. Excuse me for trying to be sociable."

"No one said you weren't sociable..."

"Except you."

The groan was out before she could stop it. "I never said that."

"But you implied it."

This conversation was going nowhere.

Fast.

"Okay, let's start over, okay?"

He nodded.

"I just got a call to narrate a book on the Civil War and..."

"Didn't you narrate that one already?"

"There's more than one book on the Civil War."

Shrugging, he said, "Go on."

"Anyway, the original narrator came down with the flu and they're on a tight schedule, so they asked me to come in and do it. So I'll go into the studio on Monday and I only have three days to get it done. That's with all the edits and everything."

"You do the editing too? Wow!"

"No," she said patiently. "I don't do the edits. There's a very talented group of people who handle that. I'm simply the one reading the book."

"And it takes three days? Seriously? Are you only reading like an hour a day or something?"

As much as she wanted to be annoyed with him, she couldn't. Most people had no idea what went into audiobook narration.

She wasn't irritated by the questions about her job–just by Drew.

Forcing a smile, Chelsea explained the process to him just like she'd explained to dozens of people over the years. "Basically, on average, it is a 2:1 ratio. So if it's a ten-hour book, it takes around twenty hours to narrate it. Remember, that includes errors, swallows, background sounds, stopping, starting, etc., so it is for sure a marathon to perform."

Thankfully, he didn't interrupt and seemed to be genuinely interested in what she was saying. Once she was done, she figured he'd move on and talk to someone else.

But he didn't.

"You must really enjoy history then."

"Why?"

"Because it seems like that's all you narrate," he replied. "I'll admit, I enjoyed studying history in school. I always aced those classes because it fascinated me to learn about how far we've come and yet how much we're still the same as some of our ancestors." He took another pull of his beer. "You ever narrate anything on the Egyptians and the pyramids?"

She had to think about that for a minute. "You know, I don't think..."

"Do you think they really built the pyramids themselves or that aliens did it?"

"What?"

"Think about it–how could they move those massive blocks without modern tools? Or toolbelts?" He shook his head. "To do all that work in a loincloth? No thank you."

"I don't think..."

"You'd look really good in the dresses the women wore back then–togas, right?"

Yeah, he's clueless.

A snarky response was on the tip of her tongue when someone came up beside her.

"There you are!" Her best friend Bianca wrapped one arm around her and hugged Chelsea tight before smiling at Drew. "Don't you two look cozy over here! What are we talking about?"

"How I would look good in the *togas* the Egyptians wore," Chelsea said, praying Bianca would get how that was a completely ridiculous statement.

Bianca studied her. "Hmm...you probably would. They're very forgiving and would hide your hips."

"Wait...what?!" Chelsea cried.

"Yeah, a toga would totally be your friend. I like to think I'd be like royalty and have a designer toga that would be more of a mermaid fit," Bianca went on. "Then I'd accessorize with a lot of jewels." She took a sip of her wine before adding, "I'd be totally hot as an Egyptian."

"I'd probably be one of those gladiators," Drew chimed in, smug smile and everything.

"Those were Roman soldiers," Chelsea murmured.

"You ever narrate a book about gladiators?" he asked.

With no other choice, she did the only thing she could.

Chugged the remainder of her wine before announcing she saw someone she absolutely needed to talk to before quickly making her escape.

Drew watched Chelsea walk away and felt mildly relieved.

He was running out of things to talk about.

Although, he would have loved to hear her theory on the whole Egyptians and alien thing.

"You're good," Bianca said with a less than sincere smile.

"Excuse me?"

"Jimmy said you were the go-to guy to keep Chelsea distracted and I didn't really give it much thought. But for the last several weeks, I always see the two of you together so...bravo." She mock-clapped and Drew had to force himself to smile.

"I thought she was your best friend."

"Oh, she is!" she gushed. "But...she really has no idea how to just relax and...you know...not bore everyone to tears with her work stories. Ugh...if I wanted to talk about history,

I would..." She paused. "What am I saying? Why would I want to talk about history? It's over, right?"

He was about to bring up his theory about how history could be from just minutes ago but immediately decided against it.

That would mean talking to Bianca more than he wanted to.

She was nice enough, but...not much going on upstairs. How Jimmy could be so head over heels in love with this woman, he had no idea. All he did know was it was time to move on and find someone else to talk to.

So he pulled a Chelsea...yeah, he knew her signature move to get rid of him...and chugged the rest of his beer and excused himself.

Clearly Bianca didn't get the similarities because she just smiled and walked away.

Thank God.

Slowly, Drew made his way over to the bar and ordered another beer–in no rush to turn and join the group of friends he was here with or to find anyone new to talk with.

Elbows on the bar, he hung his head and let out a long breath. He was in a serious rut. It was like being stuck in the movie *Groundhog Day* with Bill Murray–doing the same thing every day and every weekend and it was getting beyond monotonous. They went to the same places, drank the same drinks, had the same conversations, and went home.

Only to repeat it all again.

His beer appeared in front of him and Drew thanked the bartender. Reaching into his pocket, he pulled out some cash and threw it on the bar before turning around. So many familiar faces and he didn't have the least bit of interest in what any of them had to say.

Liar.

Yeah, okay, Chelsea was definitely interesting to talk to.

Mainly because she argued everything with him.

Every. Single. Thing.

If he said black, she said white. If he said he enjoyed something, she pointed out why it was pointless. Most of the time it was thoroughly entertaining, but tonight he could tell she was just irritated with him. Most weekends he could have dragged out that kind of conversation for at least an hour. Maybe she was as bored as he was with these gatherings and felt like he did about their little social group.

How ironic would that be? The two people with the least in common, feeling the same way?

With a mirthless laugh, Drew lifted his beer to his lips and took a long pull of it.

"There's the man!" His best friend Jimmy walked over and clapped him on the shoulder. "You must be losing your touch. You and Chelsea barely lasted fifteen minutes tonight." Then he laughed. "Are you quick in the sack too?" More laughter and another back clap.

"Conversation and sex aren't the same, dumbass."

"That's exactly what a guy who's a little too quick in bed would say."

Ugh...someday he'll grow up, right?

"Anyway," Drew said, his teeth practically grinding. "Any chance of us doing something remotely fun tonight?"

"What's the matter, quickdraw? Not enjoying yourself?"

Drew mentally counted to ten while he took another drink. Lowering the bottle, he glared at Jimmy. "Seriously, this bar is just...we're always here! Why can't we find someplace else to go? We used to do some fun shit before you started dating Bianca."

"Hey!" Jimmy snapped. "You got a problem with my girl?"

"Did I say I did?" he replied wearily. "I'm just saying there are other places to go on a Friday night besides here. Remember when we used to go to the batting range? Indoor skydiving? To concerts? Any of this ringing any bells?"

Beside him, Jimmy leaned against the bar. "Yeah, yeah, yeah...we did all that and it was great. Now we're doing something new."

"New? Dude, we've been doing this for months now. Months! That's hardly new."

"Oh, so you got any better ideas?"

"Yeah, dozens of them!"

Jimmy huffed but didn't comment.

"There are other bars, and we could do one of those crawls where we hit a bunch of them downtown, or maybe try the new cigar bar that opened up last month."

"Bianca's not going to smoke cigars."

"Maybe for one Friday night you don't go out with her."

"I knew you had a problem with her!"

Groaning, Drew twisted and placed his beer on the bar before facing his friend. "Look, I get you're all in love and all that crap, but you're not joined at the hip. Once in a while, it's okay to go out without each other." He paused. "For all you know, she might enjoy a girls' night out!"

"She does!" Jimmy argued. "Once a month the girls go out–just them."

"Seriously? Then why aren't we going out–just the guys?"

Shrugging, Jimmy looked away.

It didn't take a genius to know what that meant.

Bianca didn't want him going out with the guys.

Snorting with disgust, he muttered, "You are pathetic and completely whipped."

"Jealous?"

If he had been drinking, he would have choked on it. "Jealous? Of what? Letting some woman lead me around by the balls and tell me when I can and can't go out? Um...no. Trust me." Placing a hand over his crotch, he grinned. "These are all mine and I go where I want."

"Do you? Because I know where you are almost all the damn time, buddy. And it's pretty much wherever I am." Then he laughed. "Looks like I'm the one leading you around by the balls."

Drew snorted again. "Dude, that doesn't make either of us look or sound good." When he went to reach for his beer, he reconsidered and pushed away from the bar. "I'm outta here."

"Why?"

"I'm just not feeling it tonight. If I'm going to be this bored, I'd rather be in my own damn house."

"Drew, come on. We're just joking around!"

But he wasn't listening. "I'll talk to you later." And with a short wave, he turned and made his way to the door and out onto the sidewalk.

Knowing damn well he'd be back here again next week.

2

"I'm getting married!"

"What?!" Chelsea knew the instant the exclamation was out of her mouth that it was the wrong response. It was more accusatory than celebratory.

And her facial reaction was probably even worse.

Doing her best to smile, she looked at her best friend before launching into a very girly squeal. "I mean, oh my God! That's fantastic!" After an overly-enthusiastic hug, she sat back down and studied Bianca. "So when's the big day?"

Flipping her blonde hair over her shoulder, Bianca smiled serenely. "We haven't set the date, but I'm thinking I don't want a whole big circus of a wedding. I'd love to elope. Someplace special and romantic and with real meaning, you know?"

In Bianca's world, that could be anything from the Eiffel Tower to the concession stand at Jones Beach where she and Jimmy met.

Jimmy...ugh...

Chelsea did her best not to make a face–or gag–at the

mere thought of that guy. For the life of her, she had no idea what Bianca saw in him. He was loud, obnoxious, and almost cartoonish–like one of those guys you'd see on a reality show based out of Jersey.

Shudder on the inside, keep smiling on the outside.

"So how did he pop the question? Was it romantic? Did he get down on one knee?"

Rather than answer right away, Bianca pouted. "Didn't you see it on Instagram? Facebook? Snapchat? It was even on my blog! I posted a ton of pictures! And you haven't even asked to see my ring!" She waved her left hand around dramatically.

"Oh, uh…I haven't been online a lot the last few days. Things have been crazy at work and…"

"Too crazy to look at your phone? That's lame, Chels. Even for you."

Say what now?

"Lame? What do you…?"

"Please, you read books for a living. Boring books. How can things get crazy?"

"First of all, I don't *read* books, I narrate them. And secondly, I also work at the physical therapy clinic."

"Yawn," Bianca said, completely unimpressed.

"What's that supposed to mean?" she demanded.

With a dramatic sigh, Bianca stretched out her arm and studied her ring. "It means you spend too much time working–reading about other people's lives or helping them walk or something–and not enough time…you know…living!" She groaned. "Even when we're hanging out, you're not really focused. We all talk about it."

They were sitting in the back corner of a Starbucks, and as much as Chelsea was never one to make a scene, she seriously considered making one now. "What do you mean we *all* talk about it?"

With a careless shrug, Bianca straightened and took a sip of her latte. "You know, me, Kendall, Shauna, Robbie, Alex, Jimmy, and Drew." She shrugged. "And we all think you need to relax a bit. You're way too uptight and you can really be a bit of a downer. And seriously, all the talk about books is incredibly boring."

Her eyes wide, Chelsea had to seriously consider her options here. It was one thing to sort of bitch amongst the girls about one another–something they all did from time to time–but it was quite another when the guys got dragged into it.

Especially *those* guys.

Jimmy alone was hard to handle, but once you threw in his friends, it became unbearable.

Honestly, that was one of the reasons she knew she acted differently when they all hung out. Those guys just completely annoyed her to no end, and she knew most of the time she ended up looking and sounding like some sort of prude because she didn't think everything they did or said was hysterical.

Come to think of it, nothing they ever did or said was all that funny. Usually it was just offensive and immature.

"Alex said we should just give you a break because he knows how obnoxious the guys can be," Bianca explained.

"Oh, well...that was nice of him." *Maybe I misjudged them...*

"But Drew thinks you're just uptight and need to..." She paused and blushed. "Well, never mind. In that one instance, he was a little crude."

Chelsea saw red. "No, please...tell me what...*Drew*," she said through clenched teeth, "had to say."

Drew Russo.

Quite possibly the worst human being ever.

It was fairly safe to say her feelings for Drew were marginally worse than the ones she felt toward Jimmy. Why? Because for whatever reason, whenever they all hung out, Drew seemed to make it a habit to glue himself to her side.

He was attractive in that stereotypical Italian way–dark hair, dark eyes, charming, and always smelled good.

But once he opened his mouth, he ruined it.

At first she thought he was possibly attracted to her, but after a year of hanging out, he hadn't even attempted to make a move on her, so that wasn't it. Kendall and Bianca had teased her at first, thinking the same thing, but Chelsea assured them there was nothing there.

"Oh, come on," Kendall had challenged. "You know how sometimes guys aren't good about expressing their feelings. Maybe you're missing the signs."

"Uh, no," she'd replied blandly. "And besides *not* hitting on me, he's really kind of a jerk to me most of the time."

"That's what guys do!" Bianca had cried. "Guys are always a little mean and jerky to girls they like!"

"Yeah, in kindergarten," Chelsea argued. "Grown men–mature men–don't do that."

It had taken months for her friends to move on from that topic.

"So?" she prompted. "Go ahead. Tell me what he said."

Now Bianca looked a little uncomfortable. "He might have mentioned something about...needing a good...you know...just a night of hard..." She stopped and cleared her throat. "There are a ton of studies on the importance of a good orgasm, Chels. Have you read any of them?" Then she had the nerve to giggle. "Maybe that's the kind of book you should be narrating!"

Oh, dear Lord...

"My sex life..." *Or lack thereof* "...isn't anyone's business! Why would you even *tell* me this?" she cried. "How could you possibly think this was information I needed?"

"You asked!

Rolling her eyes, Chelsea mentally counted to ten before she spoke. "Let's just...move on. Okay?"

Bianca nodded solemnly.

"Now, show me the ring and tell me all about your plans." And plastering a smile on her face, she sat back and listened to her best friend wax poetic over all the things she wanted her engagement and wedding to be.

Most of it wasn't a surprise–they'd known each other since the third grade and, therefore, had already shared all their romantic hopes and dreams. So far, Bianca was light years ahead of achieving hers while Chelsea was...well...not.

Not for lack of trying, though.

Okay, maybe she wasn't trying all *that* hard. But her career was finally in a good place, and once she felt comfortable with it, she knew she could focus on finding a nice guy to date and go out with and...yeah...get a few good orgasms from.

Maybe.

Hopefully.

But damn would it be nice.

Stupid Drew. Now that was all she was going to be thinking about.

"So anyway," Bianca was saying, completely unaware that Chelsea zoned out. "I think it's the perfect place for a wedding. I'm going to run it by Jimmy and...if he'll go for it...I'd love to elope sooner rather than later! Wouldn't that be amazing? I mean, could there *be* a more perfect place for me to get married?"

Uh-oh...wrong time not to pay attention.

Rather than admit it, Chelsea smiled broadly and let out another girly squeal. "It is! It truly is! And it's going to be beautiful!" She let out a dreamy sigh. "All of your dreams are coming true!"

That seemed to appease Bianca because she leaned over and gave her an exceptionally long hug.

One Mississippi...two Mississippi...

When Bianca finally let her go, Chelsea reached for her chai tea and raised it. "I know it's not champagne, but...a toast. To you and Jimmy!"

She seriously almost gagged on the words.

"And your happily ever after!"

"Yay!" Bianca cried happily. "To me!"

Resisting the urge to roll her eyes, she asked, "So what's going on this weekend? Anything?"

"Again, if you had checked your phone, you would have seen the group text." Ironically, Bianca didn't resist rolling her eyes. "Jimmy and I are hosting a cocktail party at our place Friday night. We're having it catered and it's going to be amazing!"

"Wait...at your place? What about our standing Friday night at O'Dwyer's? We've been going there for years!"

Another eye roll. "Chels, this is big, okay? We want to celebrate right. And an Irish pub isn't exactly the place I want to toast my engagement with all our friends."

It was hard to argue that logic. Still, they seriously had been going to O'Dwyer's every Friday night since they were old enough to drink. It was tradition. And once Bianca had started dating Jimmy, he brought his friends along to join the party.

Much to Chelsea's chagrin. But whatever.

"Be there at eight and promise you'll refrain from talking about whatever book it is you're narrating this week, okay?"

It was on the tip of her tongue to make a snarky comment, but again, she refrained. "Not a problem. I know how much you despise hearing about history books. However, I'm auditioning to do some contemporary romances. Maybe..."

"No books, Chels. I'm serious. Can't you just hang out and be like...you know...fun?"

Sometimes it was hard to remember why she was friends with Bianca.

This was one of those times.

"Okey-dokey then. Should I bring some wine?"

Bianca waved her off. "That's all being taken care of by the caterer. Just bring yourself," she said with a smile. "And a gift! We're treating this as a mini engagement party. Fun, right?"

The only acceptable answer here was...

"Absolutely! Can't wait!"

She was just about to take a sip of her rapidly-cooling tea when Bianca reached across the table and placed her hand on top of Chelsea's.

"How long have you and I known each other?"

"Um...since forever?"

"Exactly. And I can tell when you don't approve of something."

"What? I never said I didn't approve, Bee."

"You didn't have to. Your face did it for you."

Oops...

Sighing, Chelsea slowly pulled her hand away and carefully sat back in her chair. "What is it you want me to say here?"

Bianca mimicked her pose. "I guess...just spit out what's on your mind so we can move on."

"I guess I still don't see," she began and then stopped. "Maybe you're being..."

Nope, that wasn't going to fly either, dammit.

"Chels, come on!"

"Okay. Fine. I think you can do way better than Jimmy, and I think you're being impulsive by getting engaged so soon. There!"

Leaning forward, she could see Bianca was set with her rebuttal. "First of all, we've been dating for over a year. That's not impulsive. And have you ever heard of opposites attracting? Jimmy is sweet and funny and he totally dotes on me. I get how he can be a little loud and juvenile at times, but when it's just the two of us, he's amazing! Maybe if you just got to know him..."

"If his entourage wasn't with him all the damn time, maybe I could," she countered and realized this wasn't going to get them anywhere. "Look, I'm sorry. You're right. I don't know him and it doesn't matter how I feel. As long as he's good to you then...I'm happy for you. Really." Now it was her turn to reach for Bianca's hand. "Don't hate me, okay? I just worry about you."

"I know, and I love you for it. I just wish you would relax more. Maybe if you found yourself a nice guy..."

"I've dated three nice guys this year alone and they ended up boring me to death. None of them were Mr. Right."

It was true. Sad, but true. Any of the three–David, Jeremy, or Matt–should have been right for her. Their dating profiles had said they were, but once she went out with each guy a few times, Chelsea realized there was no spark...no zing...no excitement. That wasn't too much to ask for, was it?

"Well, I think you need to spend less time worrying about me and more time focusing on finding your Mr. Right. Or at least Mr. Right Now to help you relax!"

As far as cocktail parties went, this one wasn't the worst.

It would be much better if there were more people invited.

Seriously, why did Jimmy let Bianca make everything "intimate"? That's what she called all their get-togethers and it was annoying as hell.

He snorted with disgust. Intimate? More like small and boring. If the chick didn't have friends, why did he have to suffer? Drew knew for a fact that Jimmy had a ton of friends and most of them never made it to any of their *intimate* Friday night gatherings.

I wish I hadn't made the cut...

Looking around the room, he saw the same seven faces he'd been seeing every damn weekend for almost a year–give or take a face or two. Every once in a while, someone would have a date or skip a week, but for the most part, it was always the eight of them and he was hitting his limit on how much more he could take.

With any luck, Jimmy and Bianca would get married sooner rather than later and only want to hang out with other married couples.

Hey, a guy could hope, right?

"Drew!" Bianca called out. "Come settle an argument for us!"

It was hard to stifle the groan as he walked across the room. "What's up?"

"Jimmy said no one–well, none of the guys–would want to go to some resort for the weekend and get spa treatments. I told him he's wrong, and Alex and Robbie are refusing to answer," she explained with a small pout. "You'd go though, right?"

Drew looked over at his friends and cocked a brow like, "Is this woman for real?"

"Um..."

"It's not like it used to be," she quickly reasoned. "Men go to spas and get pedicures all the time! There's no shame in it."

He held up a hand to stop her. "Why are we discussing this?"

With a dramatic sigh, she said, "Because I thought it would be fun for us all to go away for a weekend and get pampered before the wedding!"

With a shrug, he took the beer Jimmy was holding out for him. "Yeah, sure. Why not? I wouldn't say no to a massage either," he added with an exaggerated waggle of his eyebrows.

Someone snorted

Drew didn't even need to look around to know who made the sound.

Chelsea.

She was what he called The Three Bs–beautiful, blonde, and boring.

Well, mostly boring.

Why Bianca–or any of the women here for that matter–hung out with her, he had no idea. She was about as much fun as a case of poison ivy–overly serious, overly studious, and an all-around bore to be around. Maybe that was mean to think, but Drew preferred a woman with a little more personality–someone who wasn't afraid to laugh at herself–and who didn't take everything so damn seriously.

She was tedious and yet, somehow, he kept drawing the short straw whenever she had to be dealt with.

Which was every weekend.

At some point in the evening, everyone would be laughing and having a good time, and Miss Priss would have something to say about whatever they were all talking about. Usually it was to disapprove of something Jimmy and Bianca were doing. The first few times it happened, Drew didn't think much of it, but then he noticed a pattern and he wasn't the only one. Jimmy had pulled him aside and they came up with a code word for whenever he needed to step in and defuse a situation.

Cantaloupe.

Yeah, their big, manly code word was a fruit.

Chuckling softly, he took a sip of his beer. Tonight should be relatively painless. They were all here to celebrate. There was no way Chelsea–or anyone for that matter–could possibly find a reason to complain.

Jimmy moved over to his side, grinning like a fool. "Thanks for coming, man."

He shrugged with a smile of his own. "It's Friday. Where else would I be?"

"Yeah, well...I appreciate you coming and hanging out here. I know it's not our usual place and there's definitely zero chance of you hooking up with anyone..."

"Dude, I'm a big boy. I can handle a Friday night with no prospects of a hook-up. Trust me."

"You're sounding a little disillusioned. What's up with that?"

What *was* up with that?

Another shrug. "I don't know. It's getting old. I thought at this point in my life I'd be with someone and planning a future or at least thinking of it. The last few dates I've been on have just been..."

"Boring?"

"Kind of. I don't know. For years it wasn't a big deal to go out on a few dates just for the sake of messing around. Now I'd like something different. More. I see what you and Bianca have and..."

Jimmy let out a low laugh. "I still don't know how I got so lucky." He paused and took a pull of his beer. "Don't get me wrong–Bianca can be a handful and she has some serious drama issues, but at the end of the day, I just know she's it for me."

He nodded. "Everyone can see that."

"Not everyone," he muttered.

"What do you mean?"

Looking over his shoulder, Jimmy nudged Drew to move closer to the wall and away from their friends. "Okay, I know we all give her a lot of shit, but I'm afraid Chelsea's going to talk Bianca out of marrying me."

"What?!" he cried. "Why would you even think that?"

"How can you even ask? It's like she's specifically looking for me to do something wrong just so she can tell Bianca 'I told you so.' It's crazy." He took another drink. "It's like being watched over by a nun. I'm constantly on my best behavior and it's exhausting." Another drink. "And I know I'm not perfect; hell, I screw up all the damn time, and every time I think Bianca's going to realize she's making a mistake."

Drew studied his friend hard. They'd never done this–talked this real–and it was a little bizarre. So he took a minute to choose his words wisely.

"Well...screw that," he said instead. "If she doesn't love and accept you for who you are, then why are you even thinking of marrying her?" He shook his head. "I couldn't live like that–like constantly waiting for the other shoe to drop. It's got to be exhausting."

"You have no idea," Jimmy said wearily.

They stood in companionable silence for several minutes before Drew had to ask. "You're sure about this? I mean, really sure? You and Bianca?"

Nodding, he replied, "Yeah. I'm sure. I just don't know what to do to get Chelsea off my damn back." He let out a long breath before saying, "You want to know what I really think it is?"

Did he?

"Uh...sure."

"I think she sees me. Chelsea. Like *really* sees me. She's not impressed with the shit that comes out of my mouth and knows I'm a damn fraud in a lot of ways." He shook his head. "Can Bianca do better than me? Of course she can! But that doesn't mean I don't love her and I wouldn't do anything in the world to show her that!"

Well...damn.

"So...talk to Bianca about this and tell her to stop inviting Chelsea around! Seriously, it would be a win-win for everyone! I still don't get how they're even friends!"

Chuckling, Jimmy replied, "She's really not that bad. I know we all give her a hard time, but...she's a decent person– the kind who would give you the shirt off her back. Bianca's always talking about what a good friend she is, and as much as she seems to hate me, she got me the lead on the big rehab job I'm doing right now."

"You mean the house in Sag Harbor?" he asked incredulously. "That job's huge!"

"I know! Not only did she refer me, but apparently she's the only reason the homeowners picked me. They talk about how they trust her implicitly." He shrugged. "I don't get it."

"Wow..."

"That job is going to allow me to put a down payment on a house for me and Bianca."

"Maybe that's why she did it?" he suggested. "As a way of helping you out?"

"Yeah, but if she dislikes me as much as I think she does, it doesn't make sense."

"Don't look a gift horse in the mouth."

Another shrug. "Maybe she's just not good at trusting people."

"Or maybe she's just a miserable person," Drew deadpanned. "And she's looking to make her friends miserable too."

Behind them, he heard everyone laughing and turned to see what was going on. Everyone was smiling and drinking, and Chelsea was nursing her glass of wine with a serene smile on her face–like a real smile would take too much effort.

"Thanks for listening," Jimmy said. "Let's go see what everyone's laughing about!"

It was on the tip of his tongue to mention how not everyone was laughing, but...what would be the point?

If Chelsea Cooper didn't know how to relax and enjoy herself, that was her problem, not his.

3

"There's a problem."

Two weeks after the big engagement celebration and Drew didn't need to ask what–or who–Jimmy was referring to. "What's up?"

"Bianca and I are eloping this weekend."

"What?! That's awesome! Where? When? And obviously I'm going to be best man, so..."

Jimmy sighed. "Okay, maybe two problems."

Uh-oh...

Before he could ask, his buddy was explaining. "Bianca's got her heart set on getting married at some resort down in South Carolina. She made some calls, and it just so happens they have an opening for one of their super small and intimate packages this weekend and she booked it." He let out a nervous laugh before he went on. "I mean, we didn't even really talk about it, and she went and booked our wedding!"

"Jim..."

"No, no...it's great. Really. Our parents are all going to flip because they were already planning something big for like three hundred people, but I'm sure we can do both, right?" Another laugh that was bordering on hysterics–and not the funny kind.

"Jimmy, breathe. You don't have to do this. Just tell Bianca no–that you don't think it's a good idea. It's too fast! It's too soon! And...you know, your family and friends will be devastated to miss out on it." Drew let out a laugh of his own. "Well, most of your family and friends because...hey, I'll be there."

"Um...yeah...about that..."

"Seriously?" he cried. "Why not? I thought I was your best man!"

"Bianca said she wanted to do this just the two of us and then do a party when we get back, so..."

In the background, Drew could hear Bianca talking excitedly. No doubt she was calling her friends just like Jimmy was doing. He couldn't make out what she was saying, and honestly, it didn't matter. "Okay, so...what's the problem?"

"We weren't going to tell anyone–and I mean *anyone*," he added for emphasis. "But she let it slip to Kendall who's a blabbermouth for sure and we know if Chelsea finds out, she's going to show up and try to stop the wedding. Everyone's going to meet up tomorrow night as usual, and I need you to make sure..."

"You need me to throw myself on the grenade," he said miserably.

"Pretty much. I don't know if anything will happen, but when we don't show up at O'Dwyer's, people are going to wonder, and you know how Chelsea is." He paused. "I know it's a lot to ask, Drew, and I have no idea what's going to happen, but..."

"Don't worry about it," he assured. "Whatever I need to

do, I'll do. Although you should probably just say there's a family emergency out of town. Who can argue with that?"

"Normally we would, but like I said, Kendall knows, and she cannot keep a secret."

"Do I even want to know how you know that?"

"Let's just say Bianca shared some...intimate stories with her, and Kendall blurted them out the next time we were all together."

"Intimate details? Like what? I don't remember that."

"It's not important."

Leaning back in his desk chair, Drew grinned from ear to ear. "I'm going to need details or you'll have to find yourself someone else to help with this problem."

"You're a dick, Drew."

"And proud of it. Now spill."

A low growl was Jimmy's first response. Then... "As a joke, I put on a pair of Bianca's panties."

Wait for it...

"And I didn't hate it," Jimmy murmured.

Unable to help himself, Drew laughed–hard. And for a long time. Once he finally had himself under control, he said, "Fear not. I'm all over this. Tell me when you're leaving, when the ceremony is, and when you'll be back so I know what I'm dealing with."

"Holy shit, you're the best," Jimmy said with relief. "Okay, we're leaving in the morning. We've got a flight out of LaGuardia and the ceremony is Monday afternoon."

"Monday afternoon? Who gets married on a Monday afternoon?"

Groaning, he replied, "Apparently, I do. So the wedding is Monday and the plan is to fly home Tuesday night. I know it's a lot of time to cover, but hopefully there won't be any issues."

"Jim, there's only so much I can do. It's not like Chelsea and I hang out together other than Friday night. How am I supposed to know what she does for the other days?"

"I don't know...ask her to dinner Saturday night or something. Take her out east for one of those wine tastings or something."

"Are you out of your mind? She'd know something was up right away! We barely tolerate each other. Me asking her out is just going to make her think something's up."

He heard Bianca call Jimmy's name. "Listen, I need to go. Just...promise me you'll handle this."

He had no clue how, but...

"Yeah, don't worry. I've got this. Go and get married and call me when you get back."

"Thanks, Drew. You're a lifesaver."

He grinned. "I know. But you owe me."

"Anything you want, and it's yours."

"I'm going to hold you to that." He hung up and sat up straighter and tried to wrap his brain around what he'd just learned.

His best friend was getting married...eloping with his dream girl to South Carolina.

And he liked to wear women's underwear.

Wrong thing to focus on!

The main thing that really had him more than a little confused was the rush to get married. Drew was a firm believer in the institution of marriage, but he didn't get why they were rushing like this. What was so special about this place in South Carolina that Bianca jumped at the first available date? And didn't she care about her friends and family at all? All the B.S. with Chelsea aside, what about the rest of them? Wouldn't it have been better to wait so everyone could be there?

He thought about it and realized it wasn't a huge deal for him to see Jimmy get married–that's not what this was about–but both Jimmy and Bianca came from big Italian families. You don't elope; you have a big circus of a wedding! That's the way it's always been and he couldn't believe they were breaking tradition like that. Just last summer, Drew had gone to Jimmy's brother's wedding and it was like a three-day event! He just naturally assumed it would be the same way when Jimmy got married.

Plus, he totally had Bianca pegged as someone who would thrive on having the eyes of three hundred people on her for a big wedding. So what was going on? Again, why the rush?

His mind wandered to how everyone else was going to feel when they heard the news.

And not just Chelsea.

They were a close-knit group and he knew there were going to be hurt feelings. Hell, he was a little offended himself. And he knew he would kill to be a fly on the wall when the bride and groom break the news to their families.

"Better them than me," he murmured.

Raking his hands through his hair, he leaned back in his chair and tried to figure out the best way to deal with tomorrow night. He'd make sure to get to O'Dwyer's earlier than usual so he would be the first to arrive. Then, with any luck, Kendall would be the next to arrive so he could feel her out and figure out if she was going to blab the news or not. Maybe if she simply blabbed it to him, she'd feel like she got it out and then would be okay without telling anyone else.

The idea definitely had merit.

Okay, the way he saw it, as long as he kept Kendall busy, she couldn't tell Chelsea about the wedding! Why waste his time talking to a woman who barely tolerated him when he could simply do his best to prevent the information from ever getting to her? It was brilliant! And Kendall was a good-looking, friendly woman. Asking Kendall to dinner or to go out east–if it had to come to that–would be way more palatable than having to do that with Chelsea.

Problem solved.

I'm a genius.

He mentally high-fived himself before putting his focus back on his computer and getting back to work.

For the first time in ages, Chelsea couldn't wait to see everyone tonight. It had been a great week, she was going to start working with a new author next week, and hopefully this would mean she was finally transitioning from narrating textbooks and non-fiction titles to where her passion really was–fiction.

Particularly romance.

Just thinking about it had her feeling hopeful and excited and she couldn't wait to share the news with Bianca. For so long she'd been the one encouraging Chelsea to speak up about wanting to narrate something different–something she enjoyed–and now it was finally happening!

Yay me!

Stepping into O'Dwyer's, she looked around near their usual booth and didn't see Bianca. Or Kendall. Or Shauna. Feeling slightly dejected, she figured they were all running late. Looking down at her watch, however, she saw it was well after eight and everyone normally arrived long before now. She was the one who was late!

"Chelsea!"

She looked up at the sound of her name and spotted Drew waving to her from the booth. Forcing a smile, she prayed they weren't the only two here. That would mean she'd have to make small talk with him and hope the others would be arriving shortly.

"Hey," she said, smiling. "Where is everyone?"

"Can I get you a drink?" he offered, taking her jacket from her and placing it the hook next to them. "Chardonnay, right?"

"Um, yes. Thank you." He was gone before she could get an answer out of him, which was weird. Pulling her phone from her purse, she looked to see if she missed any messages, but she didn't. There had to be something up and she quickly tapped out a group text to the girls.

Hey! Did I miss the memo where we're all skipping tonight? Where's everyone at?

She stared down at the screen and willed someone to answer, but all she got was the sent memo.

Dammit.

When she looked up, Drew was sliding into the booth across from her. He slid her wine to her with a smile. "So, how was your week?"

Fighting the urge to look around and see who he was talking to, she responded, "Good, thanks. And yours?"

His hands were cupped around his beer as he smiled at her. "Yeah, mine was good too. Busy. So, what fascinating book are you narrating now? Anything I'd be familiar with?"

And for the first time in a long time, he didn't sound so... condescending about her work. Or snarky. Or...anything. He sounded genuinely interested.

"What's going on?" she demanded, sliding her wine glass aside.

"What do you mean?"

"Where is everyone and why are you being so nice?" she demanded and almost wanted to kick herself for sounding so bitchy.

If anything, his smile stayed in place. "Contrary to popular belief, I'm a nice guy," he said smoothly. "As for the rest of the group, I'm not really sure. Did you check your phone for any missed calls or messages?"

"Of course I did. The girls always tell me when they're running late, so I can't understand how they're all late and not..." She stopped and gasped, suddenly horrified. "Oh my God! What if something happened to them? What if they were all on their way here together and got into an accident? What if..." She started to slide out of the booth when Drew's stopped her. His hand was resting casually on top of hers and...she didn't hate it.

"Chelsea, calm down. No one's been in an accident," he said, his voice oddly soothing.

"But...how do you know? Did you get any calls or texts?" And his smile finally slipped before his expression turned slightly...guilty. "Drew?"

He paled and that's when she knew something was definitely up.

"I'm going to ask you again..."

"Okay, okay, okay," he quickly interrupted. "Jimmy had a bit of a family emergency and Bianca went with him. I'm not sure where everyone else is."

That was it? That's was what had him looking like he did?

"Are you sure that's it?"

"Yeah, why?"

"Because you looked way more panicked than that story would imply, so...is there anything else?" Before he could answer, her phone dinged and she breathed a sigh of relief. "Hopefully that's Kendall or Shauna responding to my text." But when she picked up her phone, she saw it wasn't a text, but a notification from Instagram. She was tempted to ignore it, but for some reason, she was curious.

It was an Instagram story from Bianca with a picture of her hand–specifically her engagement ring–with the caption, "Destination Wedding here we come!"

"What the hell?" Chelsea cried. "Is she on a plane right now?" Looking up at Drew, she held up her phone toward him. "Did you know about this?"

"About what?" He leaned forward and tapped her phone screen to bring the video back. "Maybe they're going to look at a venue or something." He shrugged. "Who knows?"

"You just said there was a family emergency, Drew. What kind of family emergency involves flying off to a destination wedding venue, huh?" Muttering a curse, she tried to slide out of the booth again when he stopped her. Yanking her hand back, she glared at him.

"What are you so freaked out about? It's a ten-second video with a cryptic message! You know how over-the-top Bianca has been about this engagement. Knowing her, she's forcing Jimmy to look at venues rather than helping his poor uncle...uh...Vito!"

"Vito?"

He nodded. "Yeah, his uncle Vito is sick and Jimmy is going to help him out. Why he decided to bring Malibu Barbie along, I have no idea."

"Hey! That's my best friend you're talking about!" Although she had to hand it to him, the name totally fit Bianca.

"Relax, Chels. All I'm saying is you're being overly

suspicious. Are you sure it's even a current video? You know she posts like a dozen stories a day on there."

"How would you know?" she asked and then, "Wait... you're on Instagram?" And she burst out laughing before he could confirm or deny. "Wow, I never would have pegged you for an IG guy! What's your handle?"

Drew's dark brown eyes went wide before narrowing at her. "Why?"

"So I can follow you! I want to see what kind of pictures Drew Russo shares on Instagram!" She laughed again, although she couldn't say why. Most people had an Instagram account. Why would she think Drew was any different?

"Hey, Drew! Did I leave my..."

Chelsea froze when Kendall approached the booth. Actually, they all did. Drew nervously looked between the two of them and Kendall was literally frozen in place.

Weird.

Drew cleared his throat and that seemed to snap everyone out of their stunned silence. Kendall looked away first, glancing at Drew. "Did I happen to leave my phone here earlier? I got all the way home before I realized it was gone."

"You were here earlier?" Chelsea asked, but no one seemed to be listening.

"I didn't see it," Drew said as he looked around. "Maybe you left it up at the bar or back by the dartboards."

"You guys played darts?"

Again, no one was listening.

Kendall turned and walked toward the back of the bar while Drew slid out of the booth and looked under the table. Two minutes later, Kendall was back.

"Found it!" she said happily. "The bartender said someone turned it in. Whew!"

"Is no one going to tell me what's going on?" Chelsea cried out, slamming her hand on the table.

Drew looked at Kendall and then at her but remained quiet. Luckily Kendall finally decided to talk.

"Yeah, so...I was here earlier and didn't know Jimmy and Bianca weren't here..." She glanced at Drew who gave the tiniest of nods. "And you were late so...I figured we all just weren't hanging out tonight." She shrugged. "No biggie."

"You could have answered my text," Chelsea reminded her. "If I had known no one was coming, I would have gone home."

Holding up her phone, Kendall gave a helpless shrug. "Obviously, I didn't have my phone or I would have."

"Oh. Right." Scooting further into the booth, she motioned to the spot next to her. "Well, now you're back so...have a drink!"

"I shouldn't. I had one earlier and once I got home, I realized how much I really wanted a quiet night in. Plus, I'm trying to find out how to get the feed from the resort for Monday!" Kendall's hand instantly flew to her mouth as Drew groaned.

Chelsea swore she was getting whiplash from looking back and forth between the two of them. "What feed? What's going on Monday?"

"Um...I should go," Kendall said nervously. "I'll talk to you later!" And then she spun and all but ran from the bar. It was pointless to go after her because Drew's hand was already poised to stop her.

With a weary sigh, she massaged her forehead. "For the

love of it, will you please just tell me what's going on? Clearly something is happening."

"I told you..."

"It's not Uncle Vito!" she snapped. "So don't even go there!"

His broad shoulders sagged as he leaned back in the booth. Both hands raked through his dark hair as he muttered a curse. "Before I say anything, you have to promise not to freak out."

"Drew..."

"I'm serious," he said tightly.

"Fine." Crossing her arms over her chest, she waited.

"Jimmy and Bianca are eloping this weekend."

"What?! But that's crazy! Where? Why? And why am I hearing this from you instead of Bianca?"

"Probably because you'd try to talk her out of it and ruin her wedding!" he shouted. Even in the loud and crowded bar, people turned to see what he was yelling about. Holding up a hand, he said, "Sorry." Once everyone stopped paying attention, he looked at her again. "You have to admit, Chelsea, you've been a real ballbuster to the two of them about their relationship. Are you really surprised they didn't tell you?"

She wasn't, but that didn't mean it didn't hurt. Bianca had been her best friend since they were eight. How could she run off and get married without her? Tears stung her eyes and she realized the last person she wanted to witness her pain was Drew.

"I should go," she said quietly, reaching for her phone and purse. He didn't try to stop her, and when she stood, so did he.

"Look, Chelsea, I'm sorry you had to hear it from me. That was never the plan. If Kendall hadn't come back..." He helped her into her jacket and even helped her get her long blonde hair out from under it. Turning around, she faced him.

"If Kendall hadn't come back..."

"You probably wouldn't have heard about it until they got back Tuesday night," he said solemnly. "I really am sorry."

Nodding, she willed herself not to cry. "Me too."

He let out a long breath as they both stood awkwardly facing each other. "You don't have to leave, you know. You should stay and finish your wine."

It was tempting–mainly because she felt like she could use a drink–but it would be better for her to be alone.

When she didn't answer, Drew added, "I get that you're upset, but if you go home all you're going to do is obsess about this situation like 'Where's the wedding?' or 'Why'd they have to do it so soon?' or 'How can I stop the wedding?'" Then he let out a low laugh. "Not that I'm saying you're going to go and crash the wedding and stop them from getting married..." He stopped and eyed her warily. "You wouldn't do something like that, right?"

"Oh, please, give me a little credit," she said testily.

However...the idea had merit.

No doubt, if Bianca was marrying anyone else this wouldn't be an issue. But no, Jimmy the Jerk–ha! Take that Malibu Barbie burn!–had to convince her to run away to get married. *Gah!* He really was the worst.

Chelsea considered her next words very carefully. "There are hundreds of places for them to go and elope, how would I possibly figure out where they picked?"

His hands slid into his trouser pockets as he shrugged.

"Bianca loathes Vegas so I know they didn't do anything as clichéd as that..."

Another shrug.

"And she doesn't even have a passport so I know they didn't leave the country..."

"Chelsea..."

"Niagara Falls makes her hair frizz so I know she'd never go there either." She racked her brain for places people normally went when they eloped. "And there's no way they'd do it in Disney World because the life-size characters freak her out."

"Seriously? Like Mickey and Minnie?"

She nodded. "Yup. It all goes back to an unfortunate photo op with Barney the Dinosaur. Ever since then, she can't stand being near anything in costume.

"Wow, that's just...wow."

"I know. Tell me about it." She paused and tried to think of more places. "Anyway, I know Bianca better than anyone. If she were going to do something like this, the location would have to have a significant meaning to her or some sort of pop culture reference."

"What the hell does that mean?"

"It means she loves places where movies were filmed–like actual locations."

"That sounds stupid."

She couldn't possibly argue with that because she had said many times how ridiculous it was to want to visit someplace just because a scene from a movie was filmed there or a celebrity couple got married there or...

Why didn't I pay more attention to Bianca's ramblings in Starbucks?

She thought about all the recent celebrity gossip and who had recently gotten married, when it hit her. "Oh, my God! I know where they're getting married!" She turned to walk away, but Drew gripped her upper arm to stop her. "Stop doing that!" Tugging her arm free, she faced him.

"Chelsea, you can't seriously be considering going to the wedding! You can't!"

"Why not? Aren't you the least bit pissed that your best friend excluded you?"

He stared hard at her. "Well, yeah, but we talked it out and I'm good with it. They're going to have a party or even another wedding for their friends and family in the future, but this weekend is just for them so...don't go ruin it!"

Ugh...why didn't anyone understand that she wasn't doing this to be mean or petty or spiteful? She was doing this because Bianca and Jimmy were wrong for each other.

"Are you saying that out of all the women in the world, Bianca is who you'd choose for your best friend?"

"Well..."

"This is crazy," she muttered before he could say another word. "I don't have to stand here and explain myself to you. Thanks for being the only one willing to hang around and wait for me tonight. And for being the only one willing to tell me the truth," she added sadly. "Have a good weekend."

Chelsea wove her way through the crowd, and once she was outside on the sidewalk, she took a couple of deep breaths to calm herself down. She hadn't considered following Bianca and confronting her in person, but there wasn't a doubt in her mind that it was the only way to go. If she tried calling, Bianca wouldn't answer, so why waste her time?

It took her a minute to get her bearings before she walked around to the side of the building to the parking lot. She was getting ready to open her door when a large hand landed on her shoulder. Screaming, she turned, knocking the hand away.

"Dammit, Drew! You scared the crap out of me!" Her heart felt like it was going to beat right out of her chest as she sagged against her Hyundai SUV.

"I'm going with you."

"Um...what?"

He nodded. "We both know you're going to try to stop this wedding, and while I don't agree with you, I also don't think you should have to face doing it alone. So...I'm going with you."

"I hate to break it to you, Ace, but...I didn't invite you, nor do I want you for company."

"Too bad because, like it or not, I'm going."

She groaned. "I don't have to wait on you or go anywhere with you. I'm just going to grab a flight in the morning. It's too late to get one right now, so I'll just get one for first thing in the morning."

Taking a step back, Drew considered her. "I'll tell you what, I'll take care of the flights..."

"Drew..."

"No, no, no...I travel a lot on business and have a crap-ton of miles I can use, so the flights are on me."

She eyed him warily. "What's the catch?"

"The catch is...when we get there, you have one hour to plead your case. If you don't convince them–and you are logical and not all...you know...crazy–then you agree to leave and let them have their day."

"Only an hour? That's hardly enough time to..."

"Either you do it my way or I'll call them both and tell them you're coming," he said quickly. "No doubt they'll have you blocked from getting anywhere near them or they'll simply move the ceremony. Either way, you won't get a chance to screw this up for them."

"Why are you such an ass?"

Now he leaned in close. "I could ask you the same thing."

Oh, how she loathed him.

"How do I know you're not going to call them anyway?" she asked.

"I give you my word," he said firmly. "Think all the bad things you want about me, Chelsea, but I'm a man of my word. If I tell you I'm not going to call, then you can rest assured that I'm not going to."

Letting out a long breath, she realized maybe he was right. "Okay, then. How do we do this?"

"We'll need to exchange phone numbers to start with, and I'll need your pertinent information so I can book the tickets. We'll meet at my place in the morning and head to the airport. Deal?" He held out his hand to her and she shook it.

And suddenly she felt like she'd made a deal with the devil.

4

"What took you so long?"

It was only eight in the morning and she was already ready to murder him. "What took me so long?" she mimicked. "You gave me the wrong address! How is it possible that you don't know your own address?"

"You're crazy," Drew replied, stepping out onto the front porch. "If I gave you the wrong address, how did you find my house, huh?"

"You said you lived on Heritage Place," she explained. "This is Heritage Place *South* and it's only by pure luck and several wrong turns that I got here!"

"Well, we need to hustle or we're going to miss our flight," he said, taking both of their suitcases to his car.

With no other choice, she followed behind him. "We should be fine. It's Saturday morning and MacArthur airport's only twenty minutes away. Our flight isn't until ten."

She was on the passenger side and he was standing on the driver's side when he shook his head. "We're not leaving out of MacArthur. We're leaving out of LaGuardia." He climbed into the car and she did the same.

"No," she said once she was buckled in. "You said MacArthur! It's in the text!" Pulling out her phone to prove her point, she pulled up their messages. "See? Right here, MacArthur."

He shrugged. "Typo. We're leaving from LaGuardia." And without another word, he backed out of the driveway.

"Why? That's so much farther away, isn't it?"

Turning, Drew looked at her like she was crazy. "Don't you know where LaGuardia is?"

"Kind of. I don't particularly like to fly and any time I do, I fly out of MacArthur. Why go all the way to the city when there's a perfectly good airport right here?"

"So you've never flown out of any other airport here?"

"Nope."

"Interesting."

"Why do you say that?"

"No reason."

They drove in silence for several minutes. He got on the Northern State Parkway and then crossed over to the Southern State Parkway. There wasn't much to see and she figured they were going to be stuck with each other for a couple of hours so she might as well try to talk with him. "How long should it take to get to the airport?"

"At this point, we've got another forty minutes or so. Then we've got to park and then race to get through security. If we make the flight, it will be a miracle."

Damn, if they missed their flight, it was basically her fault.

Even though he gave her the wrong address.

"Can I ask you something?" he asked.

"Sure."

"How did you figure out where they were getting married?"

Laughing softly, Chelsea turned to him and smiled. "I don't know if you're aware, but Bianca is a huge Justin Bieber fan."

"Um...no. I don't think it's ever come up."

"It's true. Anyway, back in September, he got married to Hailey Baldwin at this super posh resort down in South Carolina. I remember the day clearly because Bianca was glued to her phone, Instagram in particular, waiting for any pictures of the wedding to be released. She carried on about how it was the most romantic-looking place. So I took a shot at that being where they went."

"Wow," he said with a chuckle. "You really do know her well."

"We've been friends for over twenty years," she reasoned. "You get to know a thing or two about each other."

"I'm impressed." He got quiet for a minute before asking, "So was she upset that Justin got married? Did she hope to marry him herself?"

That made Chelsea laugh. "There was a time when she definitely thought it was a possibility, but she hasn't mentioned it in years, so... it was really more about it being a celebrity wedding. Bianca *loves* anything celebrity-related. It's kind of crazy."

"A little, but honestly, it kind of fits," he said casually.

"What do you mean?"

He shrugged. "She strikes me as that type, that's all."

"What type?"

"You know, shallow. Ditzy. Someone who watches *way*

too much reality TV and dreams of being on one of those shows about the housewives."

Twisting in her seat to face him more, she glared. "That's really insulting, Drew. You realize she's my best friend, right?"

"Yeah, I still can't figure that one out," he murmured. "The two of you are nothing alike. I mean, what do you even talk about when you're together?"

"Basically we talk about what a colossal jackass you are!" Straightening in her seat, Chelsea knew it would be best for her to ignore him. It was obvious they couldn't agree on anything so what was the point in even trying with him? With a huff, she reached into her purse and pulled out her phone. Maybe if she could see how much longer they were going to be in the car together, she could refrain from any more disagreements with him.

The jerk.

She pulled up her GPS and frowned. "Um...Drew?"

"Yeah?"

"You said we're leaving from LaGuardia, right?"

"About a dozen times, why?"

"Because you're going the wrong way," she stated, more than a little annoyed.

"No, I'm not."

"Yes, you are! Look!" She held up her phone next to his face but he swatted her away. "Drew!"

"Have you ever driven to LaGuardia? No, right? Trust me. I know where I'm going." He sounded just a little too cocky and that irked her all the more.

"You're on the South Shore and the airport is on the North Shore, Drew. You're driving to Kennedy Airport according to the map! If you'd just look..."

"I know what I'm doing, Chelsea," he snapped. "I've driven to the airport dozens of times!"

"To the correct one?" she mumbled under her breath and decided the best thing to do was to simply bite her tongue and see how this all unfolded. There wasn't anything she could do; she was essentially at his mercy. It wasn't like she could get out of the car and drive herself. Plus, he had her ticket!

They drove on in silence for another twenty minutes when she heard him curse.

"Problem?" she asked sweetly.

"Um...yeah, so...it seems like we're going to Kennedy instead of LaGuardia," he said begrudgingly.

"Hmm," she replied thoughtfully. "That's odd. I thought you drove to the airport sooo many times that you know everything."

"I never said I know everything," he retorted. "But...we are going to be cutting it even closer now. If there's no traffic, we could–realistically–cut across the Grand Central Parkway and be there in 15-20 minutes."

"But we'll still have to deal with parking and security," she reminded him.

"What choice do we have?"

"Why don't I look up other flights? It's not like this was the only flight to South Carolina. And what's another hour or two? The wedding's not until Monday, so we're still good."

Drew turned his head and looked at her. "You're being incredibly chill about this. Why?"

She shrugged. "I hate to break it to you, but I'm usually very chill. It takes a lot to make me freak out."

He snorted with disbelief.

"What? What was that snort for?"

"Chelsea, no offense, but you just don't strike me as the chill type. You always have a problem with something. That's not the way a laidback person is. Sorry."

"You see me one night a week for a few hours–and we never talk about anything remotely personal–and you think you know me? Arrogant much?"

"It has nothing to do with arrogance. It's observation. Plus, I may not talk *with* you about personal stuff, but I've certainly talked about you." As if he just realized what he said, he groaned.

Chelsea's cheeks heated and she was beyond embarrassed. Her conversation with Bianca came to mind.

"Seriously, you're the worst. Even when we're hanging out, you're not really focused. We all talk about it."

"What do you mean we all talk about it?"

"You know, me, Kendall, Shauna, Robbie, Alex, Jimmy, and Drew." She shrugged. "And we all think you need to relax a bit. You're way too uptight and you can really be a bit of a downer. And seriously, all the talk about books is incredibly boring."

"Alex said we should just give you a break because he knows how obnoxious the guys can be," Bianca explained.

"Oh, well...that was nice of him."

"But Drew thinks you're just uptight and need to..." She paused and blushed. "Well, never mind. In that one instance, he was a little crude."

"No, please...tell me what...Drew," she said through clenched teeth, "had to say."

"He might have mentioned something about...needing a good...you know...just a night of hard..." She stopped and cleared her throat. "There are a ton of studies on the importance of a good orgasm, Chels. Have you read any of them?"

Then she had the nerve to giggle. "Maybe that's the kind of book you should be narrating!"

"Okay, that's not what I meant. Not exactly," he clarified. "It's obvious you can't stand me or Jimmy, so I just choose not to...you know...poke the bear. It's one night a week that I go and hang out with my friends; why would I choose to try to chat someone up who clearly can't stand me?"

"And yet here we are taking this stupid trip together! Why would you even offer to do this? Although at this rate, the only thing we're going to be seeing is both coasts of Long Island."

And yes, that was a dig!

"We're going to see more than the Island! Jeez, who knew you could be a drama queen too? I thought that was all reserved for Bianca."

"Hey! Stop picking on her!"

"Just stating the facts," he argued lightly. "I call them as I see them. And from what I can see...*shit*!"

"Now what?"

"I missed the exit to the Grand Central because I was too busy arguing with you!" Another colorful string of curses was out before he seemed to calm down. "Look, can we just agree to drive in silence until we get to the airport?"

"Fine by me. I'm not the one who's directionally challenged, and talking with you only leads to things going wrong so..." She made a zipping motion across her lips and decided the best way for her to spend her time was to look for other flights. It didn't matter if he got them turned around and onto the correct parkway, there was no way they were going to park and get through security in time.

But if Captain Know-It-All thought they could make it, who was she to argue?

And really, what would be the point?

So far, everything was going to plan.

Get Chelsea lost going to his place? Check.

Go to the wrong airport? Check.

He already knew all the available flights and knew exactly how he was going to handle things once they arrived at LaGuardia. But for now, he was going to relish the peace and quiet. He knew Chelsea was fairly talkative, but normally there was a group of people around and she rarely directed any conversation toward him. Having to be in this constant state of chattiness with her was already grating on his nerves.

And they'd only been on the road for an hour.

How the hell was he supposed to survive the weekend at this rate?

Jimmy's going to owe me big time...

Taking the next exit and turning around to get back to the Grand Central exit, Drew wondered if he was really going to be able to pull this whole thing off. It was one thing to make a couple of wrong turns and go to the wrong place; it was another to pull it off all weekend long. At some point, she was going to either call BS on him or she was going to argue with him to the point that he pulled over and let her out of the car.

Who was he kidding? He wouldn't do that. Oh, he'd fantasize about it and probably wish a thousand times over that he could, but the bottom line was he wasn't a douche. No matter how much she provoked him, he would get through this weekend.

And then he'd consider finding some new friends.

To pass the time, Drew began to think of all the things he was going to ask from Jimmy as payback.

Season tickets to the Ranger games.

A weekend in Vegas.

And maybe, just maybe, he'd make Jimmy pick up the bar tab and all their meals for a year.

Yeah, all of them were great options and he liked having a plan.

He started seeing the signs for LaGuardia and had to bite his tongue to keep from pointing them out or making any kind of small talk. If he could get them parked–temporarily–then he could put the next phase of his plan into motion.

If he weren't driving, he'd be rubbing his palms together like the evil genius he was.

Drew Russo...super genius.

It had a nice ring to it.

There was the usual congestion as they approached the airport, and by the time they got to the parking garage, he could tell that Chelsea was dying to reprimand him. Rather than engage, he drove at a leisurely pace until he found the perfect parking spot. Once they were parked, he turned off the car and looked at her.

"Okay, you ready?"

Her hazel eyes grew wide. "Ready? For what? The flight leaves in fifteen minutes! It will take that long just to get to out of the parking lot and to the terminal!"

"I think that's a bit of an exaggeration."

"Seriously? You picked the farthest spot humanly possible!"

"So we're not even going to try?" he asked, doing his best to sound incredulous. "I thought you said you wanted to get to South Carolina as soon as possible. That's not going to happen with your crappy attitude."

Pulling out his phone, he checked the time, and sure enough, there was no way they would make it. But just to play it safe, he pulled up the airline app and double-checked to make sure it wasn't delayed or something.

"Damn, it looks like it's on time. That almost never happens," he said. "What do you want to do?"

Resting her head back against the seat, she sighed. "There are no other direct flights available today out of this airport." Then she turned her head and glared. "If you had just listened to me an hour ago..."

"Why look back? Ancient history, right?"

"No!" she cried. "Not right! And there's nothing ancient about it."

He shrugged. "Whatever. It's not going to change anything. What's available out of...Newark?"

"Why can't we check Kennedy? That was a fairly short drive. I know I'm not familiar with a lot of airports, but even I know that's closer than driving to New Jersey. At that rate, we might as well just drive to South Carolina!"

Snorting as he shook his head, he said, "There is no *way* I'm driving all the way to South Carolina with you." He shuddered dramatically. "At least flying would give us the opportunity to get up and walk away from each other–and the airport is a great distraction because we could each go and do our own thing! But a drive like that is easily twelve hours or more. No thank you."

"You know, you're not my fantasy travel companion either. I never should have stayed at the bar with you last night. I should have just gone home and figured this out on my own. If it weren't for you, I'd be getting my beverage service right about now!"

"Hmm...that does sound good. I could go for some coffee." He knew she had a weakness for Starbucks. "Or maybe some tea. I've recently started drinking chai tea and it's really good. You should try it."

Her eyes closed and he could tell she was losing her patience with him. "That happens to be my drink of choice and should we *ever* get to an airport, I'm most certainly going to get one for myself. But for now, can we please just focus on figuring out some kind of plan of action?"

"I guess I'll look up flights out of Newark since you can't seem to handle it," he murmured before letting out a long breath. "I mean, for someone so anxious to get going, you would think you would have had all our available options at the ready."

"I was! I was trying to find a flight out of here since this is where we already are!" she cried before she continued to mumble under her breath about what a complete moron he was.

He'd been called worse, so...

Drew already knew the flight options. And even though Kennedy was closer, and had several flights available, he wasn't going there. He had a plan for Newark, and at this rate, he knew they'd miss them too.

"There's a noon flight out of Newark. It takes an hour to get there so we'll be cutting it close..."

"It's sold out!"

"Is it? Oh, okay, let me keep searching..."

"There's one out of Kennedy at one. We can easily make that one." She was staring down at her phone and he waited for her to figure out why that one wouldn't work. "It's not direct and the connection would be cutting it close, but..."

"Nah, too risky. Flights are notoriously late taking off; we'd miss the connection for sure. Stick to Newark."

"Ugh...why are you like this?" she demanded.

"Like what? Practical? A seasoned traveler? I'm speaking from experience here. The longer we sit here and argue, the less likely we'll make the flight. Can we just go now? Please?"

"You're the driver! If you want to leave, you're the only one who can make it happen! Sheesh!"

After being overly cautious as they made their way out of the parking garage, Drew opted to take the long way to Newark, knowing Chelsea wouldn't know any better. They naturally hit traffic, he purposely got off at the wrong exit, and by the time they parked, he knew they would be cutting it close.

Again.

"I hope they still have seats available," he said, as he climbed from the car.

"Wait, you didn't buy the tickets already? I thought that's what you did back at LaGuardia!"

Shaking his head, he popped the trunk. "Nope. I wanted to make sure we made it here first before I lost even more money. I'm already eating the cost of the flight we missed."

"Oh."

Handing her suitcase to her, Drew grabbed his and began walking toward the terminal. It was really just another delay tactic, but he was ready to get out and stretch his legs anyway. They walked in silence the entire way and it wasn't until they were through the doors that he stopped and cursed.

"What? What's the matter?"

He felt around his body and made sure to look mildly panicked. "I...my wallet. I don't have my wallet!"

"What?!" She took several paces away before facing him again. "Are you for real right now?"

"Of course I am!" he lied. "We have to go back to the car." But when he turned to walk away, he noticed Chelsea wasn't following. "I'll be quick, I swear."

Will not, but you don't need to know that.

"How about this?" she began. "*You* go back to the car, and I'll go get my ticket. And if you make it back in time, you can get yours and we'll meet up on the plane, okay?"

What the...?

"Wait a minute! You can't be serious."

"Why not?"

"Because...because we're doing this together!"

"I'm not the one who forgot my wallet," she reminded him. "And frankly, I think you did it on purpose."

"What?!" he cried. "Why would I do it on purpose?"

Now she did move in close. "Because we both know you're not on board with me trying to talk Jimmy and Bianca out of this wedding. I think this is all a stalling tactic." She let out a mirthless laugh. "You didn't think I was that stupid, did you? The wrong address this morning... going to the wrong airport...missing exits...I mean, come on! It was almost comical!" She paused and shook her head. "It would have been much more believable if it had been only one or two things, but the forgotten wallet was just one step too far. Sorry, Drew, but I'm calling bullshit."

For a minute, all he could do was stare. The little minx had figured him out. And much sooner than he thought she would. Now what?

It took less than a minute for him to come clean. Why? Because he already had a Plan B ready and waiting.

"Fine. I went a bit overboard," he admitted. "But you have to know I only did it out of respect for Jimmy. He's happy and I just don't want to see you hurt him. Just because you hate him doesn't mean he isn't a great guy."

Her shoulders sagged. "Believe it or not, I don't hate Jimmy. I just don't think he's the right guy for Bianca."

"Yeah, I'm going to need to know why. You can't just throw out a statement like that with no further information."

"Drew, now really isn't the time. I've got to go get a ticket..."

"Just tell me what your beef is with him and I'll let you go."

She eyed him warily. "Now you're just trying to kill time."

Unable to help himself, he smiled. And then, much to his surprise, she laughed.

Shaking her head, Chelsea said, "I don't know whether I should be annoyed or seriously impressed."

He leaned in and said, "Impressed. Always go for impressed."

"God, you are such a jerk." But she didn't sound the least bit annoyed.

"I'll make you a deal. Forget the flight. Forget about finding another one. Drive down to South Carolina with me. Talk to me about what it is that you don't like about Jimmy and why you don't want him and Bianca to get married. Help me to understand the whole thing. Then, when we get there, I promise I'll have your back when you talk to them."

She was quiet for so long that Drew was certain she was going to turn him down. He knew he was asking a lot; knew she had no reason to even want to be in his company for that long. But he also knew he was damn curious to know what was going through her mind.

Last night at the bar was the first time he felt empathy for her. And when she showed up at his house this morning, it was the first time in a long time that he took notice of her as a woman rather than just some annoying person who was part of his social circle.

Chelsea Cooper had the potential to be a serious distraction–all blonde hair and soft curves. Unfortunately, most of the time they were together, she was wearing a pinched expression and annoyed at someone or something.

Sometimes both.

And most of the time, him.

When they first met, he had thought she was attractive and even considered asking her out. He found out fairly quickly, however, they had little to nothing in common. There were times he found her to be flat-out bitchy. And yet somehow, he was always the one who tried to smooth things over when things in the group got tense.

Maybe this time away from their little group of friends was the perfect time for them to get to know each other. It would be nice if they could hang out without being so antagonistic toward each other. Not that he was expecting a miracle, but anything was better than the relationship they had right now.

"So what do you say, Chels? You up for a little adventure?"

"Um..."

"We've got about fifteen hours of driving ahead of us, so it's not going to be easy."

"Earlier, you said twelve."

He shrugged and ignored her comment. "But if you say

yes, I swear I'll do my best to help you out with Jimmy and Bianca. What do you say?"

She moaned. "Last night, I told myself I was making a deal with the devil."

"Hey!" he said, feeling mildly attacked.

Then she held out her hand with a slow grin. "But never let it be said that I back down from a challenge."

Game. On.

5

"This is ridiculous."

"It's the perfect solution."

"It's wasting time, Drew! The GPS said the same thing! This was the longer way to go!"

"Well, it's too late now!" he countered. "We're here and that's all there is to it."

This argument was about their drive through New Jersey. Yeah, they hadn't even gotten out of one state since they'd made this stupid agreement and it was already a bumpy ride.

She had mapped out their route for the fastest way to get to their destination and no sooner had she announced it than Drew said he knew a better route.

And by better, he meant longer.

The bastard.

Right now, they were driving the car onto a ferry that left out of Cape May and would take them across to Delaware. It was a ninety-minute trip, not including the time it took to drive out of the way just for this singular purpose. And she knew it was planned on his part because he had a reservation that he clearly didn't make while she was with him–something she planned on pointing out to him later.

Once they were on the ferry and could get out of the car, Drew led her inside to the upper level where there was a lounge and snack bar. It wasn't fine dining by any stretch of the imagination, but she had to admit that she was starving. They placed their orders and found a table near the window to eat.

"This is great, isn't it?"

"It's sub-par fast food, Drew," she reminded him. "I wouldn't exactly call it great."

"I promise I'll make it up when it's time for dinner. You can pick the place. I figure we'll stop for the night in Virginia Beach."

She choked on her drink and Drew had to get up and give her a couple of swift pats on the back before she could breathe again. "Say what now?"

"What?"

"Why are we stopping for the night? That's crazy! We can drive right through! We'll trade off on the driving!"

"No can do. This has been a long day already and it's not even half over. By the time we hit Virginia Beach, it will be dinner time and the perfect time to stop. We'll have a good dinner, get some rest, and start out early in the morning. It will be another seven hours from there."

Pulling out her phone, she needed to confirm that for herself. It seemed like the time it was taking to get to South Carolina kept getting longer and longer and longer. If she didn't stay on top of him, she had no doubt that she'd find herself either in Florida or somewhere in the Midwest with his choice of directions.

"Well, drat," she murmured.

"What? What's the matter?"

"You're right."

"Well, yeah," he said, grinning. "Wait, about what?"

"About how Virginia Beach is the smartest place to stop."

He took a bite of his sandwich, his eyes never leaving hers. "Why would I lie about that?"

"Why would you give me the wrong address or pretend that you were going to the right airport? I have no idea! Although I'm beginning to think it's pathological."

The look on his face was priceless. His chewing slowed and his face flushed–clearly, he wasn't used to someone calling him out on his bad behavior.

Resting her arms on the table, she leaned in slightly. "And by the end of this trip, I'm sure that will be confirmed."

They ate the rest of their meal in silence, which was fine by her.

Once they were done, Drew led them out onto the deck to enjoy the view. It was a beautiful day out and she had to admit, this was kind of cool. Chelsea couldn't remember the last time she'd been out on a boat of any kind, so while she wasn't particularly thrilled with the company, she was going to make the most of the experience.

They were leaning against the railing, and Drew was staring straight ahead. "Jimmy and I grew up next to each other. He was born and raised in that house and my family moved in next door when I was three," he began out of nowhere. "We played on Little League teams together, were Boy Scouts together, and he's more like a brother to me than either of my own brothers."

Unsure of what to say, she simply nodded and waited for him to continue.

"I fell out of a tree once. We were trying to see who could climb higher. Jimmy had jumped down and was standing there watching to see if I could go past the limb he had gotten to." He paused. "Anyway, I reached up, lost my balance, and fell. If he hadn't been there to catch me, I would have broken my neck." Pausing again, he shook his head. "He saved my life. I don't think I've ever thanked him for that."

They went quiet again when something hit her.

"Wasn't that a scene from *Groundhog Day*?"

"What? No!"

"Yes, it was!" she said with a laugh as she straightened. "Bill Murray catches the kid who fell out of the tree and the kid never thanked him! It's exactly like *Groundhog Day*!"

"Okay, it's similar, but it did happen!" he argued.

Cocking her head, she asked, "Did it?" And there was no mistaking her sarcasm.

Facing the water again, he mumbled, "No."

"Drew, if you have to make up stuff to make Jimmy sound like a great guy, then there's a problem. And honestly, I'm not sure if it's that Jimmy isn't a great guy or, again, that you are a pathological liar." She paused. "Although, I think I'm seeing a pattern here, and God help me if both those things are correct."

He twisted to look at her again. "Fine. Jimmy and I did grow up together, that's not a lie. And he is more like a brother to me than my own."

"But...?"

"But...you wouldn't appreciate the highlights of our friendship because you're too uptight."

"Excuse me?"

"Excuse me?" he mimicked in a voice she had to assume was supposed to sound like her.

"You were saying..."

"Every milestone in my life, Jimmy was there for. He's a great friend who always has my back. There isn't a damn thing he wouldn't do for me or for anyone. Hell, if you needed a favor, he'd even do one for you–even though you've done nothing but give him grief."

She could argue how that wasn't true, but she figured she'd let him get his little speech out.

"No one makes me laugh like he does, and no one else sets me straight when I'm screwing things up," he clarified. "Is he everyone's cup of tea? No! He's loud and obnoxious and sometimes so damn immature it's almost embarrassing. But you know what? He is who he is! That's one of the greatest things about Jimmy; you never have to wonder if he's being sincere because what you see is what you get." He shook his head with disgust and faced the water again. "Most people you have to wonder if they're who they say they are or they act one way when you see them in one setting and then act completely different in another. You never have to worry about that with Jimmy. He is who he is all the damn time–even if it makes him look bad."

"Wow."

He nodded. "And you know what? Your friend is damn lucky to have Jimmy. If you ask me, *he's* too good for *her*. She's the kind of person you have to wonder about. She's the kind of person who is two-faced–sweet to your face but would stab you in the back in a heartbeat."

It was on the tip of her tongue to try to defend Bianca, but...she couldn't. Drew's description was too spot-on.

"Am I worried about the two of them getting married? Hell yeah! She's going to make him jump through all kinds of hoops and she's going to be the one calling the shots. And you know what? That pisses me off. He doesn't deserve that. Unfortunately, he's so damn head-over-heels in love with Bianca that he's not seeing things for what they are."

"Rose-colored glasses," she said softly.

"Exactly." He let out a long breath. "I never thought he'd fall for someone like her–someone superficial and spoiled–but it's obvious he sees something in her that I don't see."

"Have you talked to him about this? About how you feel?"

Shaking his head, he said, "No. If he specifically asked me, I'd tell him. But it's not my place to put down his fiancée. You know who would lose in that scenario? Me." He looked at her. "Just like you have with Bianca."

Well damn.

After that, there didn't seem to be anything else to say. He made his point and she didn't have it in her to argue and defend herself.

What exactly had she lost where Bianca was concerned? They were still friends. That wasn't going to change.

Only...it had.

If Chelsea really thought about it, she knew she shouldn't have been surprised her friend went to such drastic measures to exclude her from her wedding.

Although to be fair, everyone was excluded, not just her. That was something, right?

And maybe they didn't hang out as much as they used to, but that happens as you get older. They both had careers and other responsibilities. Plus, this wasn't the first time Bianca had pulled back because she had a boyfriend. That's happened since the seventh grade–it was the year she got boobs and enjoyed flaunting them.

It had taken Chelsea several years before she had anything to flaunt.

Self-consciously, she glanced down and realized it had been a long time since she even tried to flaunt "the girls."

Ugh...so not the time to be thinking about that...

Forcing her mind away from her boobs, she realized at some point she was going to have to get real with Drew and share why she felt the way she did. She had a feeling he would give her hell about it, but she was confident he'd understand why she was doing this.

It still seemed crazy that she was on this road trip with him. Of all the people in the world she ever imagined traveling with, Drew Russo wasn't at the bottom of the list; he wasn't even *on* the list.

She glanced over at him and felt a little guilty. Other than using some ridiculous delay tactics, he was a fairly decent traveling companion.

Well...when he wasn't speaking.

Getting to know him was frustrating, but it wasn't the worst thing in the world. And who knows, maybe by the time they were back home, they would have a new appreciation for each other.

If they didn't strangle each other first.

It was a little breezier out than she realized and she shivered. Drew turned to her as he straightened. "Come on, you're cold. We'll go back inside and grab something hot to drink. I know it's not Starbucks, and I'm sure they don't have your chai tea, but at least it will take the chill off."

That was kind of sweet.

"And I promise to stop at the first Starbucks we pass and treat you." They walked to the door and stepped back inside. "Deal?"

Chelsea couldn't help but smile. "Deal."

"Wow, there are a lot of things going on in Virginia Beach right now," Chelsea said a few hours later. They were back on the road and it was fairly uneventful.

"Oh yeah? Like what?"

"A music festival and a food and wine one. I'm having a hard time finding a room." She glanced at him. "Or did you book them already?"

He chuckled. "Why, whatever do you mean?"

"The ferry? Yeah, it was reservation only. So you clearly had a plan in place for us to miss all the flights and take this trip on the road."

"Guilty." But you know what? He was really okay with it. Everything worked out and they seemed to be on an even keel right now so...no harm, no foul, right? "And in answer to your question, yes, I have rooms booked for us already. But to be clear, I only got as far as today. Once we get to our destination, we're on our own."

"How come? I would have thought you had it all planned out."

He shrugged. "I had no idea how it was all going to go. For all we know, you may want to leave right away."

She frowned at him. "Why would I do that after driving all this way?"

"Really?"

With a long sigh, she said, "Okay, I see what you mean. If things go south fast, I'm going to want to get out of Dodge fast." She paused and then studied him. "But what about you?"

"What about me?"

"I realize you said we're in this together, but...you should know that I don't expect you to have to put up with me all the way home too. If things go poorly, then I'll take care of getting myself back."

"Chelsea, that's crazy."

"I don't think I'll be able to deal with all of the gloating and the 'I told you so,' so really, it's all about self-preservation."

Drew couldn't help but laugh. "I would totally show some self-control! Maybe just a few reminders that I told you so. Five or six tops. You can handle that, right?" He leaned over and nudged her with his shoulder as the car swerved.

"Eyes on the road!" she cried, but she was laughing with him. "You already have a hard time with directions. We don't need to add crashing to the mix. Although, that would certainly delay us more than anything."

"Hmm...tempting..."

"Drew! Don't even think of it!"

"Well, as much as I am trying to delay the inevitable, I love my car too much to sacrifice it. Believe me, you're safe."

"Good to know."

They slipped into companionable silence, and Drew began to really consider all the ways things could go down once they got to the resort and found Jimmy and Bianca. Because the truth was, he could only get them lost so much before she would either demand he get them there, or she'd ditch him and find her own way. The fact that the wedding was Monday wasn't helping. If they had the ceremony today or tomorrow–like normal people–he would have had no problem getting lost and finding delays so they'd simply miss the wedding. But Monday was pushing it.

He had a feeling Jimmy was going to be pissed at him no matter what he did. When he had asked him to essentially throw himself on the grenade, Drew was sure neither of them would have imagined things coming to this.

"Um...Drew?"

"Yeah?"

"Are we taking the Chesapeake Bay Bridge?"

"Yeah. Why?"

"Turn around," she said, and he could detect a slight tremor in her voice.

"What? Why?"

"I am terrified of bridges. I can't drive over them. Please. You have to turn around and find another way."

Glancing her way, he noticed she looked a little pale. "You're not driving, I am. And you didn't have a problem with the bridges we went over to get out of New York."

"Those are...my eyes were closed and...and I've been over them before."

Now she was breathing weird and starting to fan herself.

Neither of those were good signs, were they?

Reaching over, he gently placed his hand on her knee. "It's going to be okay. I promise. Just...put the seat back, close your eyes, and we'll be over it in no time."

"It's seventeen miles long, Drew!" she cried, swatting his hand away. "And there is nothing on either side of the bridge for miles. *Miles!* If anything happens, there's just water, and...and..."

She was spiraling and he quickly got off at the next exit and pulled into the first shopping center he came to so he could calm her down.

Although considering how worked up she was, he had no idea how to do that.

Shutting off the car, he twisted in his seat to face her. "Okay, first, you need to calm down."

"If we had just *flown*...if you had been true to your word..." She turned and glared at him. "I trusted you! I actually trusted you, you big jerk! And now I'm going to hyperventilate and die on the longest bridge in the world!" The laugh she let out was slightly maniacal. "So I guess you got your way! I won't be able to do anything to stop this wedding because I'll be dead!" She groaned. "You'll probably be able to just throw my body over the side of the bridge. No one will think to even look for me there."

"Chelsea..."

"I watch a lot of true crime documentaries! I know how the criminal mind works!"

"Wait...when did I become a criminal?" he demanded. "I'm just a guy trying to help a buddy out by making sure some crazy chick doesn't ruin his wedding!"

"Oh, so now I'm crazy!" she cried out.

"You've always been crazy!" he shouted. "This isn't new information!"

The good news was she stopped hyperventilating.

The bad news was she started to cry.

Dammit.

And not the soft, quiet sobbing kind. Nope. Chelsea was a wailer.

Awesome.

Doing his best to keep his voice soft and soothing, he reached out and placed his hand on her shoulder. "I think we need to focus on one thing at a time here," he began carefully. "If we turn around, it's going to take us three hours to get to a point where we can actually cross over to get back on I-95. And then another three hours to get back on track. Are you seriously suggesting we take a six-hour detour?"

Wait, why was he fighting this? Wasn't he just trying to come up with more ways to delay them?

Clearing his throat, he said, "But if that's what we need to do, then I'll cancel the rooms in Virginia Beach, and we'll just play it by ear and see how it goes. When we get too tired to be in the car anymore or are ready to stop for dinner, we'll just find a hotel then. What do you say?"

Her face was all red and splotchy when she looked up at him. Her mascara gave her a bit of a raccoon look, and she sniffled in a very unladylike way.

It was all he could do not to cringe.

"Six hours?" she asked weakly. "Seriously? How is that even possible?"

"You can pull up Google Maps and double-check, but I'm pretty sure that's what we're looking at."

Sure enough, she grabbed her phone and looked it up for herself, and he knew the instant she realized his math was right.

"And you know I'm bad with directions, so who knows how long it will take us," he teased, and thankfully, she smiled. "For all you know, we'll end up in West Virginia or Tennessee! I'm afraid to go west and get lost!"

Chelsea wiped at her eyes and face as she softly laughed. "You're insane. You know that, right?"

Drew motioned toward the glove compartment. "There are tissues in there if you want them."

"Thanks."

"I'm serious, Chels," he said. "I had no idea you were afraid of bridges, and if it gets you this upset, then we'll turn around and deal with the delay. It's not the end of the world, right?"

She nodded and he practically sagged with relief. As much as he didn't love the idea of adding six hours of driving to this already tedious day, it was all for the greater good. Wherever they ended up stopping for the night would be fine and he knew he'd sleep like the dead. Yawning, he almost wished they could stop for the day now.

The idea had merit.

"What if we stopped here for the night?"

"But...it's only like four in the afternoon. If you want, I can take over driving. We can change the route in the GPS and I can totally get us through this next leg. It would probably be a great distraction."

"You know there's going to be a bridge once we have to cross back over to get on I-95. I don't want you to freak out again."

She made a face at him. "Okay, so maybe I just drive for the next two hours and then pull over and you take the wheel again. What do you think?"

"I think with all the stopping and starting, we'll get to South Carolina by next Thursday," he said flatly.

"Ha, ha." She stuck her tongue out at him. "Can we take a bathroom break before we get back on the road?"

They were parked in front of a supermarket, so he figured now was as good a time as any. "Yeah, sure."

"Great. I'm going to grab some snacks, too. I could use some caffeine since we never did find that Starbucks you promised."

Damn. He had hoped she would have forgotten about that.

"Why don't you search for the nearest one and we'll stop there before we get back on the highway?"

Five minutes later, they were walking into the grocery store and toward the restrooms. Drew thought adding a Starbucks stop was a great stalling tactic.

Another stalling tactic.

The problem with all this stalling was...it was exhausting. Seriously exhausting. Any road trips Drew had ever gone on were either with his family when he was growing up or trips he took with his buddies. Both were filled with a lot of fun and games and laughter. So far this trip with Chelsea included none of those things.

Maybe it was time to change that...

They had six hours to fill thanks to this detour—although, really, the damn Chesapeake bridge was only seventeen miles long. How could she *not* be able to hold it together for twenty minutes? Thirty tops, if there was traffic.

"No," he murmured to himself. "This detour is a good thing."

After that, he made a quick run into the men's room, and when he came out, he found Chelsea at one of the self-checkouts. As he got closer, his eyes grew wide.

"Hey," she said, smiling.

"What the hell's all this?"

"Snacks."

"For how many people?"

She looked at him like he was crazy. "For us," she replied. "Why?"

"A six-pack of soda, a six-pack of water, grapes, trail mix, snack cakes, M&M's...are you sure you didn't miss anything?"

"Cookies! Oh, my gosh, how could I have forgotten the cookies? Quick, go grab some chocolate chip ones!" She gently shoved him and he nearly tripped over his own feet.

"Hey! Stop that!"

"Then go grab the cookies so I can do this all in one transaction. Hurry!"

Another shove and he walked away just because he was tired of having her hands on him.

Liar...

That thought completely stopped him in his tracks. Where the hell had it even come from? And why now? Chelsea wasn't being coy or flirting with him; if anything, she was an annoying mess who was solely responsible for ruining his weekend.

"Drew!" she called out. "The cookies are in aisle eight! Go!"

So he went and grabbed a package of chocolate chip cookies.

And some Oreos for himself.

When he walked back up to the self-checkout where she was waiting, she saw what he had and grinned.

"See? Now you'll have something you like to snack on too." She paid for everything and once they were back in the car, she got everything situated. They had a few things up front with them and the rest within reaching distance behind the seats. "I should have grabbed a small cooler or something, don't you think?"

"At the next stop," he said, knowing it would come in handy. "Now let's go get you some chai tea and me one of those caramel Frappuccinos. I love them. They're like crack."

Chelsea settled in the driver's seat and Drew in the passenger one. It felt weird to be a passenger in his own car, but he really needed a few hours not to be the one driving. But first things first...

"What are you doing?"

"Canceling our hotel rooms. No point in keeping them if we're not using them. Especially since you said there's a lot going on there this weekend."

"Oh, that makes sense."

He nodded.

"Ready?" she asked.

"As I'll ever be." He waited for her to start driving, but... she didn't. "Chels? You okay?"

"I think so."

"You think so?" he asked incredulously. "Now what's wrong?"

Her shoulders sagged but she didn't look at him. "I feel bad."

"Why?"

"I'm causing this trip to take forever." Then she did turn to look at him. "Although, you've certainly done your part in that department."

What could he possibly say to that?

"I guess I just hate how I'm this weirdo who can't handle something as simple as going over a bridge. How lame is that?"

Well...crap.

"You're not a weirdo, Chelsea. It's a legit phobia. There's a name for it, isn't there?"

She nodded. "Gephyrophobia."

"Wow. That's a mouthful."

She laughed softly. "Yeah, it is."

"So, what do you want to do?"

He found himself holding his breath while he waited for her answer, and for the life of him, he had no idea what she was going to say.

"I guess we detour and see where we end up."

"Sounds like a plan," he said right before he yawned. A nap was definitely in his future, and with any luck, his next turn behind the wheel would be a short one.

6

"Drew?"

Panic had Chelsea by the throat.

What the hell was I thinking? Why would I do this?

"Drew?" she asked with a little more force. The damn man had fallen asleep ten minutes after they left the Starbucks. She'd never seen anyone fall asleep so fast in her life. And apparently, he was a deep sleeper too.

She had driven for thirty minutes–berating herself the entire time–when she decided to be brave. Bold.

Stupid.

And turned the car around and drove straight toward the Chesapeake Bay Bridge.

Like an idiot.

"Drew!"

He started to stir and made a low humming sound that bordered on being a growl and was quite possibly the sexiest sound she'd ever heard.

Okay, now what the hell am I thinking?! Focus!

Reaching over, she slapped him on the chest and did her

best not to let her hand linger because damn, the man had some serious muscles.

Unfortunately, he simply shifted and rolled away from her.

"Son of a bitch," she hissed.

Her heart was racing, her throat felt dry, and any minute, she was going to throw up. She shouted his name and was relieved when he sat straight up.

"What? What's going on?" he barked.

"I'm going to be sick, but there's no place to pull over."

It took him a moment to get his bearings and when he realized where they were, he cursed. "What the hell are we doing approaching the bridge? We were going the other way! How the hell long was I asleep?"

"Long enough for me to make the worst decision of my life! Again!"

Drew looked around frantically and she knew exactly what he was seeing.

Cars.

Lots and lots of cars.

There was no way for her to stop without creating a dangerous situation for all the normal people just trying to get home or to wherever they're trying to go. She couldn't just stop the car and jump out! With her luck, she'd either get hit by a car or fall over the bridge when she went to lean over and vomit.

Either way, I'm screwed.

"What do I do?" she cried.

"How the hell should I know?" And yeah, he was pissed. Out of the corner of her eye, Chelsea saw him rake both his hands through his hair. "Why would you do this?"

"I thought you'd be happy! Now we don't have to lose six hours on a detour!"

"I was fine with the detour! Dealing with you driving while hysterical, not so much!"

"Okay, a little less snark would be really helpful right now!" she countered. "Talk to me!"

"I thought I was!"

"No, you're yelling! I need you to talk to me! Distract me! Tell me I'm not going to throw up all over your car or how I'm not going to die while driving over this ridiculously long bridge!"

"There's a tunnel too..."

"Seriously, Drew? What the hell? I'm trying to freak out less, not more! What is wrong with you?"

"Me? I'm not the one choosing the worst time humanly possible to try to conquer a phobia!" He muttered a rather colorful stream of curses before he seemed to calm down.

She was trembling and sweating and her heart was racing like mad. All Chelsea could do was hold onto the steering wheel in a death grip and do her best to remember to breathe.

"Can you just be a normal person for once and distract me?" she said, her voice growing more and more breathless with each word.

Raking a hand through his hair, he let out a long breath. "Okay," he began. "You're doing great." His voice was oddly soothing. "This is just a straight run and I want you to keep your focus straight ahead."

"Any chance we can switch places while the car's in motion?" she asked with a nervous laugh.

"Afraid not, Chels. But you're going to be fine. You've got this. We're already five minutes into it."

"We haven't gotten to the scary part yet, but I know it's coming."

"It's not as bad as you think it's going to be. Trust me."

"Ha! Says the man who's done nothing but lie to me since last night."

"I'm going to let that slide because I know how upset you are. But in my defense, I was doing it to protect a friend."

"And if I wasn't paralyzed by fear right now, I might think that was nice," she commented. After taking several deep breaths, some of the nausea subsided. "Okay, tell me about yourself."

"Seriously? We've known each other for over a year. What's there to tell?"

"Honestly, lots. I don't really know anything about you other than you being Jimmy's annoying friend who cocky and arrogant and is a pathological liar when it comes to protecting his friends."

She could feel the weight of his stare. "Wow, you managed to insult me on multiple levels in one sentence. That's a fine quality."

"Drew..."

"Okay, okay, okay," he said wearily. "So here's me–I'm thirty, born and raised on Long Island, I have two brothers, and I own my own company."

She tried to glance at him, but she couldn't. "What kind of company?"

"How can you not know? I talk about work all the time when we're out."

"And I usually tune you out because you have a tendency to be obnoxious," she explained. "And conceited, and sometimes just the sound of your voice irks me."

"Ouch."

"Sorry," she said quietly. "Your company?"

"Oh, right. I'm in cybersecurity."

"Cybersecurity? You mean like...software?"

"That's part of it. I get contracts to go into big corporations and work with their tech departments and train them on the most up-to-date programs and help them keep their files secure and how to identify any leaks or weaknesses in their systems."

"Wow, I'm kind of impressed."

"You don't sound it."

"Aww...does somebody need his ego stroked?" As soon as the words were out of her mouth, she was mortified. It sounded a lot dirtier than she intended. She was going to try to make light of it when she realized the tunnel was coming up. "Uh...Drew?"

"Yeah?"

"The tunnel's coming up."

"It's okay. You got this. You're doing great."

"Yeah, but...maybe there's a spot to turn off? Just a quick stop so we can switch places."

But he shook his head. "That's for authorized vehicles only."

"But this is an emergency! Certainly no one would stop us if I was sick!"

Drew reached over and placed one large hand on her knee. "You're not sick, Chelsea. You are doing this and you should be proud!"

"I hate underground tunnels as much as bridges," she murmured. "And I'm slightly claustrophobic..."

"No wonder you're still single..."

"*Hey!* That was uncalled for!"

He let out another weary sigh. "You're right. Sorry." Pausing, they both watched as the lanes narrowed down to two as they approached the tunnel.

"Ohmygod, ohmygod, ohmygod..."

"Deep breaths, you're going to be fine. This will be short. Traffic is flowing fine. We'll be through it in no time."

Unable to help herself, she slowed down. The speed limit was fifty-five, but she slowed down to almost half that. The walls felt like they were closing in on her, and all Chelsea could think of was all the water surrounding them. What if there was a breach in the walls? What if water started to leak in? They would be doomed! There was no way to...

"You know, the slower you drive, the longer we'll be down here," he said mildly, and Chelsea's foot pushed hard on the gas, sending him flying back against his seat. "Jeez! Be careful!"

"We need to get out of here! You said it yourself–the slower I drive, the longer we'll be down here and more of a chance of us dying!"

"I didn't exactly say that..."

"But it's true! Ohmygod, ohmygod, ohmygod..."

Up ahead, she could already see the light, and relief washed over her. They were going to survive. Once they were out of the tunnel and out on the bridge again, she felt like she could breathe.

"Thank God that's over."

"Why don't you tell me about you now?"

"You already know all about me."

"What? No, I don't."

"Oh, really?"

"Yeah."

"Well, according to Bianca, you guys talk about me *all the time*–saying things like how uptight I am, how boring I am, and I believe it was you who mentioned I just needed to get laid."

"*What?!*" he cried. "She told you that?"

"So you're not denying it?"

He looked ready to argue, but thankfully, he didn't. "I may have said that."

"And you wonder why I don't like you..."

"It's beginning to make some sense now..."

"Gee, what a relief."

"Okay, but again, in my defense, I was only going on what little I knew of you and what I observed. And you have to admit, you're usually...you know...kind of uptight. Just like you are now."

"Right now I'm terrified because I'm driving over a death bridge!"

"It's not a death bridge. Dramatic much? Sheesh."

Chelsea read the signs as they drove by and groaned. "Is there another tunnel coming up?"

"Um...maybe?"

"Why wouldn't you warn me?"

"Because the last time I warned you, you got pissed because I warned you!" he argued. "Man, there is no pleasing you!"

"Oh, my God...here we go again..."

"Just remember to keep going the speed limit and we'll be out in a minute."

"It will feel like an eternity."

"Like this entire trip has," he muttered.

"Hey, no one forced you to take this trip. It was all your idea. If you had just left me alone, you wouldn't be suffering right now."

"I promised Jimmy..."

"That you'd torture yourself so he wouldn't have to worry?"

"Something like that."

They were already halfway through the tunnel and she

was counting down the seconds until they were out. "After the tunnel, how much farther is it until we're back on regular roads?"

"Not far. I think just a few miles."

Nodding, she made a mental note to pull the car over at the first opportunity once they were off the bridge. Maybe she'd get sick, maybe she wouldn't, but there was no way she wanted to drive any more today.

Sunlight was streaming in and she was almost giddy. "Almost there..."

"If you slow down..."

"Nuh-uh. You told me not to slow down. You told me to keep doing the speed limit. We're almost out and almost done with this scary as shit bridge from hell with its stupid tunnels. There's no reason to slow down."

They were out of the tunnel and some of the tension eased from her shoulders.

"Yeah, but if you had slowed down, there was a rest area right at the exit of the tunnel. We could have stopped and switched places."

Now she did turn her head and glare at him. "And you just thought to mention that now?"

He shrugged. "I did try to tell you, but you wanted to argue."

"You know what? Just...stop talking! Every time you talk, bad things happen!"

"Hey, you were the one begging me to talk!"

"And now I'm the one begging you to shut up!"

Up ahead, she could see land. In just a few minutes, she could get out, breathe some fresh air, and put a little distance between her and Drew before she strangled him.

There were two lanes heading south once again and she

found herself picking up speed. Her heart rate was picking up because they were so close to being done and she was anxious for this part of the trip to be over. Once they were off the bridge, it was another mile before the first exit. She took it and pulled into the first rest area she could find–practically turning the car on two wheels. Slamming it into park, she whipped off her seatbelt and flung herself from the car.

And directly into Drew's arms.

It wasn't his intention to hold Chelsea; he was simply walking around to the driver's side.

She just happened to land in his arms.

It took all of three seconds for him to realize how hard she was shaking. Gently, he pulled her in close and carefully rubbed his hand up and down her back as he did his best to calm her down.

"You did it, Chels," he said softly. "You totally faced your fear and you made it across."

He felt her nod right before she started to cry.

Unsure of what exactly to do, Drew simply held her while she cried. It was weird, but...it was the first time he noticed how petite she was. Whenever they were out, she was in heels and somewhat dressed up, but today she was dressed casually and wearing sneakers and jeans. She fit perfectly against him with her head tucked beneath his chin, and holding her wasn't as bad as he thought it would be.

It actually felt kind of nice.

After several minutes, she seemed to calm down and pulled back a little. "I'm so sorry."

"You have nothing to apologize for," he promised. "We're good."

"God, you must hate me," she murmured, stepping out of his embrace. "All you wanted to do was help Jimmy and you got stuck with a woman with way too many issues." Turning toward him, she looked devastated. "You didn't deserve this. Any of this."

And damn if he suddenly didn't feel like shit for all the negative things he'd ever thought about her.

"Hey," he said softly, "come on. It hasn't been so bad. If anything, we'll have some funny stories to share with everyone next weekend, right?"

Unfortunately, that just seemed to make her cry again. Her face scrunched up as she turned away.

Berating himself, Drew walked over and placed his hands on her shoulders. "C'mon, Chelsea, don't cry. I was just trying to make a joke to lighten the mood. I didn't mean to upset you."

Then he realized how much he'd probably done that since they'd met.

According to Bianca, you guys talk about me all the time–saying things like how uptight I am, how boring I am, and I believe it was you who mentioned I just needed to get laid.

Hopefully that was the only conversation Bianca shared with her.

He stood there helplessly for several minutes before he attempted to lighten the mood. "What do you say we go find a hotel and just take the rest of the day off? I'll treat to dinner; you can pick the restaurant."

All she did was look over her shoulder and stare at him.

"The sky's the limit," he added with a grin. "Steak and

lobster? Done. Want to do *Grubhub* and have a whole smorgasbord of food delivered? That's cool too."

Her only response was to sniffle and blink.

"I'll book the most expensive hotel we can find and even book a massage for you if you'd like."

Because yeah, he was getting desperate.

Racking his brain for whatever else he could offer to make her feel better, he suddenly remembered something Bianca had shared with him about Chelsea.

Leaning in a little closer, he offered, "And I'm sure we get some double chocolate sundaes with marshmallow and hot fudge."

Drew noticed she swallowed hard before she spoke and he knew he finally piqued her interest.

"How...how did you know that's my favorite dessert?"

He shrugged. "It may have been mentioned before."

Wrong. Thing. To. Say.

"You mean while you and Bianca and everyone were talking about me? Was it to make fun of my dessert choice? Is it not exciting enough, like me?"

"Okay, wait...that's not what I'm saying at all. I didn't even imply that! I just happened to remember hearing how you loved that kind of sundae and I thought I'd throw it out there to give you something to look forward to!" He held his hands up in surrender. "Look, just tell me what it is I can do to help you feel better and I'll do it! Anything!"

The expression she gave him was mildly confused. He expected her to argue or to perhaps begin listing some outrageous demands, but all she did was shrug.

"Let's just go find a hotel. I feel like I need about ten hours of sleep."

Nodding, he led her back over to the passenger side of the car and helped her settle in. Then he went to the back seat and pulled out the bag of chocolate chip cookies and something for her to drink and handed them to her."

"Thank you," she said quietly.

As he walked around to the driver's side, he knew he needed to do some serious damage control. No wonder she was always on the defensive with him. He had a feeling Bianca was behind that–just another reason he didn't particularly like her–but he'd focus on that later. For tonight he needed to help Chelsea. She had gone and traumatized herself and he was solely to blame. If he hadn't thought it was a great idea to take her on this cockamamie road trip, she never would have placed herself in that position.

Fun and games and evil genius plans were over. From this point on, he was going to get them directly to South Carolina and face to face with Jimmy and Bianca.

And he'd deal with the fallout later.

Once he was settled behind the wheel, he asked, "You want to search for a hotel again or should we just wing it?"

"I didn't have much luck earlier, but I had limited my search for budget reasons. If we're not worrying about that..."

"We're not," he said firmly. "Find us rooms wherever you can and don't worry about the cost." Reaching into his pocket, he pulled out his wallet and handed Chelsea his American Express card. With a smile, he added, "I trust you."

And finally–finally!–she smiled. "I promise not to make you regret it."

It hit him at that moment how Chelsea had a great smile. Sure, her face was still red and splotchy, but it didn't change anything. Maybe it was time for them to start over–to get to know each other without any interference from their friends.

Because he had a feeling they were both going to find out they had been wrong about each other.

He knew he could admit that already.

Pulling back out onto the road and then the highway, Drew figured now was as good a time as any to start learning about her.

"So, what's it like narrating books? How did you get started doing it?"

She was staring down at the phone and scrolling through hotel choices as she shrugged. "You're not really interested in that, Drew, and it's okay. You don't have to make small talk with me."

"That's not why I'm asking. Earlier you asked about me, and we never got around to talking about you. And honestly, I am curious about what you do. I've never met an audiobook narrator before. Is that what you went to school for?"

Shaking her head, she replied, "No. I went for physical therapy."

"Wait, so you're a physical therapist too?"

"Yup. Only part-time. My cousin has his own clinic and I work there a couple of times a week. It depends on when I'm narrating. If I'm working from my home studio, my hours are flexible, but when the audio publisher wants me in their studio, I have to go with their schedule."

"Wow. I had no idea. So how did you end up doing this if you went to school for physical therapy?"

She glanced at him briefly before returning her attention to the phone. "It was kind of a fluke. Back in high school, I was in the drama club. Our director commented on how well I enunciate everything and how I should consider doing voice work when I graduate. I didn't think much of it, but the head of the drama department in college mentioned the same thing. She helped me make some recordings and I submitted them to several audio publishers." Another shrug. "I did some small parts–some children's books–and then I got picked to read for an educational publisher. It's a lot of textbooks–history, mostly. It's not overly exciting, but I'm making a living at it, so I can't complain."

"Do you want to narrate something other than history books?"

She sighed. "Sure, but it's a bit more competitive than I thought it would be. Most of the time, the author picks their narrator and then uses them for all of their books–it's nice for the reader...or listener...to associate a certain voice with their stories."

He nodded.

"I haven't been picked yet."

"If you could choose, what kind of books would you like to do?"

She was quiet for a moment. "Ooh...I found a one-bedroom suite at a fabulous, five-star hotel!"

"Book it."

"But...you don't even know how much..."

"Don't care. Book it."

"But it's only one bedroom..."

"Does it have a sleeper sofa?"

"Um...there's a couch, but I don't know if it's a sleeper."

"Doesn't matter, book it."

"Drew!" she said with a small laugh. "Let me see what else I can find!"

"I just don't want us to miss out on a room."

"I never should have made you cancel the ones you had," she said miserably. "I'm really sorry."

"Chelsea, no more apologies, okay? At the time, it was

the right thing to do. And as for this suite, I think you should just book it."

"But..."

"No buts," he interrupted. "Please book it."

"O-kay..."

A five-star hotel was much better than what he had originally booked for them back when it was all about making this trip as miserable as possible. But now that things were changing, he knew he wouldn't mind a little luxury for a night. And while it was mostly for Chelsea's benefit, he certainly wasn't going to complain.

"Are we booked?" he asked a few minutes later.

"Yup. Top floor king suite." She scrolled a little more. "They have three restaurants so I'm sure we won't even have to leave to go find something to eat."

"That sounds good to me. Maybe we'll order room service and just veg out tonight. What do you think?"

"Um...are you sure? Just the two of us?"

Laughing softly, he nodded. "Well yeah. It was going to be just the two of us even if we went to a restaurant."

"But at least there we'd have some distractions. I would have thought by now you'd be frantic to find other people to talk to."

Yeah, he was going to have to do something drastic to get her to change her opinion of him. And if room service and ice cream sundaes even began to make a dent, he'd be eternally grateful.

7

The hotel was gorgeous.

Their room was amazing.

And Chelsea felt like she couldn't enjoy any of it because she felt so damn stupid and guilty.

"Chels! Room service is here!" Drew called out.

She was in the bedroom with the door shut, trying to relax and fix herself up after her multiple breakdowns today. She shouldn't have mentioned the suite; she should have gone with two separate rooms so she could wallow in her own private pity-party without having Drew or anyone around.

"Holy crap, that's a lot of food," she heard him say.

Looking at her reflection in the mirror, she frowned. She had showered and dried her hair, but right now in her pajamas and robe without a stitch of makeup on, she began to second-guess every decision she ever made.

Especially the one that had her ordering room service so she could spend even more time alone with Drew.

"Like this is going to change his opinion of me," she murmured and forced herself to walk to the door.

Out in the main room, Chelsea found him looking out the window. She cleared her throat to alert him to her presence. He smiled and she felt an odd flutter in her belly.

Weird...

"Sorry I took so long," she said as she sat down on the sofa. The coffee table was covered with an assortment of food and drinks. "This all looks and smells amazing."

Nodding, Drew sat beside her. "Although I think eating is going to be a bit awkward like this."

It wasn't ideal, but she didn't think it would be a problem. "What if we sat on the floor? That might work better." And before she could second-guess herself, she slid down to the floor and crossed her legs, placed her napkin in her lap, and smiled up at him.

The expression on his face was priceless.

"You don't have to sit on the floor if you don't want to," she said, "but I am starving and ready to dig in."

Slowly, Drew came to the floor and eyed her weirdly.

"What? What's the matter?"

"I...I just thought you would have freaked out at the setup, that's all."

Laughing softly, she said, "Why? Because I'm so uptight?"

He groaned. "Don't tell me; let me guess...more words from Bianca?"

"And apparently from you."

Another groan. "I've got a proposition for you."

Pouring herself a glass of wine, she said, "I'm listening."

"Can we pretend like the last year never happened?"

Now it was her turn to eye him weirdly. "Why?"

"Because I think we are carrying a lot of baggage regarding how we feel about each other, and honestly, I'm beginning to realize I don't know you like I thought I did."

He paused. "And hopefully, you'll see that maybe you don't know me either."

Taking a sip of her wine, Chelsea considered his words and realized he had a point. So much of what she thought she knew about him wasn't quite right. Oh, he was still obnoxious and irked the crap out of her, but maybe without the influence of all their friends around them, they could discover something to actually *like* about each other.

"I think I like that plan," she said after a moment. Once he poured himself some wine, she held up her glass. "A toast."

Drew raised his glass and smiled at her.

"To new beginnings," she said, tapping her glass to his.

"To new beginnings," he agreed.

The wine was delicious, but her mouth was watering for everything else in front of her. They had decided to start with shrimp cocktails and she-crab soup. Both were magnificent, and they were enjoying the food so much that they didn't talk a lot. When they moved on to their entrees, Drew was the one who broke the silence.

"The crab cakes look amazing," he said.

Chelsea glanced over at his prime rib. "So does the steak."

"Want to share? Do a little modified surf and turf?"

"Absolutely!" They divvied up their dishes, and once she took her first bite, she let out a very unladylike groan. "Damn, that's good."

Drew nodded in agreement. "Hell yeah, it is." After taking a sip of his wine, he looked at her and smiled. "This is good."

She nodded. "Delicious."

He chuckled. "No, I mean this. Us. Sharing a meal. It's

good. And I'm glad you're someone who doesn't mind sharing."

Ah...that made sense. "I have no trouble sharing my dinner or even my road trip snacks. But I'm going to warn you now that I am *not* good at sharing dessert." Frowning, she glanced around the table. "We didn't order dessert?"

Laughing again, he said, "I asked them to wait an hour before delivering it. I had no idea how full we'd be or if we'd even still want dessert."

"There is always room for dessert." She took another bite of her dinner and hummed happily. "It makes Bianca crazy when I say that. She's forever reminding me how I should watch what I eat." Then she laughed. "And yet she's always eating off my plate! So stupid."

"Why doesn't she order her own food?"

"Seriously? Because she doesn't want anyone to know she actually eats." Shaking her head, she went on, "Have you ever noticed how she orders only salads but then will eat off of Jimmy's plate? She tries saying she just wants a taste, but by the time the meal is done, she's eaten a good portion of his. She does it to us girls when we go out too. We all laugh about it."

"That's insane! Why do you let her get away with it?" He paused and took a forkful of mashed potatoes and held it out to her. "You have to try these. I think they're the best mashed potatoes I've ever had."

Without thinking, she let him feed her and damn if he wasn't right. "Wow. So creamy! I should have asked if I could have them instead of the cauliflower caponata."

"Why? That looks great too!"

She held up a forkful for him to try and fed it to him.

Wow...this is getting intimate.

Pulling her fork back, she watched as Drew closed his eyes and hummed–which sounded insanely sensual.

And getting more intimate by the minute...

Chelsea cleared her throat and quickly grabbed her wine and took a long drink. "So, Drew, what's something you like to do in your free time?"

"Well, when we're not out on Friday nights with the herd..."

"Herd?"

He nodded. "I swear we're like this little herd–we all go out together and do everything together. It's a little odd."

"Why? Didn't you always go places with your friends in high school and college?"

"Yeah, but...not like this. It's like we're this core group and no outsiders are allowed to stay."

Now that he said it, he had a point. The few dates she'd had over the last year only managed to make it to one get together at O'Dwyer's, and her last boyfriend mentioned how he didn't feel welcome there at all.

"I can see by the look on your face that you know what I'm talking about." He took a sip of his wine. "I don't know if you remember, but I briefly dated a woman over the summer–Amy–and she specifically requested that we not go to O'Dwyer's after only going there once with me. Strange, right?"

"Um...not really. I just realized how my last boyfriend made the same request. He said he didn't feel welcomed at all."

"That's what Amy said too!"

"Wow. I guess there is something to it." She paused and took another bite of her meal. "Although, if it were up to Bianca, she'd have us all paired off so it would just be four couples and more..."

"Intimate?" he finished for her with a husky laugh.

"Exactly! Why is she always using that word? Why does everything have to be intimate?" She laughed and shook her head. "She makes me crazy, I swear."

"Can I ask you something?"

"Sure."

"Why are you friends with her?"

"We've been friends since the third grade," she explained, shrugging. "We just are."

Placing his fork down, Drew rested his arms on the table and studied her, his expression serious. "Chelsea, the two of you are complete opposites. What could you possibly have in common with her?"

And for some reason, she found that wildly offensive. "You mean because she's so fun and vivacious and I'm dull and boring?"

His dark eyes went wide. "No! I meant because you're an intelligent woman and she's fairly...you know...not."

"Drew..."

"I'm serious! She's kind of bitchy and controlling and... not to hurt your feelings, but...she doesn't speak very highly of you."

"What do you mean?"

"I mean when we first met, and I would say something nice about you, she would always say something negative. That's kind of why I formed the opinion of you that I did." He looked a bit regretful at the admission. "Although, to be fair, you certainly didn't help matters by always getting annoyed with me."

For a minute she didn't know what to say. Then she remembered Bianca doing the same thing to her where Drew was concerned. When she shared that, they both sat staring wide-eyed at each other.

"Holy shit," he murmured. "Do you know, when I first met you, I thought you were kind of hot. But Bianca said I didn't have a chance because you thought I was a...a...oh, what the hell did she call me? An unintelligent swine? I think that was it."

"Oh, my God! Are you kidding me? I once mentioned how I thought you were good-looking and she's the one who told me you were...a pig," she said, her cheeks turning red. "She said you only dated bimbos, and you thought I was too prudish to get a date."

The fact that he didn't correct her told her–in this instance–Bianca hadn't lied or exaggerated.

And for some reason, that bothered her.

They ate for the next few minutes in total silence. Chelsea finished her wine and poured herself a second glass–something she rarely did–but if ever there was a night that required a little more drinking, this was it.

"I know this probably won't change anything," he said, interrupting her thoughts. "But I'm sorry. I didn't know you and I made a decision based on someone else's words."

"Thanks."

"I really did used to be a bit of a pig." He rolled his eyes. "Although that's not quite how I would describe myself."

"You don't owe me an explanation, Drew."

He shifted beside her. "I know I don't, but I want to explain." Pushing his plate aside, he turned to fully face her. "Back in high school and college, I was a serial dater, and believe me, so was Jimmy. We were total frat boys, and I'm not proud of how we treated some of the girls we were with."

She sensed a but coming...

"But we're older now, and I'd like to think I've evolved... matured. Every once in a while, I slip back into that mode–

the obnoxious jerk who doesn't think before he speaks. I know it doesn't make it right, but..."

"I get it. Believe me." Then she realized that may have come off as bitchy and figured she owed it to Drew to be honest too. "I kind of hate how you've only seen me while we're out with the group. The rest of the week, I'm a different person, but for some reason whenever we're out–or I'm out with Bianca, Kendall, and Shauna–I tend to tense up."

"Why?"

"Why?! Look at them and then look at me! They're like these tall and beautiful and confident women. We've all been friends for years and I'm like the nerdy girl they keep around because they feel sorry for her."

His eyes went wide. "Chelsea, that's ridiculous. You're just as beautiful as they are! I honestly think you're *more* beautiful than any of them."

She was pretty sure her jaw was on the floor and when he started to stammer before reaching for his wine, she figured he hadn't meant to say what he did.

Or he simply didn't mean it.

Oh crap, oh crap, oh crap, oh crap...

Without thinking, Drew slammed back his glass of wine.

Sure, add alcohol. That ought to make you say less, you idiot!

"So...um..."

Chelsea reached over and placed her hand on top of his. Her skin felt warm and soft and...wait...he shouldn't be thinking things like that–especially not right now!

Damn wine.

"You...you think I'm beautiful?" she asked, her voice unusually quiet. Then she looked at him and took his breath away. "It's okay if you were just saying it to make me feel better. I know what I look like and trust me, I know I'm totally lacking compared to the three of them."

"You're wrong," he said, his own voice sounding gruffer than it normally did. "Do you know what I see when the four of you are out together?"

Silently, she shook her head.

"I see Bianca who tries way too hard to be seen. Nothing about her looks natural–like she's someone who spends hours in the bathroom watching makeup tutorials. Most of the time, she looks like a clown."

Chelsea smirked but didn't say a word.

"And Kendall and Shauna look like they're trying to do everything Bianca does, but not outdoing her," he went on. "The three of them are like...what was that movie...*Mean Girls*? Yeah, that's the one I'm thinking of. They're the girls that care more about how they look than anything else."

Her expression fell slightly and he reached for his glass and mentally cursed because it was empty.

"But you? You don't need all that stuff. You show up and you have a natural way about you that is way more attractive than anything your friends are doing."

"Drew..."

"It's true, Chels. I'm sitting right here next to you and I can see you don't have on a drop of makeup and you..." *Go big or go home...* "You're beautiful." When she started to look away, he reached out and cupped the side of her face. "They only wish they could look as good as you."

She lowered her eyes briefly before looking at him again. "I doubt that, but you're sweet to say it."

"Do you know why Bianca puts you down?" She started to look away again but he wouldn't let her. "She's putting you in your place–to make you feel small or doubt yourself–because it's the only way she can compete."

"Drew, you really don't know what you're talking about. Boys...well, guys...have always chased after her. She was the first girl in our grade back in middle school to have a boyfriend. And not just any boyfriend, the captain of the football team who was two years older. She dated a captain of one sort or another every year."

"That doesn't mean anything."

"And she was the head cheerleader, the homecoming queen, the prom queen..."

"People can be superficial," he said casually, his hand still caressing her cheek. "She probably developed boobs before everyone. That's why the guys wanted her."

"That explains middle school, but not later."

"Like I said, people–guys–are superficial. Most want to date a girl who looks good but doesn't have a whole lot to say."

"That's awful!"

He couldn't help but laugh at her indignation. "As much as I hate to quote Bianca, guys are pigs. Present company excluded."

"Just a few minutes ago, you admitted to being a pig."

"Used to be. Not anymore. I'm a reformed swine."

Her laugh was soft and feminine and...sexy. "Well, that's good to know."

Reluctantly, Drew lowered his hand and poured the rest of the wine between their two glasses. He was about to make more comparisons about her other two friends when there was a knock at the door. Slowly, he stood and stretched, almost thankful for the disruption. "Dessert," he said, looking down at her.

"Ooh...okay, let me clear some room. Or maybe we can see if they'll take some of these plates away."

Walking over to the door, he couldn't wait to see the look on her face when he showed her what he ordered for them. It took a few minutes for their dishes to be cleared away and he held their bag of dessert behind his back so she couldn't sneak a peek. Once it was just the two of them in the room again, he slowly made his way back over to the couch where she was sitting.

"So? What did we get?" she asked, trying to look behind him. "I don't remember seeing a dessert menu."

"There was one, but I wasn't overly impressed with their selection."

"Oh?"

He nodded. "So I placed a special order and the concierge took care of it."

"Ooh...I'm intrigued!" She was practically bouncing on the couch.

Sitting next to her, he placed the plain brown paper bag on the coffee table and motioned for her to open it.

"It's cold," she said, her smile growing. She pulled out the first container and let out a happy little sound. "Oh, my God! Is this a sundae?"

"It's not *Friendly's*–I know that's your favorite–but they don't have them here. So I had to ask for the best ice cream parlor in town and this was who the concierge recommended. I know it's not exactly the same..."

Before he got another word out, Chelsea was in his lap, in his arms, and hugging him.

"You have no idea how much this means to me," she said,

placing a loud smacking kiss on his cheek. She made no move to climb off of him and he certainly wasn't in a rush for her to go. "After I got out of the shower, I considered skipping dinner and hiding in the bedroom because I was just feeling so crappy. Now I'm glad I didn't." Another kiss on his cheek. "You have made this a totally great night." And yet another kiss.

Gently, he lifted her off his lap because...yeah...maybe he *was* a pig because any more of that and she was going to feel how much her nearness was affecting him.

"Dig in!" he said lightly. "Let's see how these sundaes measure up!"

Chelsea handed him his dessert and one of the spoons before she took the lid off of her own. Drew found himself holding his breath and praying he made the right choice.

"Oh...my...God," she moaned. "I think this may be better than *Friendly's*."

"Really?"

She nodded, licking her spoon.

Because clearly, she was trying to kill him.

Forcing himself to focus on his own dessert and not her, he opened his container and took a spoonful of ice cream.

And holy shit, it was amazing.

"I swear this is almost orgasmic," she said around another spoonful and Drew wasn't sure how much more he could take. Did she have any idea how sexy she was? Even sitting here in her soft robe and no makeup on and...he wondered what she had on under the robe...

No, Drew! No! Don't think about that!

But for good measure, he rested the ice cream on his crotch for a minute to try to calm things down.

"Don't you like yours?" she asked, frowning.

"What? No! It's great," he said quickly–maybe a little too quickly. "Brain freeze."

Of the little head, not the big one...

"I've got a bit of it myself, but this is too good to stop." She leaned back against the cushions and placed her feet up on the coffee table. That's when he saw her hot pink painted toes.

Cute feet, cute toes, cute robe...in another minute he was going to have to excuse himself. How had he never realized just how attractive she was? Well, he had in the beginning, but how could he have let Bianca or anyone change his mind? Why hadn't he tried harder to get to know her?

"What's your weakness, Drew?" she asked, scooping another spoonful of chocolate ice cream from the container.

"What?" he croaked.

"Foodwise. What's your food weakness?"

"Oh, uh...cake," he said, thankful she was only talking about food. "Although, if we're being honest, the icing is my favorite part."

She looked at him and grinned. "Mine too. I mean, cake is good, but the icing is better. Do you ever eat it right out of the can?"

Laughing, he said, "When I lived at home–you know, with my parents–I would. Although, my mom caught on and would just use extra icing on the cakes." He smiled at the memory. "And cupcakes were pretty much fifty percent icing."

"To me, that's the way a cupcake should be!" Another spoonful of ice cream. "There's a bakery in town that makes the best cupcakes. Sometimes I stop in there after a long narrating session and treat myself to one." She paused. "No, wait...I'm lying. The best cupcake I ever had was at Hershey Park. It was like triple chocolate and it was the size of a large muffin." She shook her spoon in his direction. "Now *that* was an orgasmic dessert for sure."

Groaning quietly, Drew wished she'd stop using the word orgasmic.

"You okay?" she asked.

"Yeah, why?"

"You just groaned. Brain freeze slowing you down?"

"Uh..."

"Power through, Drew! You can do it!"

Shoveling a large spoonful of ice cream into his mouth, he knew it was the safest way to keep him from saying something stupid.

Or seducing her.

Or...

Dammit! Brain freeze!

"Want to watch some TV?" Chelsea asked, scooting a little closer. "I know Saturday night television isn't particularly exciting, but maybe the hotel has Netflix and we can find something."

"Sure," he said, focusing on his dessert.

Chelsea stood and got the remote, and once she was back beside him–closer than she was before–she started channel surfing. "Oh, I love this show! I hate that it ended. I must have seen each episode like a dozen times, but they still make me laugh."

Drew looked up and saw she had stopped on a rerun of *The Big Bang Theory*. "I've watched this, but wasn't a huge fan."

"Want me to keep looking?"

Did he? "If you don't mind..."

"No biggie." Holding up the remote, she searched some more and stopped on an episode of *Outlander*.

"How about this? Have you ever watched it before?"

Nodding, Drew ate a little more of his ice cream. He'd

not only watched the show, he'd found–at times–he was incredibly turned on by the show.

"So, this is okay?" she prompted.

"I guess so."

Five minutes later, the main characters were having sex, and beside him, Chelsea let out a soft hum.

"I know it's not real, but...wow. These two always look like they're really doing it, don't you think?"

"Uh...yeah."

"I swear, this has got to be a bit exaggerated. I mean... people really don't do it like this, do they?"

Choking on his spoonful of ice cream, Drew coughed and sputtered for several moments. "What the hell, Chelsea?"

"What? I'm just saying, I've never been with a guy who was so...you know...enthusiastic! I get they have to make this a little over the top, but...I don't know...I was just wondering if maybe it's just me. That I'm the weirdo who's never had... enthusiastic sex."

Just keep eating...just keep eating...

She sighed. "Probably just me."

His spoon hit the bottom of the container and he panicked.

"And honestly, even in porn it's not like this. It's loud and frantic, but you can totally tell they're acting. At least on this show it looks believable–like they're really making love and we're just voyeurs taking it all in."

Oh, God...she can't possibly not realize how that sounds...

"The last guy I slept with," she said and then giggled, "I called him four and snore." Another laugh. "Literally, it was like four pumps and he was done and would fall asleep minutes later. Ugh...the worst."

Lifting the container to his mouth, Drew threw his head back and drank the last remnants just to have something to do.

"How do guys fall asleep so fast after sex? I mean, look at Jamie there on the screen. He's not going to fall asleep."

"Not all guys fall asleep right away after sex, Chelsea."

Turning to him, spoon in mouth, eyes wide, she said, "Are you sure?"

Change the subject! For the love of it, just change the subject!

Placing the empty container on the coffee table, Drew twisted and faced her. "I'm positive. I'm a guy and I don't fall asleep right after sex." He gave her a sexy grin. "Maybe after the second or third time, but definitely not after the first."

"Second or third? You mean..."

That's when he realized Chelsea's sex life was seriously lacking.

And he wanted to do something about it.

No matter how ill-advised it was.

Reaching out, he took the container from her hands and placed it on the coffee table next to his. Then he gently pulled the spoon from her mouth and put it with the remainder of her dessert.

"Drew..."

"Shh...there's something I need to know," he said gruffly before his hands cupped her face and he leaned in and kissed her.

8

*W*HY HAVE *I never kissed this man before?!*

Forget the ice cream or cupcake being orgasmic, kissing Drew was quickly approaching that status. His lips were both soft and firm at the same time–if that was even possible–and his tongue was...well, it certainly knew what it was doing, too.

Moving in closer, Chelsea's hands slowly moved up his muscular arms before gently scraping around his nape and up into his thick, dark hair. He smelled good, he felt good, and he kissed like...like nothing she'd ever experienced before.

Oh, God...what if it isn't that Drew is so good as...I'm just bad at this?

As if reading her mind, his lips left hers. She felt his warm breath against her cheek. "I can hear you thinking from here. If you want to stop..."

She never let him finish. Just as Drew's hand dropped from her cheeks, she reached up to cup his. "Don't stop," she whispered before pulling him back in for another kiss. It was hotter and wetter, and more sensual than the first.

Within minutes, he had pulled her into his lap. Her hands raked through his hair while his were rubbing a hypnotic pattern up and down her back with the occasional butt squeeze. His hands were magnificent and she wanted to feel them on her skin and not just over her robe.

Without breaking the kiss, she untied the belt at her waist and pushed the garment from her shoulders. Drew's hands immediately went to her bare legs and then around to grab her ass. She moaned into his mouth before he pulled back to look at her.

And that's when she remembered what she had on underneath.

Oh, no...

"Is that..."

Chelsea tried to close the distance between them and kiss him again, but he wasn't to be deterred. Wanting to die of embarrassment, she sighed. Leaning back, she let him get a good look at the hot pink nightshirt she was wearing.

With a giant cartoon chicken wearing a bikini and sunglasses that said, "Hot Chick."

Kill me now.

He looked up at her and then down at her shirt before he laughed softly. "Wow. I don't think I've ever..."

"You know what," she quickly interrupted, doing her best to climb off his lap with as much dignity as she could muster. "No one was supposed to see this. I was supposed to be alone in my own room and..."

She never got to finish. Drew hauled her back into his lap, his large hands on her hips, securing her to him.

"I think it's freaking adorable," he said, his voice low and seductive–like he wasn't referring to a chicken wearing a bikini. His gaze was hot and sexy. "I think you're pretty freaking adorable too."

"Really? Just adorable?"

Oh, God...why would I ask that?

"Actually, I think you're pretty damn hot, Chelsea, and I'd be lying if said I didn't want to see what you've got on under this shirt."

Maybe it was the wine, maybe it was the ice cream. All she knew was that her mind had drifted in a *very* dirty direction and she was powerless to try to change it. Feeling bolder than she ever had in her life, she crossed her arms in front of her and tugged the nightshirt up and over her head.

She saw Drew swallow hard as his eyes seemed to devour her. Her skin was both chilled and heated at the same time. Her nipples tightened and she felt more exposed than she ever had with a man.

"I love how the panties match the shirt," he said, one hand toying with the waistband. Right now, she wished she was wearing something sexier than hot pink cotton, but he didn't seem to mind.

"Drew..."

Looking up, his eyes met hers even as his fingers continued to tease her.

"Is this weird?" she said quietly. "I mean, earlier today we were fighting and making each other crazy."

The hand that wasn't tormenting her reached up and caressed her cheek. "I think we're still making each other crazy, just in a much more pleasurable way."

It should have sounded smarmy or cheesy, but it didn't because it was exactly how she was feeling. And it should have felt awkward that she was practically naked and sitting here engaging in conversation with him while he was fully dressed.

She opted to tackle one of those issues.

"You know what would be more pleasurable?" she asked.

Drew shook his head.

"If one of us wasn't quite so overdressed." The huskiness of her own voice was new and she kind of liked it.

His grin was all sex and heat–like the big bad wolf. "Well, if you think taking off your panties would make things more pleasurable, who am I to argue?"

"Drew!" Playfully smacking his shoulder, she laughed. "That's not what I meant and you know it."

Without a word, he pulled his t-shirt up and over his head and left Chelsea completely breathless. He was perfect. She knew he was fit, knew he was muscular–hell, she'd thought about it earlier today–but seeing him like this was even better than her imagination.

"Hey, Chels?" he whispered as his hands inched their way up to cup her breasts.

"Yes?" Her head lolled back as her eyes closed.

"Is this going where I think it's going? No pressure, and if this is all we do, I'm fine with it."

"But...?"

"But I'd like nothing more than to lay you down on the bed and kiss every inch of you." He paused and placed a soft kiss on the swell of one breast and then the other. "I mean, we can stretch out here on the couch, but..." Another kiss. "There's a king-size bed just a few steps away."

"Then why are we still here on the couch?"

"Hell if I know," he said as he stood with her in his arms, her legs locked around his waist.

This is my new favorite position...

Once they crossed the threshold into the bedroom, there was no going back. She knew it, and yet right now, she didn't care.

Maybe tomorrow they'd both regret this.

Or maybe tomorrow would be the start of something amazing.

Drew laid her down on the bed and immediately covered her body with his and dove in for an all-consuming kiss.

So maybe right *now* would be the start of something amazing.

Chelsea kept waiting for things to get awkward, but they didn't. Then she waited for him to rush her and make things go faster, but he didn't. And by the time she realized that making love with Drew wasn't like making love with any other man she had before, she was more relieved and turned on than she thought possible.

He shucked his jeans and socks and came back to kiss and touch her some more, and by the time he peeled her panties from her body, she thought for sure she would lose her mind.

Every touch was sensuous.

Every kiss was erotic.

And every movement of his body created friction that had her feeling like she was on fire.

"Naked," she finally said. "You really should be naked."

She never saw a man move as fast as Drew whipping his boxer briefs off.

"Wow," she said, laughing softly. "That was fast!"

"Not exactly the words a guy wants to hear when he's naked and vulnerable in bed with a woman..."

That just made Chelsea laugh harder. "Sorry. I was just impressed with how you managed to strip the boxers off without it looking awkward. If it were me and I had to be the one whipping my panties off, I'd be twisted around like a pretzel and rolling from side to side in the most unflattering positions before they came off and then I'd be breathless from the workout."

Way to be sexy, Chels...

"Anyway," she said with a small smile. "Your speed was impressive."

Grinning, he waggled his eyebrows at her. "Sweetheart, that's the last time you'll say that tonight because everything else will be slow and methodical and guaranteed to turn you inside out."

She could hardly wait.

Breathless, sweaty, and mind completely blown, Drew stared up at the ceiling and wondered how he was going to get up and walk to the living room to get something to drink. Chelsea had completely rocked his world and he felt almost too weak to move. Beside him, she was lying on her stomach, naked and smiling.

Maybe she has the energy to get up...

Waiting until his breathing was normal, Drew turned his head and studied her. "Hey," he said softly.

"Hey, yourself." She rolled onto her side and the sight of her had parts of his body perking back up. Leaning forward, she placed a kiss on his chest before sitting up and climbing from the bed. "I'm going to grab some water. Want some?"

A fantastic ass and a mind reader? What are the odds?

"Uh...yeah. Thanks!" While she was out of the room, he forced himself to move and fluff the pillows so he could sit up and lean against them. By the time Chelsea strolled back in, he was sitting up and had the sheet up over his lap.

Like some sort of prude.

There she was practically prancing around naked and

he couldn't handle lying on the bed without the sheet covering him? Inwardly groaning, he accepted the bottle of water from her and watched as she climbed back on the bed and under the sheet beside him.

But not too close.

Weird...

Silently, they both drank, and it was Chelsea who broke the silence.

"So...uh...that was new," she said with a nervous laugh.

Nodding, he said, "Yeah, but...not a bad thing, right?" Glancing at her, he could see the slight flush of her cheeks and then her smile.

Thank God!

"No, it wasn't a bad thing at all, Drew." Her voice was soft and a little husky. "I just hope this doesn't make things weird for us." She let out an unladylike snort. "Or should I say weirder."

That's when he knew he needed to get things straight between them. Twisting toward her, he reached for her hand. "We were starting over tonight, remember? The last year didn't happen."

"Then that makes me kind of slutty if I'm sleeping with you the night we met." And he knew she was only partly joking.

"Chelsea, you know what I'm saying. I think we can both agree that a lot of how we felt toward each other was because someone was feeding us some serious bullshit."

She nodded.

"Still, I'm having a hard time believing this just... happened. I don't ever do anything like this. Normally, I have to date a guy for a while–like at least four or five dates–before I consider sleeping with him."

"Okay, so then we can say we met before, but we're not

hanging onto our original feelings toward each other. How does that sound?"

"Like you're trying to make me feel less slutty. I thought guys loved slutty."

Don't answer! It's a trap!

Wrapping his arm around her, Drew pulled her in close and kissed her forehead. "You aren't slutty. You're perfect."

"Drew...you don't have to say that. I mean, I appreciate it, but...it's not necessary. We both know..."

He didn't let her finish. Silencing her with a kiss, he waited until she melted against him and hummed before pulling back. "No more of that. I may be many things, Chelsea, but I'm not a liar."

Laughing softly, she commented, "All the actions that got us here would suggest otherwise."

Carefully, he leaned over and placed his bottle of water on the bedside table before taking hers and doing the same. Then he maneuvered them until they were lying down. "Personally, I think it was all worth it." Then he kissed her again and kept kissing her until she was completely wrapped around him again.

So many things about her hit him at once–the softness of her skin and the strength of her legs, which were wrapped around him like a vice. She was extremely sensitive to his every touch and could be very vocal while making love. But the one thing that stood out the most to him was how she was so incredibly sexy and didn't even realize it.

Which might be the biggest turn-on of all.

He'd been with more than his fair share of women and most of them were beautiful and they knew it. They posed, they preened, they knew exactly what to say and do to get what they wanted from him.

Chelsea was different.

She rubbed against him and it was like hitting the launch button all over again.

And he was more than happy to comply.

"Can I ask you something?"

"Sure."

It was so late, almost two in the morning, and yet Drew didn't want to go to sleep. The entire night had been amazing and he found he really liked talking to her–way more than he thought he would and definitely more than he had in the last year.

And this had nothing to do with the sex.

Even though that was spectacular.

He loved the sound of her voice, especially right now when it was soft and a little sleepy.

"If you could narrate any book you wanted, what would it be?"

She hummed and rolled toward him. His arm was already around her, but now she snuggled closer to his side with her head on his shoulder. "I want to start narrating more fiction."

"Like...?"

"It doesn't matter," she said before yawning. "I'm very fortunate to be doing what I do already. If the opportunity came up to change, I'd do it."

"Come on, Chels, what kind of fiction?" he prompted, kissing her forehead.

"Romance. I would love to narrate some romances." She paused. "Preferably historical ones, but I read all romances. My Kindle is full of contemporary and historical ones, so if given the opportunity, those would be my first choices."

Was it crazy that he wanted to listen to her read something right now?

"Can I ask you something?" she asked, interrupting his thoughts.

"Of course."

"Do you really think I'm crazy for wanting to try to stop this wedding?"

Damn. It had been nice not talking about the reason they were on this trip, but he knew it couldn't be avoided forever, so...

"I don't know," he said quietly. "At first I did, but the more I tried to talk you out of it, the more I realized that you kind of have a point."

Chelsea lifted her head and looked at him. "Really?"

"Yeah."

"But...?"

After considering his words, Drew let out a long breath. "This has been a really great night and I don't want it to end with us arguing."

"We're not arguing..."

"But we will if we keep on this topic. Bianca's your best friend and Jimmy is mine. It's only natural that we'd defend them, and that means we're going to disagree. You're going to want to tell me why Jimmy's a bad person and not good enough for your friend, and I'm going to be doing the same about Bianca. Is that really what you want to talk about right now?"

She sighed and rested her head back on his shoulder. Drew played with her hair and prayed she understood.

"I guess you're right," she finally said. "But once we're in the car tomorrow, it's going to happen anyway."

"Then we'll wait until we're in the car. This room–this bed in particular–is a wedding-drama-free zone, okay?"

"Drew..."

"I'm serious, no wedding talk. This is our bed and we're not inviting anyone else to join us!"

Beside him, she giggled. "That sounded a little naughtier than I think you meant it to."

It was on the tip of his tongue to make a dirty joke, but he didn't. He couldn't. And for the first time since puberty hit, he didn't want to. Chelsea wasn't the kind of woman you did that sort of thing to. Plus, for all his wild ways, he never was into threesomes. Did he joke about it with the guys? Sure. The reality was, he was monogamous and enjoyed it.

Hugging Chelsea close, he placed another kiss on her forehead. "We need to get some sleep or we won't be out of here on time or get to South Carolina as scheduled." He yawned. "There's another seven hours of interstate between here and there."

"Ugh...why is it so far?"

He didn't answer because right now, it wasn't far enough. Tomorrow they'd get to the resort in Bluffton and things would get awkward–fast. He didn't want to think about it. For right now, all he wanted was to get some sleep and put off the inevitable.

Tucking his finger under her chin, he tilted her head up and kissed her properly. "Get some sleep."

"Mmm...okay."

Reaching over, he turned off the light and was asleep almost instantly.

The next time he woke up, the room was bright and he was hanging onto the edge of the mattress for dear life.

Chelsea was a serious bed hog.

Right now she was lying diagonally across the bed and all but shoving him off.

Carefully, he maneuvered himself to a sturdier spot, then reached over and gently caressed her back. She hummed adorably before rolling over and instantly wrapping herself around him.

Clearly, Chelsea only had two sleeping positions–get the hell away from me or boa constrictor.

She began kissing his chest.

I guess the boa constrictor has its perks...

One hand anchored into her hair as he glanced over at the clock. It was only seven-thirty, so they had plenty of time before they had to check out. And really, who didn't enjoy morning sex? All his attention beyond that moment was on Chelsea.

Kissing her.

Touching her.

Making love to her.

It was slow and lazy and oh-so-good.

The next time he looked at the clock it was after eight and he felt like he needed another couple of hours of sleep.

"Can we order breakfast?" she asked sleepily.

"Only if we can order it telepathically. I don't think any of my limbs work anymore." He lay motionless, eyes closed. "But if you can do it–and I am seriously conflicted on whether or not it will hurt my feelings if you can get up and make the call–I wouldn't say no to some bacon and eggs and a gallon of coffee."

Chelsea laughed softly, placing a kiss on his cheek before rolling off the bed. It was the second time in the last eight hours that she had been the one to get out of bed first. And the sight of her walking around naked was just as spectacular this morning as it was last night.

A guy could get used to this...

She walked out of the room without seeming the least

bit shy about her nakedness, and a minute later, he heard her ordering breakfast. Part of him felt bad about not doing it for her, but he was too deep in orgasmic bliss to really care.

"Thirty minutes," she said, waltzing back into the room and going over to her suitcase. "I'm going to go grab a shower."

That perked him up.

"A shower, huh?"

Nodding, Chelsea walked with an armload of her things across the room. "Yup."

Shower sex was always fun...and they did have thirty minutes...

Kicking the sheet off, Drew stood and stretched.

"What are you doing?" she asked.

Walking over to her, he held her gaze. "It would really be wrong to waste the water," he explained. "Two of us showering at once would be the responsible thing to do."

Her smile was slow and knowing. "You think so?"

"Yeah, I do." When they were toe to toe, he reached up and cupped her face in his hands. "I promise to wash your back if you wash mine."

"Well...far be it from me to be irresponsible," she said sassily. "Plus, I'm a sucker for a good, hard...back scrubbing."

They nearly tripped over each other in their haste to get into the bathroom and into the shower.

But thirty minutes later, Drew opened the door for room service with a very satisfied look on his face.

9

“What are you reading?”

Chelsea glanced up from her Kindle and looked at Drew like he was crazy. “Why?”

He shrugged. “Just curious.” They’d been on the road for over two hours and she thought he’d be tired of talking with her. So far today they’d covered places they’ve traveled to, favorite foods, concerts they’d seen, and favorite movies.

Right now, she wished he was tired of talking with her.

She was exhausted and her throat was a little sore from all the talking.

And her body was a little sore from all the sex.

All. The. Sex.

Holy crap. She never knew sex could be so...exciting, arousing, fun, exhausting...the list of adjectives was endless, and more than anything, she was blown away by it all. The fact that Drew wanted her was more than a little shocking.

And how much she wanted him in return, even more so.

Normally, Chelsea, Bianca, Kendall, and Shauna would get together once a week and share this kind of exciting news, but there was no way she was going to tell them about her night with Drew. She wasn't ashamed of it, but for some reason, it just felt like it was more private–like she didn't want anyone knowing the intimate details of their night because it was special.

Probably only special to her, but...she'd worry about that later.

"You fall asleep over there?" he teased. "Come on. Fess up. What are you reading?"

Groaning, she leaned back in her seat. "It's a rom-com by one of my go-to authors."

"Oh yeah? What's it about?"

"Drew..."

"No, come on! Just tell me. I'm tired of listening to music. Read to me."

Her eyes nearly fell right out of her head. "Are you high? I'm not reading to you!"

"Do you have one of your books on there–one that you've narrated–that we can listen to then?"

Sighing loudly, she argued, "No, I don't, and even if I did, I wouldn't play it for you."

"Why?"

"Because they're mostly history books! Listening to one of those puts us at risk of you falling asleep at the wheel and killing us. I know you don't want me getting to the wedding, but that's a bit of a dramatic way to stop me, don't you think?"

He laughed even as he shook his head. "You want to know why I really want you to read to me?"

"I don't know. Do I?"

Turning his head slightly, he grinned at her before putting his attention fully back on the road. "I like the sound of your voice."

That was...surprising. "Really?"

"Yeah. Really. Why? You know you have a great voice. That's why you're a narrator."

Chelsea had to admit it was one thing for people to say that of her in her professional career, but it was the first time anyone said it to her on a personal level.

"Wow."

"Humor me. Just read me a little something. We're going to be at a good place to stop for lunch soon. There's a Cracker Barrel coming up in Rocky Mount. I figured we'd stop there for lunch if it works for you."

She was a little hungry, so...

"Yeah, that sounds great."

"So it's only a few more miles up the road. Read me a little of what you're reading to pass the time."

"You're not going to let this go, are you?" It wasn't really a question.

"Nope."

Groaning, Chelsea scanned the page. "I really only just started it."

"Doesn't matter."

Chuckling, she shook her head. "You're not going to believe this, but it's about a couple of strangers on a road trip."

He laughed with her. "Stop! You're making that up."

"Why would I lie?"

"I don't know! Don't you think it's weird that we're on a road trip and don't know each other all that well and you're reading a book on the same topic?" He paused. "Wait, is this one of those thrillers where one of them kills the other and takes off with the car?"

"What? No! That's insane!"

"Whew! Just checking."

"I told you it's a rom-com."

"Ah...like a chick-flick, except in a book. Got it."

"Do I really need to read this? Aren't we there yet?" She looked up and saw the Cracker Barrel was five miles away and mentally cursed.

"I'm waiting..."

"Fine," she grumbled and then reached for her bottle of water and took a long sip.

Then she cleared her throat and made a big production out of putting the water bottle back in the cupholder.

"Chelsea?"

"Hmm?"

"Quit stalling."

"Ugh...you are the worst."

All he did was laugh.

Looking down at the screen, she let out a long breath and began.

There was a flash of lightning, and the rain was really coming down, and at this point, Finn knew he would be smart to grab a car and then find a hotel and start driving first thing in the morning. With a sigh, he sat back and stared out the window until they pulled into the rental car parking lot.

"Holy crap! Did you see that?"

Finn looked out the front window toward the building and saw...wait...what was he seeing? "What the hell is that?"

The driver laughed awkwardly. "Looks like a bride–or at least, someone in a wedding gown."

And sure enough, that was what they were seeing. Whoever they were, they fell getting out of the car and were now in a heap of white satin on the pavement. Finn quickly climbed from the car–thanked his driver–and immediately ran over to help her.

At her side, he held out a hand to her and noticed the guy who was with her coming around to do the same. "Hey, are you okay?" Finn asked, noting the dirty gown and the curses flying out of the woman's mouth. He pulled her to her feet and held on until she was steady. The rain was pouring down on them both and he did his best to guide them up onto the sidewalk and through the doors of the rental office.

She was a little breathless and pointed toward the car she'd just vacated. "My bag," she said, shaking her hand. "My bag is still in the back seat!"

"No problem," he said, hoping to calm her. "I'm sure your husband will bring it in."

Pushing him aside, she walked back out the door and slapped a hand on the trunk of the car as it was about to pull away. Finn watched with mild curiosity as she opened the back door and grabbed her bag before slamming the door shut again.

Okay, not her husband, he thought.

Because he had manners, he moved to open the door for her. "Thanks," she muttered, shaking the rain off herself–and onto him. He wanted to be mad, he seriously did, but what would be the point?

"So...wait...they both show up at the car rental place at the same time?" he asked.

"Uh-huh."

"Why is she in a wedding dress?"

"Runaway bride. Found out her fiancé–well, ex-fiancé–not only cheated on her, but also knocked up his assistant."

"Wow! Okay, go on."

So she did.

With a shrug, he walked over to the agent at the counter and did his best to smile. "Hey...Carl," he began, reading the agent's name tag. "I would like to rent a car."

The agent smiled but it didn't quite meet his eyes. "Then

you've come to the right place!" he said in a semi-flat tone. Finn would bet good money this was an exchange that was had all day, every day at a car rental office.

Beside him, the bride stepped up and said the same thing to her agent–an older woman named Tammy. He looked over and gave her a small smile and wasn't surprised when she didn't give him one back. Any bride trying to rent a car while still in her wedding gown couldn't possibly be having a good day.

Finn handed over his license and credit card and waited. Carl was typing, Tammy was typing, and there was no other sound in the place. Finn looked around and saw the place was a little run-down, and there weren't any cars in the parking lot.

That's when he started to worry.

The cars could be around the back, couldn't they?

"Um..."

"Oh, uh..."

Both agents spoke at the same time as they glanced nervously at each other. "Is there a problem?" he and the angry bride asked at the same time.

"Well, it looks like," Carl began.

"There seems to be," Tammy started.

"Oh, for the love of it!" the angry bride snapped. "What's the problem?"

Finn had to hand it to her; she was pretty fierce, even he stiffened up at her tone. Deciding that one of them should be respectful, he looked at the agents and smiled. "Is there a problem?" he asked.

"We only have one vehicle available," Carl said.

"Oh, well...okay." This didn't seem to be a problem for him since he got here first. "I'll take it."

"Wait, wait, wait," the angry bride said, moving closer to him. "Why do you get it? We got here at the same time."

"Actually...we didn't," he corrected. "I got to the counter first, and that was after I held the door for you to come back in."

If looks could kill, he'd be a dead man for sure.

"Look, um...I know this is a bad situation," he reasoned, "but it can't be helped. It's been a really bad day and I need this car."

"Oh, really?" she asked sarcastically, motioning to her ruined gown. "And do I look like someone whose day has gone well?"

"Uh..."

"Because it hasn't!" she cried. "If we're going to get into some sort of contest over whose day was worse, believe me, buddy, I'd win!"

He was beginning to see that.

Beside her, Drew laughed. "Man, I can totally picture this in my head as you're reading it! I can see it being in a movie for sure!"

"I can too," she agreed, smiling, and more than a little relieved they were getting off the exit for lunch.

"Promise me something."

"Sure."

"When we get back on the road, you'll read some more–and hopefully there will be some sexy parts."

"I'm not reading the sexy parts out loud."

"Consider it practice."

"What?!" she cried. "Practice?"

"Yeah, you know, for when you audition for doing more than narrating textbooks. If you can read the sexy parts in front of me, you should have no problem reading them for a microphone."

"I already don't have a problem reading for a microphone," she said wearily. "Why are you like this?"

"You mean helpful?"

"I mean crazy! We have the radio! There's even talk radio! Why do I have to read a book to you?"

"I already explained that," he said patiently. "It's your voice. I love it." His mouth snapped shut as he suddenly seemed to realize what he said and possibly feared how she might take it.

Rather than draw attention to his comment, Chelsea did the only thing she could–changed the topic to food. "I've never eaten at a Cracker Barrel before. I hope they have fried chicken!"

After lunch, Chelsea took over the driving.

Actually, she had insisted on it.

Part of Drew thought it was simply a way to get out of reading to him. He didn't understand what the big deal was. It was something she did for a living–something she was comfortable with–so why was it such a big deal to read for him? Rather than argue, he took advantage of the break and napped briefly. He seriously thought he'd sleep longer considering how little they had slept last night, but he kind of hated missing out on this time alone with her. Once they hit South Carolina and got to Bluffton, it was going to be a fiasco.

He just knew it.

And on some level, he knew Chelsea knew it too.

His phone chimed with an incoming text and he considered ignoring it. No doubt it was going to be Jimmy, and he didn't want to get into the whole situation via text with Chelsea sitting beside him.

Another chime.

Although, if he didn't respond, Jimmy would call and then what would he do? With a small groan, he pulled out his phone and read the message.

Jimmy: Dude, what's going on? You've been radio silent. Did everything go okay with Chelsea?

Glancing to the left, Drew prayed she wouldn't ask who he was talking to.

Drew: Yeah, Kendall spilled but everything's fine.

Jimmy: Seriously? She didn't freak out?

Drew: I didn't say that

Jimmy: So what the hell are you saying?

But before he could respond, Jimmy was typing again.

Jimmy: I'm calling now

Drew: Don't! Can't talk! I'm in the car with her right now!

Jimmy: WHAT? WHY?

Drew: Long story, but basically she was going to fly down and I offered to go with her. You know, to try to defuse the situation

Jimmy: So you're flying? You just said you're in the car

Drew: I managed to make us miss our flight so we're driving down

Jimmy: WTF, Drew! You were supposed to keep this from happening! You promised!

Groaning, he scrubbed a hand over his face and tried to

figure out what to say. At this point, nothing was going to be easily conveyed via text.

"Everything okay?" she asked.

"What? Oh, um...yeah."

"It's Jimmy, isn't it?" Again, not a question.

"How did you know?"

"You were typing pretty furiously over there. I'm surprised he hasn't reached out to you sooner."

"Yeah, me too," he replied miserably.

Drew: What did you think I was going to do? Lock her in a closet until Tuesday? I'm doing the best I can!

Jimmy: Well your best sucks and so do you

"Oh for fuck's sake," he murmured. Then glanced at Chelsea. "Sorry."

"Nothing to apologize for. I'm just sorry you're in the middle of this. If you had just let me be..."

"Yeah, yeah, yeah...that ship has sailed and I wouldn't be here if I didn't want to be."

She snorted and he didn't take it as a good sigh.

"What? What was the snort about?"

"Drew, you're here because Jimmy told you to be." She shook her head. "Don't try to pretend it's anything else. He told you to babysit, and you did."

And for some reason, that logic pissed him off. "It was my choice."

"Not really. Like I said, he told you to..."

"I don't do everything Jimmy tells me to!" he argued. "And I kind of resent you implying that."

"I wasn't implying. I was stating a fact."

"You don't know what you're talking about! That's not

the way things are. I have never..." He was cut off by the sound of a text coming in.

"Better get that and see what Jimmy has to say," she said sweetly.

So many comebacks were on the tip of his tongue, but just as it had minutes ago, more incoming texts were practically blowing up his phone.

Jimmy: So where are you?

Jimmy: And just so you know, Bianca's crying

Jimmy: Thanks for ruining our wedding

Jimmy: Seriously? You're not even going to respond?

Jimmy: Answer me!

Part of him wanted to prove Chelsea wrong and not answer the text, but...that would be a little petty, and right now, he really wanted to answer the text.

Drew: We're in North Carolina. Just went through Fayetteville

Jimmy: Shit. So like three hours away

Drew: I guess

Jimmy: Can't you stall? Break down? Take the wheel and turn the car around?

Drew: Okay, can you just relax? Chelsea and I have been talking and this isn't going to be as bad as you think.

Jimmy: Says you

Drew: Yeah, says me. When have I ever lied to you?

Jimmy: When you said you were going to

keep her away and now are driving her directly to us

Drew: She would have been there sooner if it weren't for me

Jimmy: Yeah, you're a hero

Drew: WTF, man?

"You're angry typing again. Why don't you just call him?" Chelsea suggested.

"Because I'm not going to get into it with him with you sitting right here," he snapped and went back to texting.

Drew: If you had manned up – or better yet, if your damn girlfriend had done the decent thing and talked to her friend rather than sneaking off like a damn baby – none of this would have happened!

Jimmy didn't respond right away, and for some reason, that made Drew nervous.

Ding!

Jimmy: Say that to my face when you get here and I'll show you how I can man up

Great. Just freaking great.

With a snort of disgust, he turned his phone off and tossed it on the floor.

"Trouble in paradise?"

If they weren't in a car doing seventy on the interstate, Drew would have punched something–not Chelsea, but definitely something.

"Thanks to you, not only are we walking into an openly hostile situation, but I'm going to have a throwdown with my best friend."

"And you're afraid you're going to lose?"

Slowly he twisted in his seat until he was facing her. "Excuse me?"

"I mean, Jimmy's definitely bigger than you. Bulkier too. I bet he could seriously kick your ass."

"He is not bigger or stronger than me!" he countered angrily. "I can bench way more than he can. He's gotten soft from all his girly weekends with Bianca. Trust me, I was feeling bad because I didn't want to have to mess him up before his wedding."

She snorted quietly, but he heard it.

"It's the truth!" he yelled. "I may not think this wedding is a good idea either, but I'm not looking to ruin it!"

"Trust me, you won't."

It seemed like a perfectly innocent comment to make, but...

"What's that supposed to mean?"

"I'm sure if they tell the photographer to be careful about taking pictures of Jimmy's hands, they should be fine."

"You seriously believe he'd win in a fight with me? Is that what you're saying?"

She shrugged and made some little noncommittal sound.

Seething, he needed to get out of the car and just...he needed a few minutes. "Get off at the next exit."

"Why?"

"Just do it!"

"Okay, okay...sheesh. If you need to use the bathroom, just say it. No need to freak out."

"I don't have to use..." He stopped himself. "That's not why, dammit! Just get off at the next exit and find a place for us to switch places."

"Oh, no," she countered, shaking her head. "No way.

You are not getting behind the wheel while you're all freaked out. Did you learn nothing yesterday?"

"Yesterday?"

"Yeah, when I was driving while freaking out? Was that enjoyable for you as the passenger?"

"No, but..."

"Then there's no way I'm switching places with you. Maybe when you calm down I'll think about it..."

"Think about it? It's my damn car!"

"But I'm the one driving."

"Chelsea!"

"Drew!" She mimicked his tone and that just pissed him off even more.

Raking his hands through his hair, he growled with frustration. "I wanted to get out and just work off some of this aggravation! Maybe walk around a bit! Is that too much to ask?"

"As a matter of fact, it is," she replied primly.

"Excuse me?"

Nodding, she explained, "You're being completely unreasonable right now. For all I know, we'll pull over and I'll go use the restroom, and you'll leave me there! Then what the hell would I do, huh? You've essentially kidnapped me, and then I get dumped on the side of the road somewhere in the backwoods of North Carolina? Um...no thank you."

"Kidnapped you?" he cried with disbelief. "Kidnapped you? How the hell did we end up there?"

"You lured me into your car under false pretenses, took me to multiple–and incorrect–destinations, and..."

"Hey, you're free to leave at any time," he snapped. "No one's holding you against your will. As a matter of fact, you were free to walk away at any time! You could have gone into the airport when we were there, but you didn't."

Ha! Think about that, missy!

"Oh, really?"

"Yeah, really."

"And you would have just let me go and not tried to stop me?"

Dammit.

"Okay, fine. I would have tried to stop you. But never at any point have I told you that you couldn't leave. And, may I remind you, you didn't seem to mind staying with me last night! Last night you were more than happy to be with me!"

All over me...whatever...

Gasping, she glared at him. "I cannot believe you're throwing that back at me! How dare you!"

"Yeah, well...you know I'm right, Chelsea. And you know what?"

"What?" she snapped.

In that moment, Drew knew he wasn't really mad at her. Well...he sort of was, but he was more pissed off at himself. She was right; Jimmy always was trying to tell him what to do, and he never seemed to appreciate all the shit Drew did for him. This entire situation had gotten out of hand, but he had no idea what to do to reel it in.

His entire body relaxed slightly. "I don't regret a thing about last night," he said after a minute. "It was an amazing night and I was having a great time with you all day until Jimmy interrupted." Letting out a long breath, he leaned back in his seat so he was facing forward again. "I'm sorry, Chels. This whole situation is just crazy."

She didn't respond right away and he thought she was going to keep arguing with him, but when she did respond, she surprised him.

"Can I let you in on a little secret?"

"Sure."

Glancing at him, she had a small grin on her face. "I've been having fun, too."

"Really?"

She nodded. "Yeah. Really."

He relaxed a little more.

"And you want to know something else?"

"What?"

"Now that they know, I kind of want to stop someplace else for the night and make them wait. You know, prolong their misery since they're both too chicken to do their own dirty work."

And right then and there, he fell a little in love with Chelsea Cooper.

10

"This is naughty. Very, very naughty."

"Mmm...but so good, right?"

Humming with pleasure, Chelsea closed her eyes. "I never knew...I didn't know..."

"Stick with me, Chels. I know what I'm doing."

She had to agree.

If this trip lasted much longer, she didn't know if... "Hey! Did you take the last strawberry?" she demanded. They were watching the sunset while having dessert for dinner on the beach at The Isle of Palms. Barefoot, toes in the sand, and enjoying decadent treats they picked up while strolling through town, and the rat bastard ate the last glazed strawberry. "I was saving that!"

Beside her, he chuckled and handed her the half of the strawberry he hadn't eaten yet.

Actually, he fed it to her.

"Next time, call dibs." His voice was low and gruff and so damn sexy that she was practically in a puddle on the damn blanket.

It was quite the one-eighty from earlier today. After

their argument, Chelsea had driven for another hour before they changed places. It was then that they decided to do as she suggested and take a detour for the night.

And turned off their phones.

Chelsea wasn't normally a mean person, but so much about her relationship with Bianca hit her–the way it was seriously unbalanced and how little her friend must think of her to pull a stunt like this. Granted, she knew there was kind of a good reason for Bianca opting to run away and elope–namely, Chelsea's open aversion to the whole thing–but maybe she wasn't the only one opposed to it?

They had basically grown up together and she knew Bianca's whole family very well. On more than one occasion, she remembered Bianca's father not being impressed with the things Jimmy did. Or maybe she was remembering it wrong for her own purpose. There was no way she was going to turn her phone on and call them and open that dialogue.

Sometimes ignorance was bliss.

And this situation was far from blissful.

Well, not the current situation she and Drew were in. That was pretty damn awesome.

"You have to try this salted caramel cheesecake," he said, holding up a forkful for her. Turning her head to him, she opened her mouth and let him feed her. The flavor burst in her mouth as the creaminess of the cheesecake melted on her tongue. Unable to help it, she moaned, and beside her, Drew chuckled softly. "Right? I'm not usually one for salted caramel, but that was...what was the phrase you used last night?"

"Orgasmic," she said, licking her lips. "I'm not sure that was orgasm-worthy, but it was pretty darn close."

She felt him move closer, his breath warm against her ear. "Are you looking for more orgasms?"

Hmm...that was a loaded question...

Smiling, her head fell back slightly. "That depends."

"On?"

"Are we talking public orgasms or private ones?"

Drew's tongue teased the shell of her ear before he answered. "I think I can give you both."

Oh, my...

"Both, huh? Someone's ego certainly doesn't need stroking," she said, sounding breathless to her own ears.

"All men need their egos stroked." Another swipe of his tongue. "Among other things."

And God help her, she wanted to stroke all the other things.

"How fast can we load up this food and be back at the hotel?" Chelsea was practically panting by now, and public orgasm be damned. She wanted them all, and she wanted them privately.

Drew placed a finger on her lips, and with her eyes still closed, she opened her mouth and sucked.

Chocolate icing.

Lots and lots of chocolate icing.

Maybe I do have time for a public orgasm...

He began kissing her neck as she sucked the chocolate from his finger. It was all a little heady, a little weird, and when Drew gently bit her throat, she was thankful for the mouthful of chocolate because she certainly would have cried out, and everyone within a mile of the beach would have heard her.

When she felt herself relaxing, Drew slowly pulled his finger from her mouth and placed a soft kiss on her cheek.

"We can be back at the hotel in ten minutes." Chelsea went to get to her feet, but he stopped her. She turned and looked at him questioningly. "Once we're back in the room, we'll see what other desserts we can use to make you come again."

Desserts were quickly rewrapped and tossed into the bag, and there was probably a pound of sand in their blanket, but neither seemed to care in their haste to go. Fortunately, their hotel was right here on the beach so they really just needed to walk back up the sand and over the long wooden walkway that led to the hotel property.

Chelsea found she was giggling like crazy and her laughter was contagious because Drew was laughing too–like they were sneaking off and afraid of getting caught.

Which...they kind of were, but no one was going to catch them.

Walking across the lobby, they made it to the elevator before Drew hauled her in close. "The things I want to do to you," he whispered in her ear, causing her to shiver with delight.

"The things I want you to do to me," she replied as the elevator doors opened. Luckily no one was inside and they had the space all to themselves–and hopefully all the way to the top floor.

All four stories of it.

She wanted Drew to kiss her, touch her, but there was something incredibly exciting about him keeping just enough distance between them that was also oddly arousing. Anticipation was building, and when the elevator doors opened on the fourth floor, he took her by the hand and led her to their room–a trail of sand flowing behind them from their blanket.

Once they were in the room with the door closed, everything dropped to the floor–the blanket, the bag of desserts, and Chelsea's bra.

Although how Drew got that off of her so quickly, she wasn't quite so sure...

Lifting her, she wrapped her legs around his waist and let out a small cry when her back hit the wall. His gaze was hot and so damn sexy, and all Chelsea could think of was how she thought last night was a fluke–that it was just going to be a one-night thing. But looking at him now, she knew that wasn't possible. One night would have never been enough. Hell, two nights probably won't be either. They may annoy the crap out of each other most of the time, but clearly it was working for them.

He didn't kiss her yet, though. He was studying her until she started to squirm.

"Drew?"

She saw him swallow hard. "You make me crazy, Chelsea."

And she couldn't help but grin. "Funny, I was just thinking the same thing."

"One minute I want to strangle you, and the next, all I want is to get you alone and have my way with you."

She blushed. "I'm more than okay with that."

"Yeah?"

Nodding, she said, "Yeah."

But still he didn't kiss her. "I feel a little guilty though."

"Drew," she whined. "We promised not to talk about Jimmy and Bianca again..."

One finger came up and covered her lips. "Not about that. I'm talking about how I've treated you in the past. How stupid I was for not taking the time to really get to know you."

Wow...that was incredibly...depressing.

Honestly, the last thing she wanted to think about right now was their history and former dislike of each other.

"Right now, Drew, I'd really like you to get to know how much frosting you can lick off of me before I beg you to make love to me."

Then she mentally crossed her fingers and prayed he would take the change of subject and run with it.

The searing kiss he gave her told her what she needed to know.

Mission accomplished.

Their room was large and as he carried her across it to get to the bed, he tripped on the corner of the area rug, banged into the coffee table, and Chelsea's foot knocked the lamp off the nightstand, but neither seemed to care.

On the bed, she whipped her shirt off while Drew kicked off his sneakers. She shimmied out of her jeans while his shirt went flying.

"Grab the cake," she said breathlessly. "I'm definitely going to want more of that icing." Then she winked at him. "You should try some too."

He leaned down and gave her another thorough kiss. "Baby, I already planned on licking it off of you." With a wink of his own, he turned and ran across the room–without tripping this time–and grabbed the bag of desserts from over by the door. Chelsea was down to her panties and breathless with anticipation as she watched him place the bag on the bed before his jeans and boxers came off.

Yeah, this was way better than driving straight through to Bluffton. Right now, Jimmy and Bianca could be getting married and she wouldn't care at all. They might be making a mistake, but at this moment, Chelsea knew what she and Drew were about to do was the best decision in the world.

Possibly in the history of the world.

"I should warn you," she said, hoping she sounded serious. "I'm extremely ticklish."

Drew loomed over her. "And you should know that I promise to be extremely gentle."

"Oh. Okay, then."

His tongue ran from her belly button up around her nipple and onward to the shell of her ear. "And thorough."

One of them might not survive this.

But what a way to go.

"I'm regretting not having dinner."

"We did have dinner, but it was cake and sugary goodness."

"Yeah, but now it's almost midnight and I'm starving." And as if on cue, Drew's stomach rumbled from hunger.

"Maybe we can do *Grubhub* or *Uber Eats* or something. Although we still have snacks in the car..."

"Oh, God. No more cake." Groaning for dramatic effect, he rolled toward her. "I'll get my phone and see what's available at this hour." And this time, he was the one to climb from the bed naked and walk across the room to get his phone. When he turned around and walked back toward the bed, Chelsea was resting on her side watching him.

And smiling.

He took that as a good sign, that she liked what she was seeing.

And maybe he sucked in his gut a little and flexed his muscles.

"There aren't a lot of options at this hour, but we can definitely get some burgers from places that are more like pubs than fast food." He looked up at her. "Is that okay with you?"

She sat up, holding the sheet over her breasts. "Definitely. You pick the place and order any variety of bacon cheeseburger and fries, and I'll be happy."

"A girl after my own heart," he laughed as he sat back down on the bed, tapping out their order. "Drinks?"

"As much as I want to say milkshake, I think I'll be fine using the soda machine down the hall."

"Yeah, me too." He finished the order and placed his phone back down on the nightstand and maneuvered himself so he was lying back beside her. "Thirty minutes."

"Sounds about right." She stretched, and it was so tempting to pull the sheet down so he could see her properly, but it was probably smarter for them to put some clothes on. Last night's room had a separate bedroom with a door; this room was just one big open space. As if reading his mind, Chelsea stood and walked over to her suitcase. "The driver will just have to deal with me being in pajamas." She pulled something from her bag and held it close when she turned around to face him again. "Or do you have to meet them down in the lobby? I thought that's the way some hotels do it."

"Honestly, I didn't even think about it. Let me call down to the front desk and ask." Sitting back up, he used the hotel phone to call down. He heard Chelsea go into the bathroom and thought it was cute how she was suddenly modest. He had licked and tasted every inch of her, and the images of her writhing on the bed were permanently burned into his brain.

"Front desk. How can I help you?"

"Yes, this is Drew Russo up in room 415. We just ordered food that's going to be delivered. Do we need to meet them down in the lobby or will you let them come up to the room?"

"You'll need to meet them down in the lobby, sir."

"Oh, uh...great. Thanks." He hung up and groaned. Going down to the lobby required more of an effort for him to get fully dressed again. Just as he was resigning himself to it, Chelsea walked out of the bathroom.

"Do you need to go to the lobby?" she asked.

"What is that on your shirt?"

"What?"

"That's a different nightshirt from last night, isn't it?"

"Um...yeah."

"Why?"

After walking around and picking up the clothes they had discarded of hers earlier, she turned to face him. "Because hotel beds are just...I don't know...icky. I refuse to wear the same pajamas twice after sleeping in one of these beds."

"Well, you really didn't wear last night's one to bed. It only made it as far as the living room."

"Yeah, but then it spent the night on the hotel room floor." She shuddered. "There was no way I was putting that back on."

"But what if we're here for another couple of nights? Then what?"

She shrugged. "I guess then I'll have to keep sleeping naked. Will that be a problem?"

"Not for me," he said with a lecherous eyebrow waggle.

Best motivation to drag out this trip ever.

Tonight's nightshirt had a cartoon moose wearing a bathrobe and slippers with the phrase "I need a mooseage" under it. It took him a minute to get the pun, but then he chuckled. "That's funny."

"Yeah, I kind of have a thing for quirky pjs," she said with a small laugh. "I know it's ridiculous, but..."

Standing, he walked over and wrapped his arms around her. "It's not ridiculous at all. It's cute. And I never would have pegged you for wearing something like this."

"You mean you thought I wore flannel, grandma pajamas?"

"I wouldn't say grandma..."

With a playful shove, Chelsea stepped out of his arms and walked over to the door. After picking up her purse, she walked back over and pulled out a couple of dollar bills. "For the vending machine. If you can grab a soda and some water, that would be awesome." Then she looked him up and down. "But you should probably put some pants on first."

"You mean I can't just walk down to the lobby like this?" He feigned indignation. "Just what kind of place is this that a guy can't walk around naked to go pick up his food?"

Chelsea put her purse down on the coffee table before coming back over to him and patting his shoulder. "The normal kind. The question is, what kind of places do you normally stay at where they do allow it?"

He snorted. "Please, I would never stay at a place that allowed that."

"Right..."

"It's true!"

"Sure, because you would hate strutting around showing off your body," she said sarcastically. "And you would definitely hate seeing women walking around doing the same."

Without answering right away, he scooped his boxers off

the floor and slid them back on before doing the same with his jeans. "Have you ever gone to a nude beach?"

"No! Why would you even ask that?"

Her outrage was adorable.

So was her blush.

"Because if you had, you would know that most people who go to the nude beach should *not* go to a nude beach."

"You mean..."

He nodded. "Yes. The nude beach is not filled with supermodels and bodybuilders. So I can pretty much guarantee any place that allowed you to walk around buck naked would not be filled with guests who *should* be walking around naked."

"Ah. Gotcha." She walked closer and placed her hand on his chest. "Well, just for the record, you could walk around naked and no one would be offended by it. You've got a great body."

Wow...he felt...holy crap...

Oh, God...am I blushing?

"Then I think you should know that you would make the perfect naked companion for me. I think a lot of guys would love to see you walking around like that."

"Stop," she said with a small laugh. "No one wants to see me naked."

"I do," he argued. "I just saw you naked five minutes ago and I can't wait to see you that way again." He paused. "Hell, if it were up to me, we'd eat naked!"

"Oh, no. That's not something I'm going to do." This time her laugh was a little more of the nervous variety. "I was hoping we could eat out on the balcony. There's a little bistro set out there and we could listen to the sound of the waves and look at the stars." She stopped and shook her head. "Sorry. You probably don't want to do that. I mean, we're just..." Without another word, Chelsea turned and walked over to the sliding glass doors and looked out.

Walking up behind her, Drew wrapped his arms around her waist and rested his chin on the top of her head. She fit perfectly against him like that. "We're just what?"

She shrugged but didn't answer.

If he had to guess, Drew would say she was probably going to say they were just messing around. He was sure it must feel that way to her. It wasn't like they had talked about feelings, and when they weren't in bed together giving each other mind-blowing orgasms, they tended to be fighting.

But that didn't have to mean this wasn't something more, did it?

"I'd like to sit out on the balcony with you," he said softly, moving to rest his cheek against hers. "I think that sounds great."

She twisted slightly and looked at him. "Are you sure? I know you said you'd rather we eat naked..."

"I was just being a guy, Chels. And believe it or not, I like your idea better."

"Really?"

He nodded. "I wish we had wine like we did last night. Even though we're just eating pub food, it would have been nice to sit outside and eat and have a nice glass of merlot or something." He kissed her cheek. "Let's plan that for tomorrow night when we're in Bluffton. What do you say?"

Her smile was so sweet and so beautiful. "I think I like that plan very much."

They stayed like that staring down at the beach and listening to the waves crashing until he got the text that their delivery was on its way. He kissed her cheek one more time before stepping away and throwing his shirt and sneakers back on.

"I'll be right back!" he called out on his way out the door.

In the elevator, something hit him–he felt good. Happy. Really happy. Although to be fair, he was normally a happy person, but this felt different. He was having fun with Chelsea on this trip–way more fun than he had anticipated and it wasn't all sex-related.

But it was certainly a perk.

It was hard not to think about what was going to happen tomorrow though. Right now they were sort of in this bubble where it was just the two of them and it was like an adventure. Tomorrow it was all going to hit the fan, and for the life of him, he had no idea how it was going to play out.

When Jimmy had called him Thursday night and asked him to essentially do whatever he could to keep Chelsea away from the situation, he never imagined things going like this.

Not even close.

It was still weird to think about all the time they'd spent hanging out together and talking to each other for a damn year without ever getting to really know each other. He learned more about her in the last two days than he had all year!

That was sad, right?

And part of the reason was that he listened to Jimmy. And Bianca. And pretty much everyone else for far too long. Very rarely had he formed any opinions on his own that his friends hadn't influenced, and that was beyond eye-opening.

It was also infuriating.

The thing that pissed him off the most was how he

thought he was beyond all of that. Back when they were younger and growing up together, it was one thing to let your friends' opinions influence the people you liked and hung out with. But at his age, it was just embarrassing. How many other people had he blown off who he could have had a decent relationship with? And not just women, but other guys he could have hung out with?

And Chelsea had seen it and figured it out just from their weekly get-togethers. She had managed to look beyond the surface and see something that he hadn't. And what had he done? He'd just written her off as being a bitch without even trying to figure out why or if that was truly who she was.

Just thinking about the things he'd said about her to Bianca–the things Chelsea had found out about–filled him with disgust.

And regret.

He needed to make it up to her–to show her that he wasn't that guy. Drew knew he wasn't perfect, and on some levels, he was always going to be a little immature and say stupid things, but he didn't want them to be about her. He had a feeling she dealt with that sort of behavior a lot from their group of friends and he wasn't going to let that happen anymore–not while he was around.

So yeah, that was going to make their confrontation with Jimmy and Bianca even more awkward than it was already going to be.

The elevator opened in the lobby and he met the delivery guy and thanked him before immediately turning around and getting back on the elevator. The entire trip down and back took less than five minutes and yet he felt like he'd had a life-changing revelation on it.

He only prayed that it was a revelation he was going to actually learn something from.

Up on their floor, he stopped at the vending machine and grabbed two sodas and two bottles of water before going back to the room. When he stepped inside, the room was dimly lit and there was no sign of Chelsea.

"Chels?"

"Out here!"

Walking across the room, he stepped out onto the balcony and found her sitting at the little bistro table with her feet up on the railing. She had put her robe on over her nightshirt, her head was thrown back and her eyes were closed. Even in the moonlight, he could see she was smiling.

"I love this," she said softly. "I love listening to the sound of the waves."

Placing the bag of food on the table, he sat down beside her. "Maybe we can sleep with these doors open so you can hear it all night. Plus, we might be able to catch the sunrise in the morning."

Lazily, she turned her head, opened her eyes, and looked at him. "You don't think it will be too cold?"

"I promise to keep you warm."

"Damn, where was this guy for the last year?' she teased, but there was no malice in her tone.

"That's what I'm trying to figure out too," he admitted.

11

"I THINK I'm going to be sick."

"I told you not to eat that second chocolate croissant."

"It's not because of that."

"Or to wash it down with a Yoo-Hoo."

"Please. Those things are delicious, and again, it's not breakfast that's making me sick," Chelsea said wearily. And Drew knew exactly what she was talking about and was just trying to make light of the situation.

Bless him.

They had left Charleston a little before ten this morning. It was only a two-hour drive to Bluffton and they had been driving for a little over ninety minutes already. The closer they got to their destination, the worse she felt.

And with the way things had been going between her and Drew, she didn't want to ruin it by vomiting all over his car.

There would be no way to recover from that level of disgusting embarrassment.

"Do you need me to pull over?"

It was on the tip of her tongue to tell him she wanted

him to turn the car around and to simply forget about going to Bluffton all together. Coming here had been a mistake. There was no way she was going to win or accomplish anything other than pissing off Bianca and potentially ruining their friendship, but...

Drew reached over without taking his eyes off the road and took her hand in his. "Whatever you need to do, Chels, we'll do it."

"What if I said I wanted to go back to the beach?" she asked carefully.

"Then I'd say we'll get off at the next exit."

Huh. She thought for sure he'd try to talk her out of it.

"What if I said I changed my mind and I want to go home?" Carefully, she glanced his way.

"Then I'd say okay, but let's find a few different places to stop on the way back and we're skipping the Chesapeake Bay Bridge."

Wow. Again, not the response she was expecting.

"What if I said I was in the mood for waffles for lunch?" And this time, she fought a grin.

"Hmm...to that I would have to say not a chance."

"Seriously? You're okay with turning around and driving all the way home but you draw the line at waffles? That makes no sense!"

He squeezed her hand. "One has us continuing our adventure; the other has all kinds of consequences that would require my car having to be professionally cleaned."

"I didn't mean I'd really get sick. It was just nerves."

"Yeah, I'm not willing to take that chance."

"Drew..."

"Chelsea..." he mimicked. "Look, what is it you want me to say here?"

"I don't know." And now she was pouting.

"It seems to me the closer we get that you're having second thoughts about this whole thing."

"I am."

"Okay, then. We can always turn around," he explained. "Or we can go and wish them well and possibly stay and be part of the wedding. Or at least be there to offer our congratulations."

That was true, but...did she want to? Would it be too hard to hold her tongue if she had to actually watch them say their vows?

"Honestly, Drew, I don't know what I want to do. I feel like such an idiot for making us drive all the way here and then turning around."

"You're not an idiot, Chelsea. You're worried about your friend and fear she's making a mistake." He paused. "If you ask me, you're brave."

"Um...what?"

Drew nodded. "It's true. I've been struggling with the whole thing–even just the dating thing. When Jimmy announced that he was proposing, I wanted to say something, but all the guys were congratulating him and I thought it was just me who felt the way I did." He sighed. "Then I was too afraid to say anything and piss Jimmy off and...you know...ruin the friendship."

"What bothers you about it? Them," she quickly corrected.

Releasing her hand, he put both of his on the steering wheel. "I know it's petty, especially since we pretty much learned this weekend not to judge a book by its cover, but... it's her. It's Bianca." His grip on the steering wheel tightened and she could tell he was tensing up.

"Maybe you just..."

"No. I've tried. Believe me, I've tried. I've gone and

hung out with just the two of them, I've done work for her salon, and no matter what the situation or where we are, she's just..." He growled. "She's the worst! She dresses like Malibu Barbie and tries to come off as being all sweet, but if you don't fawn all over her, she completely shifts gears and turns into Bitch Barbie."

"Okay, I don't think that's a real Barbie..."

"Chels, please. You know what I'm saying. She's one of those plastic, shallow people, and at the end of the day, she only cares about herself."

Wow. Part of her really wanted to defend Bianca, but... she couldn't.

"At first, I thought Jimmy was a nice guy," she began quietly. "I mean, he was friendly, polite, and...I don't know... after a couple of times of hanging out, I noticed how he's kind of crude, kind of loud, and just nothing like the kind of guy I imagined Bianca being with–let alone marrying."

Beside her, Drew chuckled. "Jimmy's definitely crude, but it doesn't make him a bad guy."

She groaned because it was time to come clean. He deserved to know the truth before they went and ambushed their friends.

"I have to tell you something," she said solemnly.

He looked at her oddly. "Sure. What's up?"

"It's about..." She let out a long sigh. "It's about Jimmy and...how I really feel about him."

Chelsea's side slammed into the car door as Drew cut across three lanes of traffic and off the exit ramp. He pulled into a gas station parking lot and threw the car into park before he faced her. "If you're going to tell me that you've got a thing for Jimmy and this weekend was about some sort of...of...I don't know...weird way of getting him to notice you, I will freak the fuck out!"

"What?! *No!* That's *not* what I was going to say!"

"Did you sleep with me because of Jimmy?" he asked through clenched teeth.

Part of her wanted to laugh at how this had escalated so quickly, but she didn't think Drew would find the humor in it. "Okay, first of all, relax. What happened between us this weekend had absolutely nothing to do with Jimmy. Trust me."

"Then what the hell are you talking about?" he demanded.

"If you'd shut up for five seconds, maybe I could explain!" Gah! She hated when she had to shout. "As much as I'm not a fan of Jimmy's personality, I don't totally hate him," she admitted. "It's not only that I don't think he isn't right for Bianca...I don't think she's right for him. I think she will slowly wear him down and just...I don't know...I see how he already kowtows to her. That's not what she needs."

Drew let out a mirthless laugh. "Does she know that?"

"Definitely not. I think right now he's bending over backwards to please her, but she's going to suck the life right out of him..."

Another laugh. "You said suck him."

Reaching out, she punched him in the arm. "And that's one of the reasons I never enjoyed hanging out with the two of you! Your crude and juvenile comments are not always appreciated!"

"You're right; that was crude. Sorry." But he was smirking so she knew he wasn't really sorry and she chose to ignore that fact.

"I think Jimmy is an amazing businessman. I recommend him to a lot of people because I've seen the quality of his work. But I'm telling you, Bianca's going to start making demands on his time. She's going to want them to buy a house and have all the upgrades known to man. Jimmy's going to be working just to support her. It's not going to be fair to him."

Drew was frowning and he didn't say anything for a solid minute.

"Wait," he finally said. "You're genuinely concerned for him, aren't you?"

"That's what I've been trying to say!" she cried. "Haven't you been listening at all?"

"Um..."

"Look, I could be totally wrong here. Maybe things go on between the two of them when no one else is around that we don't know about."

"God, I hope that's true..."

"Drew!" she whined. "Can you please be serious?"

"I was! I am!"

"Okay, whatever." She waved him off. "Maybe I'm not seeing the big picture right now, but what I *do* know and what I *do* see is just...this can only end badly. And when it does, she is going to take him for everything he has."

"Again, why are you even friends with her? I don't get it!"

"It doesn't matter. We've known each other forever, so..."

"So...what? It's habit? That's not the way a friendship works." He paused, shaking his head with disgust. "She doesn't respect you, and it seems to me like you don't really like her, so why not just walk away?"

"You know what, it doesn't matter. Let's just go."

"Go? Home? To Bluffton? Where are we going, Chels?"

"Where do you think we should go? I mean, am I going to just end up making a fool out of myself if we go to see them?"

"This isn't about me," he said, sounding completely reasonable. "We've already established that I'm not confrontational where Jimmy is concerned. You're the bold one in this relationship."

She rolled her eyes. "Drew..."

"It's true! You think it's easy for me to sit here and admit that you're bolder and braver than I am? And just to be clear...only in this situation, okay? In any other part of my life, I am a freaking rock star! A superhero! Just...not this one."

And for some reason, that made her laugh.

Hard.

Until tears were streaming down her face.

Drew cleared his throat. "It wasn't *that* funny..."

Waving her hand in front of him, Chelsea did her best to catch her breath. "I'm sorry! I know it's not, but I suddenly had this mental image of myself in like a Super-Girl costume with the flowing red cape and I was protecting you from Jimmy and Bianca!" More laughing. "I swear I don't know why, but it just popped up and made me laugh!"

"Yeah, ha-ha, very funny. Drew's a wuss. Great."

She heard the hurt in his voice and it almost instantly sobered her. Reaching out, she took one of his hands in hers. "You know what this means, don't you?"

"Yeah, that I'm one step away from needing to curl up with one of my grandmother's afghans with a pint of chocolate chip ice cream while watching some sappy chick flick like *The Notebook*." He hung his head and shook it.

Oh, for the love of it...

"Oh my God! Will you stop!"

"Why? We both know it's true."

"Actually, we don't. And while you paint a very vivid

picture, I was going to say that we need to go to Bluffton. I need to do this and let the chips fall where they may."

He instantly straightened, his dark eyes going wide. "Really?"

"Unfortunately."

"Chelsea, if you don't want to...no one's going to know but me." He put her hand on his chest and held it there. "No one will ever know. I promise."

"That means a lot to me," she replied softly. "But...this is something I have to do. I've been in the background long enough."

"What exactly does that mean?"

And with a weary sigh, she knew they weren't driving away just yet.

For some reason, Drew had to know the answer.

Had to know why someone like Chelsea was friends with someone who clearly didn't value their friendship. But the longer they sat there in silence, the more he wondered if it was something she really wanted to share.

"It's okay if you don't want to tell me," he said when he couldn't take the silence any longer. "I didn't mean to push."

"You're not," she said sadly. "But...you're probably going to think much differently about me by the time I'm done."

"I seriously doubt that."

The look she gave him was both sad and challenging. "Remember you said that."

All he could do was nod.

"Bianca has always been the outgoing one, while I was

always more reserved and quieter. I'm not shy–not really. I enjoy meeting new people and being sociable, but I tend to be more of a people-watcher."

There wasn't anything for him to say, so he waited for her to continue.

"As I've said, Bianca and I have been friends since the third grade, but we didn't meet Kendall and Shauna until middle school. The three of them became cheerleaders while I joined the drama club. I was kind of relieved that they still wanted to be friends with me; after all, they were part of the popular crowd and I wasn't. It intimidated me to be invited to the parties they went to, but Bianca always insisted I go."

Drew had his own theories on why, but he kept them to himself.

"By high school, we started to drift apart–I began to pull away because we didn't have anything in common, but in typical Bianca fashion, she would cry and tell me how I was her best friend, and I'd feel bad and cave. She'd come to all my plays and everyone would make a big fuss over her when she'd show up at the cast parties."

"Probably because she enjoyed the attention."

So much for keeping my theories to myself...

She laughed softly. "Yeah, I figured it out eventually." With a shrug, she continued. "We both went to SUNY Cortland with the intent of becoming physical therapists."

"But...she works in a salon now doing hair. How did she go from PT to cosmetology?"

"I don't think she ever had an interest in becoming a therapist. She thought she could ride my coattails and I'd get her through college, but it didn't work out that way. She barely managed to graduate, and while I went on to get my certification, she opted to go home and go to cosmetology school. That's really what she was born to do. We both know how obsessed she is with her looks so..."

"That totally makes more sense."

"When I moved back home after I finished my education, I kind of thought we would run into each other occasionally, but...man, she just showed up and acted like she'd been waiting for me to come back. It was weird."

"Where were Kendall and Shauna?"

"They had gone to school locally, so they were always around."

"Ah."

"It was like I had moved on but they didn't. But I went out with them because...I don't know...it was something to do. They're all just so...aggressive when we go to clubs or whatever. So I became the designated driver, the practical one. When we go out, it's just easier for me to fade into the background and not stand out too much because whenever there's any attention on me, things just go wrong."

"How?"

"Before Jimmy came along and Bianca was single, any guy who hit on me, Bianca would come and flirt with. I lost count of how many guys walked over to talk to me and ended up taking her home."

"Seriously?"

She nodded. "Yup."

"Man, if I didn't already dislike her, that story just sealed the deal."

"Are you crazy? I'm the loser who couldn't keep a guy's interest!"

Was she for real? "No, that's not even a little bit true, Chelsea. *She* is the loser who only feels good about herself by making others feel bad about themselves. She's a narcissistic sociopath and you don't need her! I guarantee it, if you went out with a different group of friends, you'd meet a guy and no one would swoop in and leave with him!"

Wait...why am I encouraging this? I'm the only one who can swoop her! No other guy's allowed to swoop!

"Somehow, I greatly doubt that. And besides, it's so much harder to make new friends at our age. This is just... it's comfortable."

"It's dysfunctional," he corrected. "You're essentially in an abusive relationship."

"It's not *that* bad."

"Okay, she's not physically hurting you, but psychologically? Um...yeah. Big time."

"You don't understand..."

"That's the thing, Chels, I do. I *do* understand. So many things are making sense now that I'm getting to know you! I get the whole staying in the background and not wanting to be in the spotlight stuff. I do. But can you honestly say that's where you're happy? When you were away at school and Bianca was gone, did you stay in the background? Because I have to tell you, someone who is in the drama club and acts on stage and...and does amazing book narrations doesn't sound like somebody who deserves to be treated like they don't matter."

"It's not like that," she said, but they both knew it was a weak defense.

This was getting them nowhere, and as much as he wasn't looking forward to the confrontation with Jimmy and Bianca, now he really wanted it. Not for him, but for her. She needed to go stand up for herself, and she needed someone to be on her side to support her and cheer her on.

Drew Russo, male cheerleader!

Um...yeah. No. That was so not the title he wanted, but the sentiment was the same.

"So here's the thing, Chels," he began carefully, "we will do whatever it is you want. Go home, go to the beach, hell, we can drive across the damn country if that's what you want. But I think we need to go to Bluffton and talk to Bianca and Jimmy and get this whole thing settled. You need to do this."

Her shoulders sagged and her expression turned sad. "I think you're right."

"I'm going to be right there with you, okay? You don't have to go talk to her alone. I won't leave your side." He squeezed her hand. "You got this."

She let out a long breath and then another. "Yeah. It's time."

"Good girl." Kissing her hand, he turned and straightened in his seat, pulled out of the parking lot and got them back on the interstate. They only had maybe another twenty minutes of driving and he wanted to do whatever he could to distract her. "So uh...the book you were reading–the one you read out loud to me the other day–have you read any more of it?"

"I finished it earlier. How come?"

"I'm just curious how it all went," he said with a grin. "I mean, obviously they both end up in a rental car together, but where did they go? How soon until they slept together? Did they end up seeing each other again once they got to their separate homes?"

Chelsea laughed softly even as she shook her head. "You know, you could just read the book yourself."

"Seriously? Do I look like the type of guy who sits around reading romances?" He snorted dramatically. "I was simply curious about how it all went down."

"Of course they end up together. It's a romance. The happy ending is guaranteed."

"But they didn't just drive and fall in love and get married. That would be the world's most boring story. Something exciting had to happen along the way."

"Well...there might have been some sexy time while on the High Roller in Vegas."

"Nice."

"Ever been to Vegas?"

He nodded. "Twice. Would love to go back." Then he was the one shaking his head. "I had thought we would do that for Jimmy's bachelor party but...I guess not."

"Yeah, we had always talked about a girls' weekend either out in the Hamptons at one of those spa resorts or going into the city and hitting up all the places where *Sex and the City* was filmed. Bianca's a huge fan."

"Sounds about right."

"That's always been her thing–wanting to get as close to someone famous or going to famous movie locations. She's gone to the *Today Show* more times than I can count so she can get on camera. It's exhausting."

"She's exhausting."

"Same thing."

"What about you? If you could go to a famous movie location or someplace famous, where would you go?"

"It's always been my dream to go to England. London, actually. I want to see Buckingham Palace in person." She looked at him and smiled. "I truly believe if given the opportunity, Duchess Kate and I would be great friends."

"Friends with royalty, huh? I never would have pegged you for being into that."

"Then I want to have my picture taken while walking the crosswalk at Abbey Road."

"Beatles fan?"

"Oh yeah. But their early stuff–you know, anything before Sgt. Pepper's."

"That was definitely their best time."

She smiled. "Most people argue with me on that."

"Why?"

"I don't know. Something about how diversified they were and enlightened in their later years." She shrugged. "Their earlier stuff just speaks to me. Makes me smile."

"I get it." He paused. "You know, that's something we haven't talked much about on this trip."

"The Beatles?"

"No, music. We briefly talked about it, but not anything in depth. Like...who's your favorite band of all time?"

"Drew?"

"Hmm?"

"I know what you're trying to do."

"Is it that obvious?"

Nodding, she said, "Yup."

"Damn."

"But you know what?"

"What?"

"It's working." And her smile was one of sweet relief and gratitude, and it made Drew feel like he had slain a small dragon.

But the bigger one was only minutes away.

12

"Well, well, well...I knew you'd pull something like this," Bianca said as she stood in the doorway to her suite, hair up in hot rollers, and wearing a white satin robe with "bride" embroidered on it. Then she glared at Drew. "And you're useless. I told Jimmy not to trust you."

Chelsea was ready to turn and run, but Drew placed his hand on the small of her back and it gave her strength.

Or it was shoving her forward–right now she couldn't be sure which.

"We can either talk about this out here for all the other guests to hear, or you can invite us in," Chelsea said, thankful her voice wasn't shaking. "Your choice."

"Oh, please, we both know you're not going to make a scene," Bianca commented, sounding bored. "Look, I get it. You don't agree with this wedding. Fine. Message received. Now if you'll excuse me, I'm scheduled to get my makeup done in fifteen minutes."

"Um..."

"Where's Jimmy?" Drew asked, his tone harsh.

Bianca's eyes went wide before narrowing. "He's not

allowed to see me before the ceremony. Everyone knows it's bad luck," she huffed.

Part of Chelsea wanted to scream and demand to know why her friend was such a bitch, but the other part wanted to just wish her luck–sarcastically–and walk away. It was just a matter of which part was going to win out.

"Sorry you drove all this way and wasted your time," Bianca said as she took a step back into her suite. "But then again, it's not like you have much of a life anyway."

And screaming it is!

"What is wrong with you?" Chelsea cried out. "What have I ever done to you to make you treat me like this? I was genuinely *concerned* for you! I actually *cared* about your happiness! And this is how you talk to me? How you treat me?" She growled with frustration. "Seriously, if you think so damn little of me, why are we even friends?"

Crossing her arms over her chest and looking defiant, Bianca simply said, "I felt sorry for you."

Wow. On some level, she wasn't surprised, but deep down she thought her friend would at least be tactful enough to sugarcoat it.

"You were always needy, Chels. Then the older you got, you became boring. We all know it. Hell, Drew says it more than any of us!"

"Oh no," Drew interrupted, coming to stand beside her as he glared at Bianca. "You are *not* going to deflect this onto me. I knew nothing about Chelsea except all the shit you were constantly telling me!"

"You still said it..."

"Yeah. I did. And you know what? I was wrong. All weekend, Chelsea and I have been talking and she's not boring! She's freaking brilliant–far smarter and more exciting than you'll ever be!"

"How dare..."

"Oh, shut it," Drew snapped. "Every word out of your damn mouth makes my head hurt. And you know what else? I feel sorry for Jimmy. I used to think he was lucky–that he found a great girl and was getting everything he wanted. Now I pity him. You're just a shallow, manipulative bitch. And on top of that..."

"Um, Drew?" Chelsea whispered.

"What?"

"Kind of stealing my thunder here."

"Oh. Right. Sorry." He took a step back and motioned for her to go on.

"Now, where was I...?"

Bianca yawned.

A dozen different insults were on the tip of her tongue and she was bristling with anger and pent-up nervous energy, but instead of unleashing all her anger, Chelsea opted for a different approach.

"You know what?" she said sweetly. "Go get your makeup done. I'm sure it's costing you a fortune to be here and having your hair and makeup professionally done can't be cheap either. I guess Jimmy's business is doing better than I thought." She shrugged. "So...we'll let you get to it. Congratulations."

Before she turned away, Chelsea saw the stunned look on Bianca's face and did her best not to appear too smug. Drew looked at her like she had lost her mind, but she simply held her head high and walked away.

They were down the hall and waiting for the elevator before he spoke.

"What the hell was that all about?"

"What do you mean?" she asked, pushing the down button.

"You just...you clammed up! Wished her well, for crying out loud! What happened to your...your thunder? Telling her off? Putting her in her place?"

Then she did look at him, in all her smug glory. "Yelling and insulting her were getting us nowhere. If anything, she was sort of enjoying it. But once I was the one being indifferent, she shut up." Her smile grew. "It will make her crazy. I got into her head."

The elevator doors opened and they both stepped inside. Once they were closed, Drew looked at her with a lopsided grin. "Wow. You're a bit of an evil genius."

She shrugged. "I do what I can."

The doors opened in the lobby and they stepped out. "I have to admit, it was all very anti-climactic. I was hoping for a more of a scene. Or at least for someone to get slapped."

"You were probably hoping for us to strip down to our underwear and conveniently fall into a pit of Jell-O."

His bark of laughter echoed through the lobby as he put his arm around her. "Sweetheart, you know me so well!" They were walking by the check-in desk when Drew stopped.

"What's the matter?"

"We drove all this way," he began. "And we got done much faster than I imagined."

"O-kay..."

"Why don't we stay here tonight?"

"Oh, Drew...I don't know. I think it would be weird. Don't you think it would be a little awkward? What would we do if we ran into the two of them?"

Pulling her closer, he said, "Would it be awkward or would it make Bianca crazy to see you enjoying yourself without her acting as puppeteer?"

"I wouldn't exactly call her a puppeteer."

"Please, she's the puppet master!" He made a motion like he was controlling a marionette.

"Drew?"

They both turned at the sound of his name being called and Chelsea inwardly groaned when they turned and saw Jimmy walking toward them. When she went to put some distance between the two of them, Drew held her close. Honestly, both men looked more than a little annoyed and she had no idea what was going to happen.

Or if she wanted to be this close to the action.

Somehow, she didn't think they were going to strip down to their underwear and wrestle either.

"I didn't think you'd have the nerve to show up," Jimmy said.

Here we go...

Drew shrugged casually. "We were almost here anyway, so we figured we'd see it through."

Jimmy glared at her before returning his attention to Drew. "What the hell are you doing, man? Why are you here? I thought we were cool. I thought you were my friend."

"Listen, Jimmy," Chelsea said, feeling the need to explain herself. "Don't be mad at Drew. This is on me. I was the one who made him drive here."

He snorted with disbelief. "Oh, I know you're the cause of all this, but I thought–as a *friend*–that Drew would have taken care of things like I asked him to. But judging by how chummy the two of you look, I guess I can see why he changed sides."

"Hey!" she cried indignantly.

"Jimmy..." Drew warned.

"No, I get it now," Jimmy said with a mirthless laugh. "I asked you to basically throw yourself on the grenade, and instead, you literally threw yourself onto–and into–Chelsea. Good to see the bro code is still strong."

Chelsea gasped and Drew lunged.

And security came and hauled them all outside.

There was a lot of yelling, a lot of shoving, and when the hotel manager stepped outside to see what was going on, all Chelsea could do was shrug.

Things had gone horribly, horribly wrong and she had no idea how to fix it. It was wrong to involve Drew in her battles and now she was going to be the reason he and his best friend stopped talking to each other. And as much as she wasn't really a big fan of Jimmy's, she kind of felt bad for him. Not only was he marrying a woman who was going to essentially ruin his life, but he was going to lose Drew too.

Letting out a weary sigh, she put her fingers in her mouth and blew. The loud whistle did the trick and everyone froze and looked at her.

Wow...wasn't expecting 100% compliance. Now what?

"So...um...I think we all need to calm down," she said nervously. Then she turned to the manager and the security guards. "We're very sorry for being so disruptive. Things escalated faster than they needed to. We promise to keep it down."

It took several minutes for them to leave and once it was down to just the three of them again, Chelsea looked around and spotted a gazebo over to the side of the resort that she thought would be perfect for them to go and hash things out.

Both men begrudgingly–and silently–followed her. Once they stepped into the intricately-designed structure, she had to force herself to focus on Drew and Jimmy and not how completely adorable this gazebo was.

"Okay, now that you've both gotten out some of your aggression, how about we try having a grown-up conversation?"

"I've got nothing to say to you," Jimmy snapped. "You ruined my wedding!"

Chelsea wasn't sure if he was talking to her or Drew, but figured it was safe to assume it was her. When Drew went to speak, she stopped him.

"I wouldn't say it was ruined..."

He simply gave her the death glare.

"Okay, you may not believe this, but...I was more concerned for *you* than for Bianca," she blurted out."

"What?"

She nodded. "I think we can all agree that I haven't been particularly quiet in my dislike of you, but at the end of the day, I think it has more to do with who you are with Bianca than who you are as a person."

Jimmy blinked at her but looked a little less hostile. Chelsea looked at Drew and he gave her a small nod.

"I don't think it's a crime not to like someone," she went on. "Everyone's different and personalities can clash. I think that's the case with you and me. However...I see the way you are with Bianca, and the two of you are a train wreck just waiting to happen."

And he was back to looking hostile.

"You don't know her like I do," she explained. "Bianca is manipulative and needy and will do anything to get her own way. And I watch you cater to her and she is just going to run right over you."

Okay, and less hostile again.

"You're a talented man with a successful business that's only going to continue to grow. Eventually she's going to resent you for not paying enough attention to her even as she's going to be demanding more money for the things she wants. Is that really what you want for your life? Do you ever tell her no?"

It took a minute, but Jimmy eventually shook his head.

"That's what I thought." Looking over at Drew, she sighed sadly. "I...I don't know what else to say. Maybe it's your turn."

"I hate to say it," Drew began carefully, "but Chelsea's got a point."

Jimmy's head snapped up. "You too?"

"Yeah. Me too." Letting out a long breath, he raked a hand through his hair and watched as Chelsea took a few steps back. "I didn't want to say anything because it's your life. But after driving with Chelsea and talking with her, she voiced all the same concerns I had. It can't be a coincidence, right?"

Muttering a curse, Jimmy started to pace and Drew had no idea where this was going. Would anything they said make a difference? Was there going to be a wedding? He hated the thought of being the reason they called it off, but... maybe it wasn't the worst thing that could happen.

"Look," he began, hoping he sounded diplomatic. "You know her better than I do. And I'm sure there are things that happen between the two of you that I'm not seeing. Hell, I hope I'm wrong, Jimmy. I really do. I just want you to think about this before you jump into a marriage." Shaking his head, he let out a small laugh. "I still can't believe you ran off to elope."

Jimmy's laugh sounded the same as Drew's. "Yeah, my folks are going to be so pissed."

"Then why are you doing this?"

Leveling him with a look, he replied, "Why do you think? Bianca wanted a chance to get married at the same place Justin Bieber did." He shuddered. "I thought she was kidding when she brought it up. I mean, who does that? Who runs off and gets married someplace just because some teen heartthrob got married there?" Another shudder. "The next thing I knew, we were on a plane and had an appointment with a wedding planner." He groaned. "Why the hell would she think I want to emulate some guy's wedding whose music I don't even know?"

Okay, so his friend wasn't nearly as far gone as Drew had feared.

And clearly not a fan of the Biebs.

Thankfully.

"And at the appointment? Bianca badgered the poor woman for details about Bieber's wedding because she wanted our ceremony to be as close to it as possible! She was pulling out her phone and trying to pinpoint all the places she wanted us to be so her Instagram pictures would be similar."

"Why didn't you stop her?" he demanded, unable to believe how crazed Bianca was.

Or how much she must love Justin Bieber to basically want to clone his wedding.

Jimmy guiltily glanced at Chelsea and that's when Drew knew his answer–he never tells Bianca no.

Wow.

"You have to know that I'm sorry, Jimmy," Drew said solemnly. "I never imagined things would go this way. But... maybe you need to go talk to Bianca before you do something you're only going to regret."

"Yeah. Maybe." He sighed wearily. "What about you? You staying or heading home?"

He looked over at Chelsea and remembered the conversation they were having before his friend interrupted them. Turning back, he said, "We've been driving for days so the plan was to hang out tonight and then hit the road in the morning."

"Oh, okay. Cool."

They both stood there awkwardly. Drew slid his hands into his pockets and Jimmy did the same. "So...uh...what do you think is gonna happen?"

"I think Bianca's going to have a damn fit if we don't get married here today," he said miserably. "Part of me thinks she cares more about where she gets married than to who."

"Whom," Chelsea murmured, and Drew shot her a look that said, "Really?"

"Jimmy, I...I'm sorry. I really am."

And for a minute, he thought they were going to be okay–that maybe this trip had been the right thing to do. But then...

Jimmy's expression hardened again as he took a step toward Chelsea. "You," he said, his voice a near growl. "You just couldn't let this go. Everything would have been fine if we didn't have to worry about you. And then you go and poison Drew's mind against me, too? Like cutting Bianca down wasn't enough?" He let out a snort of disgust. "I never understood why the two of you were friends, and I can guarantee after this, you won't be. I hope you're happy." When he turned to walk away, Drew grabbed him and spun him around.

"Don't take this out on her!" he warned. "I told you, I was already feeling like you were making a mistake. Chelsea just happened to be brave enough to say something about it."

"Yeah, great. She trash talks her only friend and ruins her wedding while destroying our friendship." He laughed. "Real brave."

This time when Jimmy tried to walk away, Drew let him.

It took a solid minute before he felt like he was calm enough to face Chelsea, and when he did, he felt awful. She was sitting on one of the benches in the gazebo, bent over, and her face in her hands. Drew walked over and sat beside her. "You okay?"

"Oh, yeah," she mumbled. "Just freakin' peachy." When she groaned, he reached over and put his arm around her.

"Okay, but to be fair, we kind of knew this was how it was going to go, right?"

"I knew it wasn't going to go well, but I wasn't expecting quite so much..." She straightened. "They were both just so mean! Maybe they do deserve each other. Ugh...why didn't I just stay home? I ruined everything!"

It would be a big fat lie if he said she didn't because... well...she did. But he still felt like he had to say something.

Anything.

???

How can my mind be completely blank?!

Say something!

Oh, God...this is getting awkward.

"Um...you know what? It doesn't matter what they think about you, Chels, the important thing is that you...you know...you love yourself."

She shoved his arm off of her as she straightened. "Are you seriously quoting Justin Bieber to me right now?"

"Um...what? No! Sorry!"

"Ugh...you just did it again!"

Drew jumped to his feet. "Did what again? I have no idea what you're talking about! I don't even know any Justin Bieber songs!"

She stood and started to walk away. "Right."

He had to go after her; that was a no brainer, but damn she was a fast walker. He jogged past her and blocked her path when he stopped. "Can we please just calm down and talk? I hate seeing you this upset." She struck a defiant pose–much like Bianca had earlier–but he wasn't deterred. "None of this is a surprise. We said we'd come and say what we had to say and let the chips fall where they may, remember?"

Frowning, she mumbled, "Maybe."

"And," he went on, "we were in the middle of making plans to stay for the night when we got interrupted. So why don't we go see about a room and then figure out what there is to do around here and get a recommendation for dinner? Come on, what do you say?"

He could tell she didn't want to agree with him–that she wasn't quite done feeling bad–but he was going to make sure she changed her mind. "We can even find out where the best ice cream place is and go there for dessert."

Sighing dramatically, she said, "Fine. But we are having a real dinner tonight. No dessert for dinner."

"Technically, it was a pre-dinner thing since we ordered food and eventually ate dinner. It was just technically the next day."

"Why are you like this?" she whined, but she was fighting a smile, he could tell.

"Like what? Delightful? Charming?"

"Full of yourself? Um, yeah."

They both laughed as they walked back into the hotel

lobby. "You think they're even going to let us get a room for the night?"

"Judging by the stink eye the manager is giving us, I'm not so sure."

"I guess I'll just have to be delightful and charming to him too."

She groaned. "Please don't. We'll definitely get thrown out then."

He stopped walking and stared at her. "Why would you even think that? What do you think I'm going to do?"

"All I'm saying is that this is the South. They have manners here that are just a wee bit more...genteel than yours."

"Genteel? What the hell is that?"

"Listen to how you speak," she said calmly. "Do you hear anyone else talking like that?"

"Like what? I don't freaking get it. What the hell's the matter with the way I talk? They don't like it, they can fuhgeddaboudit it." Her shocked expression instantly relaxed into a smile. Hugging her close, Drew kissed her soundly. "Got ya."

"You are so weird. Sometimes you are the sweetest man in the world. Other times, I swear you could be a reject from the cast of *The Jersey Shore*."

"I'm not even going to dignify that with a comeback. I'm classier than that."

"Says you."

"Watch it, Chels," he teased softly in her ear. "I'll make you pay for that when we get to the room."

She hummed in that throaty way he was beginning to love. "What room? We still don't know if we'll even get one."

"You think this is the only hotel in the area? If they turn

us down, I promise to have us in another room within thirty minutes or else."

She laughed. "Or else what? Are we talking sex or pizza delivery?"

"Why not both? Pizza in bed! How great would that be?"

"Oh, no..."

They started walking toward the front desk, his arm around her waist. "And this time, I *will* get you to eat naked. Trust me."

13

He had found them a room.

And they were currently naked and in bed.

Eating pizza.

And it wasn't nearly as scandalous as she thought it would be.

"What time do you want to get on the road in the morning?" she asked, reaching for her second slice.

"I know I should say early, but...right now the thought of getting back in the car for the long drive is beyond unappealing."

Yeah, she knew what he meant. With her original plan, Chelsea would have been back at work tomorrow. While they were waiting for their pizza, she had called her cousin and told him she wouldn't be in until Thursday.

God, what an idiot she was. All this trip accomplished was killing her friendship with Bianca, losing money because she had to take so much time off of work, plus all the expenses for the road trip–even though Drew paid for that first night, they split the cost of the hotel and meals after that. It was all just so depressing. Why hadn't she just kept her damn mouth shut? If Bianca wanted to make a mistake, why was it any of her concern? They had talked about this briefly and she had already known the chances of her changing her friend's mind were slim to none.

Sighing, she took a bite of her pizza.

"What's the matter?"

"Hmm?"

"You just sighed," Drew commented. "I know it's not New York pizza, but it's not that bad."

Once she finished chewing, she tossed her slice down and looked at him. "It's not the food, it's...everything. I have total remorse and there isn't anything I can do about it."

"About everything?" he asked, and she heard the hurt there and was quick to clarify.

Reaching for his hand, she squeezed it. "Not about this. Not about us." She sighed again. "I don't know what I was thinking coming here. There wasn't going to be any scenario that was going to make everyone happy."

"Why does everyone have to be happy? I mean, sometimes what's best isn't the popular choice. Jimmy and Bianca could get married and be happy today and tomorrow and for the foreseeable future, but we all know this isn't going to end well. If they don't get married, we'll be happy for now but...it's going to be a damn shit show for a while. Feelings have been hurt, things have been said that can't be taken back and we have to just deal with it."

"Maybe."

Turning her hand over in his, he squeezed. "No maybes. You know you had to stand up to her. If anything, that was long overdue. She didn't respect you and you deserve better."

She felt herself blushing. "Thanks."

"You're welcome."

They ate for a few more minutes in silence before she asked, "What about you?"

"What about me?"

"What's going to happen with you and Jimmy?"

He waved her off. "Please, that was nothing. He'll be pissy for a while, but we've been through far worse. Guys tend to be way more forgiving. He'll give me shit for a while and I'll do the same, but this isn't a deal-breaker for us."

"Wow. You're lucky."

"It's not luck, Chels. True friends–real friends–can have disagreements and still be friends. Even huge disagreements. Unfortunately for you, Bianca's definitely the type to hold a grudge."

"Tell me about it."

"The best way to handle someone like that is to just move on. She's going to be expecting you to come groveling back because she thinks she improves the quality of your life. She's a classic narcissist."

All she could do was nod because Drew was completely right.

"What about Kendall and Shauna?" he asked.

"What about them?"

"Are they like her? Is she like...their leader? Are they like Skipper and Midge?"

"Who?"

He rolled his eyes dramatically. "You know, Malibu Barbie's friends."

Unable to help herself, she laughed.

Snorted actually.

"Ah, *that* Skipper and Midge." She paused and grinned. "Do I even want to know why you know who Barbie's friends are?" she asked, still giggling.

"I have a ton of girl cousins," he admitted. "And I may

or may not have had to play with them and be Ken when they came over."

"Oh my goodness! That is awesome! You played with Barbie dolls!" Falling back against the pillows, she laughed even harder. "And not even the manly ones like G.I. Joe! You were Ken!" More laughing.

"They used to make me play dress-up with them too..."

"Stop!" she said around more laughter. "You're killing me! Was there makeup?"

"Yeah," he grumbled. "And so many damn tea parties and dancing."

Rolling onto her side toward him, she slapped him on the knee as tears were streaming down her face. "There was dancing?"

"Spice Girls. I was..." He groaned."

"Oh, no. You can't stop now. Which Spice Girl were you?"

"Sporty."

"This is the greatest thing ever!" she cried happily.

"Okay, you can stop being so amused now," he murmured.

Sitting up and doing her best to look serious. "Is that what you want? What you really, really want?"

Throwing his pizza down, he lunged for her, pinning her on her back. "That is not funny."

That just made her laugh harder. "It is so funny that I can barely breathe!"

When he started to tickle her, she screamed but couldn't stop laughing. "Cut it out, Sporty Spice!"

Probably the wrong thing to say since he just tickled her more. "I can do this all night, Chelsea!" he teased, but his fingers lightened up a little and now they were more like soft caresses. "You give up?"

Did she?

His hands moved to her ribs as he poised himself to start to seriously tickle her again and she knew she only had one option.

Holding her arms up, she said, "I surrender!"

Relaxing, Drew leaned back, straddling her. "Okay then. Good."

"Whew, that was...I mean, it felt like...hmm. What's the word I'm looking for?" she wondered out loud. "Oh, I know, it was like *zig-a-zig-ah*!"

He clearly knew when to admit defeat because he rolled off of her and picked up his discarded slice of pizza. "Fine. Laugh. I don't care."

After she caught her breath, Chelsea sat up and looked at him innocently. "Thank you."

"For what?"

"That was the perfect distraction. This whole day just... well, it got to me and it felt good to laugh."

"The whole day?" he asked incredulously. "There have been some high points, you know."

She patted his shoulder. "Yes, you've been wonderful, but you know what I mean, Drew. This is all just...it's huge! Bianca's been a part of my life for so long and I have no idea how to just...*not* have her in my life."

"Maybe..."

But she held up a hand to stop him. "You said it yourself. She holds grudges. I don't think I want to go back to the way things were before and then have this hanging over me too." She let out a long breath. "I think I have to just do what I did earlier and learn to be okay with simply walking away. If I make any attempt to fix things between us, she'll make me pay for it and use it against me forever. I don't want to live with that kind of pressure."

"And Kendall and Shauna? Will they still be your friends?"

Shrugging, she said, "Probably not. As much as it pains me to admit it, you were spot on where they're concerned too."

"Skipper and Midge?"

"Actually, Skipper was Barbie's sister. Midge was a friend."

"Not really the point here, Chels," he said wearily. "You know what I mean."

"Yeah. I do. They'll side with her. If anything, she's probably called them both already to tell them what an awful person I am. It won't be the first time, but hopefully, it will be the last."

"Well that just sucks."

"Tell me about it." They finished eating and it was still relatively early in the afternoon. "Let's talk about something more pleasant. What should we do for the rest of the day? Go sightseeing?"

"We can totally do that. Although I did get a look at the spa menu. After all the time we've spent in the car, it might be nice to go for some massages. What do you think?"

"That sounds glorious! Can we really do that?" She thought about all the costs of this stupid trip already and decided to throw caution to the wind. One more expense wasn't going to kill her. If anything, she'd just work double at the clinic next week to try to make up for it.

"Want me to call and see if we can get an appointment?"

"Definitely. We deserve it!"

Why the hell did I have to tell her about the whole Spice Girls thing?

Drew forced himself to relax as the massage therapist began working on his lower back. They secured appointments for themselves–and not a couple's massage session, even though that was an option. For some reason, he felt like he needed a little time to himself to relax and think some things through. He wasn't kidding earlier when he said the whole thing today had turned into a shit show. It all played out pretty much how he thought it was going to, but that didn't make him feel good.

Fighting with Jimmy was something that happened with more frequency than he would ever admit. Like Chelsea and Bianca, they were growing apart in so many ways, but the bonds of a lifelong friendship were hard to break.

Probably going to be a lot easier now...

It wasn't like his friend was a bully like Bianca. Jimmy was going to be pissy about this for a long time, but he'd get over it. And Drew knew he was going to be fine with the wait. Maybe a little distance and time apart would be a good thing for both of them. Their lives were going in different directions and he couldn't help but wonder if this was what was supposed to happen. How could either of them become the people they were supposed to be if they were constantly holding on to the guys they always were?

But...why can't we be both?

"You're very tense," the therapist commented. "You need to clear your mind and relax."

Easier said than done.

Drew let out a long breath and tried to simply focus on the sounds and smells in the room–the soft music, the smell of peppermint and lavender...

Probably should have mentioned I'm not a fan of lavender...

"Just let me know if the pressure is too much or not enough," the therapist said, interrupting his thoughts.

"I've been in the car for almost two days straight. I'm not sure if I need a deep tissue massage or a relaxing one," he explained. "Whatever you think I need, go for it."

After that, he forced himself to focus on the massage and reaping the benefits of it and hoped Chelsea was doing the same. Then his mind wandered to their earlier conversation–pre-Spice Girls and Barbie–and he could still see the sad look on her face. This whole thing was going to be harder for her to get over. He had a feeling the drive back home was going to be like one giant therapy session and he knew he was no Dr. Phil.

Maybe I should look up some of his quotes to use just in case...

And that had him thinking about going online and checking in at work. He may be the boss, but this was the longest he'd been away from a computer in a long time. It wouldn't be the worst thing to take an hour or so once he was back in the room to make some calls and make sure there was nothing pressing that he needed to help out with. Hopefully Chelsea would be so relaxed that she'd want to nap or something.

Hell, they were both going to need to shower before they went anywhere because the amount of oils this guy was using on him was going to make it difficult to put any clothes back on!

Then he thought of Chelsea all oiled and up and thought work could wait a little longer.

By the time his hour was up, Drew felt much better and definitely more relaxed. He thanked the therapist and went to the changing room to get dressed. The spa robe was pretty plush and he considered taking it, but...stealing wasn't his thing.

Stretching, he slid his shoes on and was about to turn to leave when he spotted Jimmy.

Shit.

"You're still here," his friend said, and he couldn't tell if he was annoyed or not.

"Uh, yeah. We decided to stay the night and head home tomorrow." They stood there in awkward silence until Drew knew it would be best to just walk away. "See ya, Jim." He walked out of the room and stood there for a minute and realized he felt okay.

No drama, no fighting, just...nothing.

Weird.

He went no more than a few steps when the door opened and closed behind him. "Drew?"

So close...

Looking over his shoulder, he said, "Yeah?"

Slowly, Jimmy walked toward him. "That was pretty intense earlier, huh?"

They started walking down the long hallway and out of the spa. "Yeah, it was."

It was a strained conversation at best, and once they were out in the lobby, Drew was more than a little anxious to part ways.

"Listen, I...I know you tried," Jimmy said after a long moment.

"Tried?"

He nodded. "Yeah, to help with Chelsea. I never should have put that on you. I know how you feel about her and believe me, if Bianca hadn't told Kendall about what we were doing, none of us would be here right now."

"I guess..."

Looking around, he asked, "Want to go get a drink?"

"Uh..." Honestly, he didn't.

Jimmy motioned to a small sitting area surrounded by a ridiculous amount of oversized potted plants. "Can we just talk for a few?"

"Sure."

It wasn't until they were seated that he spoke again. "I hate this shit. In all the years we've known each other, we've never let a woman get between us."

Drew nodded. "True."

"So why now? What's the big freaking deal this time?"

Wait, was he referring to Bianca or Chelsea?

"I mean, how can you defend her?"

Okay, Chelsea.

"Because she's not wrong, Jimmy. This whole thing...you just got engaged, for crying out loud! Why didn't you put your foot down and tell Bianca that you wanted to wait?"

He raked a hand through his hair. "Yeah, I know. Like I said earlier, it just snowballed. And she's so happy...how could I disappoint her?"

"How can you keep giving her everything she wants? Eventually you're going to have to disappoint her. Everything can't go her way. No one person can be the only one winning. That's not how relationships work."

Leaning back against the oversized chair, Jimmy sighed. "Ugh, I hate talking about this shit. We're not a bunch of girls. I wish you had just kept all this to yourself."

"Yeah, well...you involved me when you asked me to try to stop Chelsea from finding out."

Shaking his head, he said, "I knew Kendall would blab. Personally, I think Bianca did it on purpose."

"Did what?"

"Let it slip about the trip. She knows Kendall is the world's biggest blabbermouth."

"But why?"

"To piss Chelsea off," he said with a smirk. "I think she just wanted to make her crazy and show her that all her opposition didn't bother us."

"But clearly it does."

He shrugged. "Yeah. A little. I mean, what did I ever do to Chelsea for her to hate me?"

"She doesn't hate you, Jim. She refers you for jobs all the time, doesn't she?"

"Yeah..."

"She just thinks you and Bianca aren't a good fit. That's all."

"Seriously? Because she acts like she hates me."

"Well, hate's a strong word. It's...well...you're not her favorite person to hang out with."

"That's not the way Bianca describes it."

"Yeah, well...I learned that Bianca seems to have a way of not describing things in the best way where Chelsea's concerned."

"What's that supposed to mean?"

"Jimmy, come on..."

"No," he demanded. "What the hell does it mean?"

With no other choice, he told him about the multiple conversations he and Chelsea had and all the ways Bianca had described them to each other. When he was finally done, he waited to see how Jimmy was going to respond. His expression was hard and his glare was heavy.

"I wouldn't lie to you," Drew finally said, hoping to prompt his friend into saying something.

"I think this girl must have either a magic mouth or vag," Jimmy sneered.

"Excuse me?"

"Look, I appreciate that you took one for the team and slept with Chelsea. I mean, that had to be some desperate measures for you to have to do that. But she must have been a great lay for you to take her word over mine."

Drew couldn't speak even if he wanted to. He couldn't believe what Jimmy was accusing him of.

"I'm going to let this all slide since you're obviously still wearing sex goggles. Once we get home and you get rid of her, I know you'll go back to being reasonable." His phone chimed and he held up a finger to Drew. It was Bianca calling, and Jimmy was promising to come back to the room right away. "I love you too, baby," he cooed before hanging up. He stood and looked down at Drew. "Get all you can out of this girl while you're on the road and then get your head out of your ass." He clapped Drew on the back. "But seriously, dude, I owe you one. Sleeping with Chelsea was a brilliant way not only to distract her but to get me the information I need to make sure she doesn't worm her way back into Bianca's good graces. You're a good friend."

And then he was gone.

Drew had no idea how long he stayed in his seat, completely dumbfounded.

What the hell just happened?

How had they gone from nearly punching each other out a few hours ago to Jimmy thinking he had slept with Chelsea for the sake of saving this ridiculous wedding?

Groaning, he rubbed his forehead. All the relaxing he had done during the massage was gone, and, if anything, he was way more tense than he was an hour ago.

Biggest waste of money ever.

Slouching down in the chair, Drew had no idea what to do. It pissed him off that he didn't defend himself–and Chelsea–but while Jimmy was going on and on and on, he just couldn't seem to find the right words. Did he even tell Chelsea about this or did he just keep it to himself? After all, no good could possibly come of it. It wasn't like she was going to talk to Bianca or Jimmy any time soon.

If ever.

Okay, that was one issue down, he thought. The best thing to do was to simply pretend that this conversation never happened.

Now he just needed to take a few minutes to relax before going up to their room. No doubt she'd take one look at him and immediately see that he wasn't the least bit relaxed.

Quick, think relaxing thoughts!

That was easier said than done. On average, Drew knew he was a pretty chill guy, but now that he was trying to force himself to relax, he had no idea how to do it!

"It can't be that hard," he muttered. People always say things like "Go to your happy place" so...

I'm out on my boat for a day of fishing. Drinking a cold beer and the fish are biting like crazy. All the guys are there and we're laughing and joking.

Jimmy calls out, "Hey, guys! Did you know Drew slept with Chelsea to help me out?"

He immediately tensed back up and cursed. That was clearly not the way to go. After taking several deep breaths and letting them out slowly, he opted for a different approach.

I'm at home and enjoying a big bowl of macaroni and cheese–a classic! The Rangers game is on and they are kicking the Islanders' asses. The announcers are doing the play-by-play commentary when Sam Rosen looks right at the camera and says, "And the Rangers are leading seven to one! It's been one hell of a game! And speaking of games, did you all hear about the game Drew Russo is playing? He slept with Chelsea Cooper to save his best friend's wedding! He's our MVP of the game!"

Scrubbing a hand over his face, he hissed, "Shit." Something had to give–had to help. So after another round of deep breaths, Drew leaned back in the chair and forced himself to relax and think of only pleasant things.

A cold beer.

Sex with Chelsea.

Ice cream sundaes.

Eating frosting off of Chelsea's naked body.

Playing a perfect golf game.

Shower sex with Chelsea.

"I'm screwed," he said after a minute. He could sit in this damn spot all day and she was going to be on his mind and this stupid situation was going to eat away at him. The only thing left to do was to go up to the room and pray that Chelsea wasn't done with her massage yet. Then he could shower and make those business calls and do his best to use that as a distraction.

Standing, he stretched. And as he made his way to the bank of elevators, he felt like this might actually work.

14

"SON OF A BITCH!"

That was the third time she'd stubbed her toe on the damn desk chair, and yet she still didn't think to move the stupid thing out of the way. At this rate, she'd have to hop on one foot while trying to make her speedy exit.

Tossing the last of her things into her suitcase, Chelsea prayed she could get done and be out of the room before Drew got back. Her heart was hammering like mad in her chest and several times she had to will herself to not get sick.

Sleeping with Chelsea was a brilliant way not only to distract her but to get me the information I need to make sure she doesn't worm her way back into Bianca's good graces. You're a good friend.

That one statement had been playing on a constant loop in her head ever since she'd overheard it.

It had been a complete fluke that she and Drew had gotten done with their massages at the same time. She had been about to call out to him when she noticed Jimmy walking with him. Then her curiosity had gotten the better of her, and stupidly, she stood behind a wall of plants and listened to their conversation.

With trembling hands, she closed the suitcase and quickly made her way out of the room. As much as it would be completely normal to go down to the lobby in the elevator, she didn't want to run the risk of running into Drew. With no other choice, she went to the end of the hall and down the emergency stairs.

Ugh...I really should start going to the gym again. Going down the steps should be much easier than this.

Huffing and puffing, she paused at the ground floor and made a mental note to look into renewing her gym membership.

Carefully, she opened the door and looked out to see if anyone was around. When she noted she was somewhat alone, she stepped out and went out the side door. Leaning against the building, she pulled out her phone and immediately pulled up her Uber app and requested a car.

"Oh, thank God," she sighed when one was only two minutes away.

Those two minutes felt like an eternity, and she was certain that any minute Drew was going to come running out of the building looking for her. She hadn't left a note, but he'd have to be an idiot not to notice she was gone. When he got up to their room and all her stuff was gone, she would hope he'd realize what happened.

But he wouldn't have any idea why.

"Once I'm in the car, I'll text," she muttered. "Maybe."

Her ride arrived, and she tried to sprint but ended up looking more like an idiot walking over hot coals because her toe was throbbing. Giving up on even trying to be smooth, she got to the car and threw herself into the backseat. She refused to look back and kept her eyes closed for several minutes while she tried to calm herself down.

That's when her phone started to ring.

Drew.

It would be childish–well, *more* childish–for her to ignore his call, so she answered.

"Hello."

"Hey," he said, but she could hear the uncertainty in his voice. "What's going on? Where are you?"

Letting out a long breath, she explained about getting out of her massage and seeing him with Jimmy.

"I heard your conversation."

"Shit."

"Yeah," she said blandly.

"Why did you stand there and listen? Why didn't you let me know you were there?"

"Seriously? Why didn't you defend me or tell Jimmy he was wrong, huh?"

"You were eavesdropping!" he yelled.

"And you've been lying to me all this time!" she countered. The driver glanced at her in the rearview mirror, but she didn't care. "I believed you, Drew. I didn't trust you at first, but I thought we were past all that. I thought I had been wrong about you all this time." She shook her head and willed herself not to cry. "But it turns out I was right all along."

"Chelsea, please. Just let me explain..."

"There's nothing to explain. You lied. You used me." She let out a mirthless laugh. "You convinced me that I shouldn't trust my friends, but the joke's on me. Clearly, I can't trust anyone. Especially you."

"Chels, come on. That's not true! Jimmy took me by

surprise! I was completely freaked out by everything he said, and when I was about to speak up, he left!"

"Convenient."

"Okay, yes, I could see where the timing would seem suspicious to you..."

"It would be suspicious to everyone."

He sighed loudly. "Can you just tell me where you are? We need to talk about this."

"Why? So you can go tell Jimmy and Bianca more stuff about me? Want to make sure you put the final nail in our friendship? Well, ...screw you, Fredo!"

"Fredo?"

"Yeah, Fredo," she said tartly. "Or better yet, Pettigrew."

"Are you having a stroke right now?"

"Oh my God! How are you not getting this? Fredo? *The Godfather*! He was a big fat traitor to the family! You should be real familiar with that movie considering you're Italian. That trilogy is probably gospel to you."

"Hey! That's offensive and stereotyping!"

"And Peter Pettigrew from *Harry Potter and the Prisoner of Azkaban*? He was a big fat rat! Any of this ringing any bells for you?"

"Yeah, I'm not really a big Harry Potter fan..."

"Just another reason why you are the absolute worst. I swear I don't know what I was thinking hooking up with you. It seriously must be Stockholm syndrome." She shuddered at her own stupidity.

Again.

"Stockholm...we've been over this, Chelsea! I did *not* kidnap you and that's not something to joke around about!"

"That's exactly what a kidnapper would say."

"Ma'am?" the driver asked nervously. "Are you okay?"

She waved him off. "I'm fine now. Thank you."

"Who are you talking to?" Drew asked. "Are you down in the lobby?"

"It doesn't matter where I am," she argued. "I'm no longer any of your concern."

He let out another long breath. "You're being dramatic and a little like your old self."

If he was within reach, she'd strangle him right now.

"Yeah, thanks. That really makes me want to keep talking to you," she said sarcastically. "Goodbye, Drew."

"Chelsea, wait!" he yelled, and she must be a glutton for punishment because she actually stopped herself from hanging up."

"What?" she snapped. "What else is there possibly to say?"

"Just...he was wrong. You have to believe me. Nothing that happened between us had anything to do with Jimmy or this wedding or anything. It was about the two of us finally connecting."

For a minute, she started to weaken–started to believe him.

"It wouldn't have mattered what I said to Jimmy at that moment. You would have only heard what he said and nothing else."

Again, she was ready to strangle him.

"I guess we'll never know, will we?" she said sadly. They were both quiet for a moment. "Look, this is all for the best, if you think about it."

"I don't see how."

"Now your friendship with Jimmy is safe. We both know this wasn't your fight, Drew. You just got dragged into it. Now he thinks you're some kind of hero and I'm finally out of their lives."

"Chelsea..."

"No, really. It's okay. I hate that it all happened this way, but...you helped me." And damn did it pain her to have to admit that.

"What?"

"It's true. You gave me the push I needed to break up with Bianca. We both know I wouldn't have done it on my own. I'm too much of a damn pushover." Her voice started to shake and she took a few seconds to regain her composure. "So, thank you. Now I can move forward and stop feeling bad about myself because of how Bianca treated me." Swallowing hard, she saw the first signs for the Savannah airport. It was a shockingly short drive. "I need to go, Drew. Have a safe trip home."

"Chelsea, please..."

"Goodbye, Drew." She hung up before she could change her mind and immediately turned off her phone. It wasn't a long-term solution because she'd have to turn it back on eventually, but for right now, she could handle the silence. There were so many details she needed to work out and they were all overwhelming.

First, she had to find a flight home.

Probably should have looked that up before I rode all the way here...

Then she'd have to figure out what life was going to look like in the coming weeks. She had no doubt that Bianca already told Kendall and Shauna about what happened, so she was essentially going to be friendless for the foreseeable future.

Ugh...now I'll really need to join the gym just to meet new people.

And probably the biggest hurdle she was going to have was getting over Drew. It was hard to believe how this short weekend really affected her. For a year she thought she hated him, but once they got past all of the animosity, Chelsea realized there were strong feelings there that had nothing to do with hate.

Of all the times for me to fall in love...

And yeah, painful though it was to admit, she had no doubt in her mind that she was already in love with Drew Russo.

Damn him.

Why did he have to turn out to be an even bigger jerk than she ever imagined?

And why did he have to break her heart so damn soon?

The knock on his door had Drew lunging for it–hopeful it was Chelsea coming back to him. He pulled it open and wanted to slam it shut again.

Bianca.

Oh good. Bridal Barbie is here.

Wearing a blindingly white strapless dress that was way too tight for a wedding dress–at least, what he thought of as a wedding dress–Bianca waltzed into the room like she owned it. "Where is she?"

"What?"

Turning on her ridiculously high heels, she looked at him with annoyance. "Where is Chelsea?"

Drew leaned against the open door and hoped she'd take the hint that she wasn't welcome here. "She's not here."

"Oh, please. Jimmy told me the two of you were sleeping together. Don't try to tell me she got a separate room." She snorted with disgust. "Look, I'm getting married in fifteen minutes and I need to know where she is. Now."

Crossing her arms over her already pushed-up breasts, she glared at him. "Well?!"

"I'm not sure what part of 'she's not here' you're not getting, but look for yourself. Her stuff is gone and so is she." And man did it hurt to say that out loud.

Stomping around the room while huffing and puffing, Bianca made a big show of searching the room–even opening the dresser drawers and looking behind the bathroom door. She spun around and faced him. "Well, where is she?"

All he could do was shrug. "I don't know. Gone. On her way home, I'm sure."

"But...I'm getting married!"

"Uh...yeah. I know. We *all* know," he said impatiently. "Don't you need to go?"

"How can I? Chelsea's supposed to be my maid of honor!"

Drew was fairly certain his eyes were bugging out and his jaw had to be on the floor. Was this woman for real? Swallowing hard, he pushed away from the door and knew he couldn't hold back. He'd made that mistake already today and he wasn't going to do it again.

"Your maid of honor? You're kidding, right?" he snarled, stalking toward her.

Bianca stumbled back a foot. "No," she said weakly. "Why?"

"Besides the fact that you were ridiculously hateful to her earlier, you mean? Or how about the fact that you've always been a total bitch to her? Hell, in the year that I've known you, you've never said one nice thing about her! You were pissed off that she even showed up here, so why on earth would you think she would be anything for you?"

"Um..."

"Are you really this cruel or are you just damn clueless?" he demanded, his voice rising with each word.

"I...I should go..."

"Chelsea's gone and it's all your fault!" he shouted. "This whole damn thing is your fault! You create drama everywhere you go! You're a damn narcissistic sociopath!" With his own snort of disgust, Drew stormed over to the door and opened it again. "Get out!"

Bianca seemed uncertain. "Drew, you have to realize..."

"I don't *have to* anything," he said, his teeth clenched. "I knew I had you pegged right from the beginning. Chelsea was right about you. I only wish Jimmy was smart enough to dump your selfish ass. Now get out." When she didn't move fast enough for him, he added, "Now!"

Once she was gone, he slammed the door. Honestly, he would have preferred to punch something, but there wasn't anyone around. It would be wrong to call Jimmy just for the purpose of hitting him, right?

Walking over to the bed, he collapsed on it. "I need help." Closing his eyes, his mind spun with all the ways this day had gone downhill. Earlier, when they were still in the car, he never should have left the decision up to Chelsea; he should have put his foot down and said to hell with her needing closure. At the time, it seemed like the mature and responsible way to handle things, but now? Now he wished he had turned the car around and taken them someplace else. They'd probably be out to a nice dinner right now and then go back to their room for another amazing night.

Now he was alone and even though hardly any time had passed, he was already hating it. He missed her. He needed her.

He was quite possibly in love with her.

"Damn." Groaning, he realized he had no idea what to

do with himself now. It was too late to start driving home, and even the thought of driving all the way back to New York alone made him feel even worse. If he left first thing in the morning, he could realistically drive home in one day. It would be fourteen hours' worth of driving, but it was better than stopping for the night along the way and being alone. He'd rather get the damn drive out of the way and sleep in his own bed tomorrow night.

Alone.

There was another knock at his door and he knew it wasn't going to be Chelsea. Sighing wearily, he got up and walked over to open the door and found Jimmy standing there looking just as tired as he was. Without a word, he shoved the door the rest of the way open and walked away, figuring his friend would just follow him inside.

"What did you say to Bianca?" Jimmy asked, his tone mild and fairly unconcerned.

"Don't you have a wedding to get to?" Sitting down on the desk chair, he raked a hand through his hair and wished like hell this whole situation was over.

"Right now, Bianca's fixing her makeup because you made her cry. Where's Chelsea so we can just fix this mess and move on?"

"I already told her that Chelsea left." He motioned to the whole room. "Her stuff's gone. She heard our conversation and left."

"Why?"

The longer this went on, the more Drew realized that maybe Jimmy and Bianca were perfect for each other after all. They were both clueless.

When his friend continued to stare at him blankly, all he could do was rub his head. "Because she heard what you said."

Still no reaction.

"And she thinks I only slept with her to help you out!"

And...still nothing.

Jumping to his feet, Drew advanced on Jimmy. "And it's not true! How are you not getting this?"

If anything, now there was total confusion on his face. "Then why didn't you say something down in the lobby?"

"Um, when? You talked non-freaking-stop and then left!" He began to pace. "And on top of that, everything you said just took me by surprise and I couldn't collect my thoughts quickly enough." Turning, he faced Jimmy. "I didn't sleep with Chelsea for any reason other than I wanted to! I learned a lot about her on this trip, and I've always found her attractive." Groaning, he added, "But like an idiot, I listened to you and everyone else and formed an opinion of her that turned out to be completely untrue!"

"Now you're just thinking with your dick," Jimmy stated. "Because she's crazy. I mean, look at what she did today alone! Now Bianca's without a maid of honor!" He shook his head. "Wanna be my best man?"

That was it. Any minute, his head was going to explode.

"No, I don't want to be your best man! I don't want anything to do with this ceremony!" He started pacing again. "All this wedding has done is ruin everything! Friendships are over and Chelsea's never going to talk to me again and it's all because you can't say no to Malibu Barbie!"

"Hey!" Jimmy shouted and then stopped and blinked. "Wait...Malibu who?"

"Oh my God! Bianca! You can't say no to Bianca!"

"Why'd you call her that Malibu thing?"

"I'm not doing this with you right now," Drew said, beyond frustrated. Taking Jimmy by the shoulders, he spun him around and shoved him toward the door. "Go! Leave! Go make the biggest mistake of your life! I'm done!"

"Biggest mistake? But..."

Drew didn't let him finish. He gave him that last final shove out the door before slamming it shut.

The first thing that came to his mind was how he now completely understood Chelsea's frustration with him over the phone earlier. He had been just as clueless as Jimmy and the whole scenario that just played out in his room was painful.

Before he could second-guess himself, he pulled out his phone and typed out a quick text to her.

Drew: Hey. I don't know if you'll read this but you have to know—again—how sorry I am. I just told Jimmy off and said that he was making the biggest mistake of his life. Not sure it will change anything but...I wanted you to know.

He stared at the screen and waited for any sign of Chelsea responding, but all it said was "sent".

Drew: I miss you. I was really looking forward to road tripping back to Long Island with you.

After he hit send, he knew it would be pointless to wait for a reply. He was sure that she turned her phone off and even if she hadn't, he was probably the last person she wanted to talk to.

Or at least in the bottom three.

There wasn't much of anything else for him to do. Sightseeing held zero appeal without Chelsea and he wasn't in the mood to go out to eat by himself. The only thing to do was to order some room service, try to get some sleep, and get on the road as early as possible in the morning.

Feeling good about having a plan, he walked over and picked up the room service menu and sat on the side of the bed. His foot kicked something and when he crouched down and looked under the bed, he spotted Chelsea's Kindle. Smiling, he picked it up and placed it on the bed next to him. Within minutes, he had decided on treating himself to a kind of mixed bag dinner–crab cake appetizer, a bacon double cheeseburger with fries as his entrée, and a slice of chocolate cream pie for dessert, along with a bottle of beer, a bottle of soda, and a bottle of water.

"And I'm not going to feel weird about it at all," he murmured as he picked up the phone to place his order.

When he hung up the phone, he turned on the bed, leaned against the pillows and picked up the Kindle. The right thing to do was to put it in his suitcase and mail it to her when he got home.

But he was never particularly good at doing the right thing, so...

Turning it on, he looked at her collection of books–which was quite eclectic. There were more romances than anything, but even they seemed very diverse judging from their covers. Historical romances, contemporary ones, and–again, based on the covers–some pretty sexy-looking ones. After that, there were a few biographies, a couple of thrillers, some cookbooks, and one lone self-help book for introverts.

That one single book made his heart ache for her.

How many times had he joined in the jokes about her–about how she was uptight and nerdy and awkward–and all that time, she was struggling with who she was and just trying to fit in.

"I'm such a jackass."

Clearly, no one was going to argue that fact.

And not only because he was alone and talking to himself.

The last several days had taught him a lot about himself, and he didn't like what he found out.

He was a jerk.

He was selfish.

And he let what could have been the greatest relationship of his life go because he was too afraid to defend it when it mattered most.

"Add loser to the list and that ought to make it complete."

Looking at the time, he saw he had about thirty minutes before his meal was to be delivered. The Kindle was in one hand and he used the other to reach for the television remote. It would be easy to kick back and watch some TV, but...maybe he should broaden his horizons and do a little light reading.

Some romance reading.

Scrolling through the titles, he found the one Chelsea had started reading to him the other day and decided he was going to check it out from the beginning and find out for himself how their road trip ended.

"Hopefully better than ours."

15

I miss you.

"Ugh...stop reading this."

I miss you.

"I'm totally going to delete this."

I miss you.

"Tomorrow. Tomorrow, I am definitely going to delete this."

The reality was that she knew she was never going to do it. She was a glutton for punishment and reading Drew's texts was her current form of torturing herself.

"I should really get a hobby."

Reading had been her hobby, but somewhere along the way in her haphazard packing that last day, she lost her Kindle. There were plenty of paperback books in her living room, but she was really more of an e-reader girl when she was reading for pleasure. With no other choice, she grabbed her laptop and bought a new Kindle through Amazon. Once the sale was complete, she slammed the computer shut and sighed.

She'd been home for two days and life was fairly uneventful.

In other words, boring. She was bored out of her mind.

Unwilling to deal with the fallout from her argument with Bianca, Chelsea had simply avoided reaching out to Kendall and Shauna, and considering she hadn't heard from them either, she knew she made the right choice.

But it still made her sad.

She also hadn't heard any more from Drew since his last text when he told her how he'd told Jimmy off. As much as she didn't want to admit it, she was proud of him. It seemed they both had crappy best friends, and as much as she hated to think that she was the cause of him and Jimmy fighting, part of her felt like they deserved to suffer a bit too.

Misery loves company and all that crap.

And as much as she wasn't looking for a new best friend or anything–sort of a BFF embargo–Chelsea knew she couldn't stay holed up in her house forever. Eventually, she was going to have to go out for something other than work and start socializing with new people.

"I'm exhausted just thinking about it," she groaned, leaning back on her couch.

Although, she was working at the clinic for the next four days–even took the dreaded Saturday shift that so many therapists tried to avoid in their urgent care office. It was better than staying home alone, and it would make up for some of the time she lost while on the road with Drew.

Eventually, she would stop beating herself up over her bad decision. It had to get better. Maybe in time, she wouldn't look back on it and feel like kicking her own ass for being so damn stupid–and not just with trying to stop Bianca from getting married, but for falling for a guy like Drew.

Drew...

And maybe her heart would stop aching at the thought of him.

"I am such a cliché." Forcing herself up off the couch, she walked to her bedroom and got ready for work. Today she was pulling the 12-8 shift and then the next three days were twelve-hour shifts. She was hopeful that the mental and physical exhaustion would help her sleep because so far nothing else worked.

"It will get better," she told herself.

And kept telling herself for the next week.

By the following Friday, she was just about dead on her feet when she walked through the door. There had been a package on her front porch and her stomach clenched when she saw that it was from Drew.

Tossing her purse on the entryway table, she studied his messy handwriting as she kicked off her shoes. From the size of the envelope, she had a feeling it was her Kindle.

Although why it took him over a week to send it to her was still a mystery.

Sitting down on the couch, she opened the bubble mailer and pulled out her tablet. A sheet of folded paper fell to the floor and for a moment, she contemplated ignoring it. It was obvious it was a message from him and she wasn't sure she could handle reading it.

Sadly, she was incredibly curious and immediately picked it up. She closed her eyes and took several deep breaths before she allowed herself to start reading.

Chelsea,

Hey. So I found your Kindle in the room Monday night while I was ordering dinner. I had meant to get it back to you sooner, but...I started reading one of the books and couldn't stop.

"What?!" she cried. "Seriously? Get your own Kindle, you jerk!"

I'm sure you're pissed off right now because I held on to it for so long, but between the long drive home–which took me almost 15 hours because of an accident on the Jersey Turnpike–and getting back to work, I didn't have a lot of free time to finish. And I really needed to read the book in its entirety.

"Again, buy your own copy!"

I have to admit, I saw a lot of similarities between the characters in the book and us. Did you when you read it? Or am I crazy? I'm sure you'd just say I'm crazy because you want to disagree with me and that's okay. I really miss our disagreements. Hell, I just miss talking to you.

"Dammit, I am *not* going to cry."

Anyway, I'm sorry I kept this for so long, but thanks for introducing me to a whole genre of fiction I never would have picked up on my own. I saw there's another book in the series coming up and I can't wait to read it. Maybe by the time it comes out, you won't hate me so much and we can have a little two-person book club and talk about it.

"It's not the worst idea in the world," she said, fighting a smile.

Take care of yourself, Chelsea. I really hope you're doing okay and if you ever want to talk and give me another chance, I'm here. I miss you.

Love, Drew

It was stupid how her heart skipped a beat at the word love, but...that didn't mean anything, right? The word love, not the heartbeat skipping. That could lead to some serious cardiac issues, but...

"Oh, my God! Stop thinking like such a damn dork!"

But she did make a mental note to maybe make an appointment with a cardiologist.

"This is why I currently have zero friends and no boyfriend." With a snort of disgust, she tossed Drew's note onto her coffee table and stood. Before the whole wedding debacle, she would be getting ready to go meet everyone at O'Dwyer's. Now she had nothing to do but make a sad dinner for one and watch some TV.

"No such thing as Netflix and chill for one."

Then she realized there was and it wasn't something she was going to do.

Like ever.

Okay, that was a little extreme and it wasn't like she didn't believe in some self-love, but...not with Netflix on in the background. With a little more moaning, she went to the kitchen to see what there was to cook. After several minutes and nothing inspiring hitting her, she opted to be a little frivolous and order takeout.

"You're saving money by not having a social life. Might as well splurge on Chinese food." Walking back to the living room, she picked up her phone, pulled up the *GrubHub* app and placed her order. With nothing else to do, she sat down and picked up Drew's letter again.

If you ever want to talk and give me another chance, I'm here. I miss you.

Sighing loudly, Chelsea considered her options.

For starters, she should let him know she got her Kindle back. Chances were, he was hoping for at least a confirmation of that. It wouldn't be the worst thing in the world for her to send him a simple text just letting him know...what... that the U.S. Postal service did its job?

Okay, maybe not *exactly* that, but...just to thank him for getting it to her.

She put the letter down and picked up her phone and stared at it.

"It's just a text," she murmured. "Not a marriage proposal. It's not a big deal."

And yet, her fingers never moved.

Ugh...why was this so hard? This wasn't anything personal; it was just an act of common courtesy. It was no different than writing a thank you note except instead of mailing it, she was sending it via text. No big whoop.

Easy peasy.

It wasn't like she was sending him naked pictures of herself or attempting to sext with him. Looking down at herself in her plain khakis and navy polo shirt, she frowned.

Definitely not sexting attire.

And that was before anyone got to the plain cotton underwear she had on underneath.

"Okay, stop focusing on your lame underwear and put your attention on sending this stupid text!"

Still, she stared hard at her phone.

It took a solid five minutes where she battled internally between fear and loathing before she finally swiped the screen and brought up Drew's last text.

I miss you.

Chelsea: Hey. Just got home and got the Kindle. Thanks for getting it back to me. I had just ordered a new one. So...thanks.

She hit send before she could second-guess herself but then...she second-guessed herself.

Did that sound too sarcastic? Was I being snarky because he held on to it for so long that I had to go buy a new one?

"I am seriously the most awkward human being ever."

Her phone dinged with an incoming text and she was so startled that she dropped her phone.

"Smooth, Chels. Real smooth."

Even though she knew it had to be Drew, it took her a minute to confirm it.

Drew: Damn. Now I'm sorry I didn't get it back to you sooner. I'll reimburse you for the cost of the new one.

Chelsea: That's really not necessary. It wasn't that much money and it's always good to have a spare.

Drew: Seriously? Why would anyone need a spare Kindle?

Chelsea: Why? Because they don't exactly last forever. I read a lot and there's a ton of books on there already.

Drew: Well, there were definitely more than I would have imagined, but I wouldn't say a ton. More than I've ever read, that's for sure.

Chelsea: And you opted to go with a rom-com?

Drew: That's totally your fault. I probably would have gotten the Kindle back to you the day I got home, but you piqued my interest with that story so I had to read for myself how it ended.

Was it wrong how much she was enjoying this? The banter? The easy back and forth? She could hear his voice in her head and it was oddly comforting.

Chelsea: Were you surprised? All romances have a happy ending.

Chelsea: I mean, in books. All romance books have a happy ending.

Drew: Yeah, it wasn't that I thought I was going to be surprised. I was just curious how they got there.

Chelsea: Ah. Gotcha.

He didn't respond right away and she figured they were done with the conversation. She had thanked him, they made small talk, and now they were done.

Drew: What are you doing right now? Can I call you?

Or maybe not quite done.

Her heart rate kicked up, and she knew it shouldn't be a big deal for him to call, but...it was. Texting was safe. She had control and no one had to know that she was a hot mess right now. Drew knew her better than she ever realized. He'd be able to hear it in her voice that she wasn't comfortable and having extreme anxiety.

Drew: I'm guessing you don't want that.

Chelsea: Why do you say that?

Ugh...why would you even ask that, dummy?

Drew: Because you're stalling and you didn't respond right away.

Chelsea: Oh.

Drew: I almost didn't ask but...I wanted to be honest with you. I'd love to hear your voice and know that you're doing okay.

Chelsea: I'm okay. Really.

Liar.

Drew: I'd still love to talk to you, but I understand.

Oh, God. How could she possibly explain that she was too embarrassed and horrified at her behavior to talk to him or even face him? She knew he'd tell her she was crazy and that everything was fine, but...it wasn't. As much as she regretted not thinking things through with going after Bianca and Jimmy, she knew she'd get over it.

She was practically over it already.

But the way she had fallen into bed with him and in love? Um, yeah. That was going to take a whole lot longer to recover from.

Especially since he clearly didn't feel the same way.

How do you know?

Well, for starters, he didn't make any effort to come after her when she left him at the resort. He hadn't come to see her when he got home and...dammit, she just knew!

Drew: Chels? You still there?

Chelsea: Yeah. Sorry. I wasn't sure what to say.

Drew: Believe it or not, I don't know what to say either. At least not via text. Can we maybe meet for coffee sometime? I swear I don't want to pressure you, but we went through a lot on that trip and I hate the way it ended.

Chelsea: The trip or us?

She hadn't meant to hit send, but it was out before she could stop it. Then she held her breath as the little dots danced on the screen.

Drew: Both.

Tears stung her eyes and Chelsea was glad she was alone.

Chelsea: Me too.

Drew: Then don't let that be the end! I know

we can't do anything about the trip, but we were over before we even had a chance to start.

Chelsea: It's not that easy, Drew.

Drew: I know and I swear I'm not making light of it and I know I said I don't want to pressure you, but I think we owe it to ourselves to at least talk face-to-face. Please, Chels.

Her doorbell rang and she was never so thankful for a disruption.

Literally saved by the bell.

Standing, she put her phone down and went to answer the door and get her food. With a smile and a murmured thank you, she accepted the bag and closed the door.

And stared at the phone like it was a ticking time bomb.

Placing her food on the coffee table, she calmly went and grabbed a plate and silverware along with something to drink. When she sat back down on the couch, she knew she needed to answer Drew.

Even though it was with something he didn't want to hear.

Chelsea: I can't, Drew. Not yet. I'm sorry.

Chelsea: I need to go. I've got plans and have to get ready. Take care.

She turned off her phone and tossed it to the other end of the couch and forced herself to eat when all she wanted to do was cry.

"Dude, what is going on with you? I mean, for crying out loud, you look like you're at a funeral instead of a bar!"

It wasn't the first time Jimmy had asked that question in

the last several weeks, and it probably wouldn't be the last. Honestly, Drew couldn't figure out why this thing with Chelsea was bugging him so much. It was clear she wasn't interested in seeing him or even trying to figure out if what they had that weekend could have been more.

Even though he knew it could.

And that's why he was still in a funk.

It wasn't a weekend fling; they weren't screwing around. What he felt for her was deeper than that, and no one was more surprised than him about it.

Over the last two weeks he had reminded himself more than once that they only had three days alone together. *Three!* He shouldn't feel this way after what was essentially a long weekend. But the logical side of him was quick to counter with the fact that they'd known each other for a year.

A year of verbal foreplay.

If any other woman had rejected him so blatantly, Drew was quick to move on. But...he knew Chelsea was in protective mode. And how did he know? Because she was still responding to his texts.

Beside him, Jimmy sighed loudly. "I'm going to shoot some darts. You coming?"

"In a minute," he murmured, looking around as if he expected her to walk through the door of O'Dwyer's like she had almost every Friday night for a year.

"Whatever. I'm getting a board."

Once he was gone, Drew walked over to the far corner of the bar and pulled out his phone, and before he could change his mind, he pulled up the ongoing conversation with Chelsea.

Drew: Hey. You around?

Please say yes. Please say yes.

After a minute, she responded.

Chelsea: Yeah. Working late tonight. Between clients and grabbing a quick cup of yogurt. What's up?

It would be totally expected for him to jump right into asking her out or trying to get her to meet up with him, so he decided to kill some time first.

Drew: Yogurt? Ew...

Chelsea: What's wrong with yogurt?

Drew: It's gross

Chelsea: No it's not!

Drew: It is! It's like sour white goo. Gross.

Chelsea: That is not even a little bit true. This is Greek yogurt and it has blueberries. It's yummy.

Drew: Not a fan of blueberries either. That's not your dinner, is it?

Chelsea: It's the snack that's holding me over until dinner.

Drew: When are you out of there?

Chelsea: 8:30

Drew: Seriously? I didn't think clinics were open that late

Chelsea: Normally we're not, but it was a special request so I volunteered

Well damn. She probably did it to have something to do on a Friday night since she wasn't here.

Looking up, he glanced around the bar and saw all the usual members of their group–Kendall, Shauna, Alex, Jimmy, and Bianca...yeah, they were all here.

Maybe it was time he got Chelsea up to date on that situation.

Drew: So Jimmy and Bianca didn't get married

Chelsea: ???

Drew: Apparently all the things we said to them made them both stop and think

Chelsea: So they broke up?

Drew: No

Chelsea: Oh.

Drew: It's a whole big thing. Can I call you later when you get home?

Chelsea: We've been over this...

Drew: Yeah, yeah, yeah, you don't think it's a good idea

Chelsea: Exactly

Drew: And yet you're still talking to me

No response.

One Mississippi. Two Mississippi. Three Mississippi...

Drew: Aren't you the least bit curious about what's going on?

Chelsea: Okay, maybe a little

Drew: What time are you going to be home?

A smile was tugging at his lips because he knew she was trying to find a way to get out of it, but her curiosity was getting the better of her.

Chelsea: After nine

Chelsea: Probably closer to 9:30. I plan on grabbing some takeout on the way home

He wanted to offer to pick some up for her and meet her

at her place, but for now, he was happy that she was going to talk to him.

Drew: Great! I'll talk to you at 9:30

Chelsea: K. Gotta go. Client should be here any minute.

Drew: Talk to you later

She didn't reply and it didn't matter.

Feeling better than he had in weeks, he pushed his beer aside and went back to where Jimmy was waiting to shoot some darts with him. It would be a great way to kill the next hour before he left because there was no way he was going to call Chelsea from the bar. He was going to be home and sitting on his own couch with no distractions.

She was enough of a distraction.

And maybe, just maybe, they could put all this crap behind them and start over.

Or just...start.

16

"*Oof!*"

Faceplanting on the bathroom floor seriously wasn't part of the plan.

Coming home, showering, and putting on something other than her boring cotton panties was.

When her client didn't show–the rat bastard–Chelsea had all but sprinted from the building and then sped across town to get home. It was another *GrubHub* night and she had come to terms with it.

She knew the plan was for Drew to call her, but she had a feeling he might show up at her place instead.

And she wouldn't hate it.

Even though she would pretend that she did to his face.

Secretly, she wanted to see him–or not so secretly. She was completely open and honest with herself about how much she missed him. And if everything he'd been saying about missing her was true and if he really was sincere about wanting to take her out someplace...if he said any of those things to her face, she'd cave in a heartbeat.

Which was why coming home and showering was so important.

And so was the shaving of pertinent areas.

A girl can't be too prepared, right?

Now, as she struggled to get to her feet, she prayed she wouldn't be sporting a fat lip along with her favorite sexy underwear.

Moving in close to the mirror, Chelsea inspected her face and almost sagged with relief before glaring at the rogue shoe she had tripped over. In her haste to get in the shower, she had stripped all over the bathroom.

Lesson learned.

Quickly, she brushed her teeth, moisturized from head to toe, and cursed the fact that she hadn't had a pedicure in almost a month.

"First world problems, Chels. Focus!"

After that, she slid on the sexy undies along with a nightshirt that had a cartoon sheep walking upright in slippers and a sleep mask, with the words "Sheep Walker" underneath it. It was pretty darn cute if she did say so herself, and hopefully Drew would get to see it.

Why put on the jammies instead of clothes? Well–and she thought it was a fairly brilliant move–if Drew *did* happen to show up, he would think he was surprising her. Would she be all dressed just to be hanging out alone at home? No. Chelsea felt it added some authenticity to the situation.

Or maybe she was genuinely going insane and needed to talk to a shrink.

"Authenticity," she murmured. "This is all completely normal."

Her food was due to arrive any minute and she still had to dry her hair.

"Decisions...decisions..." Opting to put on just a little makeup–not too much, mind you–she kept her hair up in a towel until after her dinner was delivered. Then she could blow it dry quickly before she ate.

Everything was coming together. All she needed was to *not* freak out and try to relax.

Easier said than done.

Twenty minutes later, she shook out her hair, pulled on her robe and studied her reflection. She looked good but not like she was trying too hard. She felt like *should* Drew show up, he would never know all the effort she put into looking like she hadn't put in an effort.

Yeah, I definitely need help. I should look up psychologists tomorrow and make an appointment.

Out in her living room, she turned off the overhead light and left on one small lamp that sat on her end table. Then she set up her dinner–Chinese again–on the coffee table, before turning on the TV and immediately putting on HGTV. It didn't seem to matter what show was on; she'd watch it.

It was barely nine o'clock so she knew she could eat in peace without having to rush–which was good because The Property Brothers deserved all of her attention.

Hell, they deserved everyone's attention.

"Those are some fine-looking men." She took a forkful of sesame chicken and watched as the brothers walked across the screen on their way to help a family of four find a new home. "I would totally let them find me a new home." Then she paused. "If I had money to buy a home." Yeah, her condo was a rental, but someday she hoped to own a place of her own.

And perhaps own it with her husband.

"If I ever get one of those..." she added with a weary sigh.

Pushing that thought aside, she focused on her dinner and the Scott brothers. And when her phone rang at exactly 9:30, she wasn't sure if she was surprised so much time had passed or pissed off that Drew was actually calling and not ringing her doorbell.

Muting the TV, she picked up her phone and saw his name on the screen.

"Hey," she said, hoping she sounded neutral.

"Hey," he replied, sounding very relaxed. "Is now a good time?"

"Yeah, why?" They had agreed on 9:30 so...

"I just wanted to make sure you got home and had time to eat before we got on the phone," he explained. "So if you need to finish eating and want to call me back, that's fine."

Well, that was kind of sweet.

"No, I'm good. I just finished."

"Great! So how was the rest of your night? Did everything go okay with your last client?"

"Oh, um...they never showed."

"Seriously?"

"Yeah. Seriously. And that was after they called begging for this after-hours appointment!"

"That's just rude."

"I agree. That's the last time I agree to do something like that." She shook her head and got comfortable on the couch. "I emailed my boss and let him know because I'm starting a new narrating gig next week and won't be back in the clinic until Thursday."

"Is there anything he can do? Can he fire the client?"

Laughing softly, she replied, "Unfortunately, no. But he can still bill them since they didn't call in advance to cancel. That usually gets their attention so they don't do it again."

"Still, it kind of sucks that you had to stay late when it wasn't necessary."

"I guess, but it's not like I had anything else to do." Chelsea immediately snapped her mouth shut and wanted to kick herself for admitting such a thing. "I mean..."

"No, no...I get it. For what it's worth, you weren't missing anything tonight. The crowd was kind of lame and everyone's being weird so..."

"So they didn't get married, huh?"

"Yeah. I didn't find out about it until a little over a week ago."

"Really? But...why? You were still there at the resort. You didn't go to the wedding?"

"There wasn't a wedding to go to," he said slowly, as if explaining it to a child. "And...okay, basically, after you left, it was a bit of circus."

Was it wrong how that made her smile?

"Why?"

He began to explain how Bianca came to the room looking for her and she almost choked on the imagery.

"You're lying!" she said, but she was laughing.

"I'm really not! She waltzed in like she was the freaking queen or something and was expecting you to just be sitting there waiting to be her maid of honor!"

Sadly, it wasn't all that hard to believe. It was typical of Bianca.

"I'm not going to lie; it was very satisfying to throw her out after I told her off."

"Well, thank you for defending me. You still should have gone..."

"Then Jimmy showed up," he interrupted.

"Oh?"

"And we fought and I told him that I wasn't with you to help him. I told him I was with you because I was attracted to you–that once we didn't have his fiancée acting like a puppet master, we found out that we actually liked each other." He paused, his voice gruff and very, very yummy. "I told him I didn't agree with what he was doing and then I threw him out."

He had already told her that part via text, but she still couldn't believe it. "Really?" she asked quietly.

"Yes, really. Chels, I feel like we've let other people dictate this relationship–even when it was barely a friendship. Can't we..."

This time she was the one to interrupt. "I promise to circle back to what you were about to say, but I still don't get how they ended up not getting married."

She heard him sigh and felt a little guilty for not letting him say what he wanted to, but she had to know the full story before she could allow herself to think about the two of them.

"Jimmy went back to their room and Bianca was crying. He was pissed off and said he'd had enough. He told her this whole wedding thing had done nothing but cause trouble, and that wasn't how he wanted them to start their lives together."

"Oh, God. Bianca must have flipped!"

"She didn't talk to him for a week, he said. Apparently, when she got home and talked to her parents, they were upset because they had no idea she tried to elope!"

"They're a pretty close family so I'm sure they would have been devastated to miss out."

"So when Bianca finally called him, Jimmy laid down

the law a bit and told her she needed to quit playing games and manipulating people to get what she wanted."

"No!"

"Yup. And before you say that maybe that's just his version of things, the two of them came over to my place to talk to me and she admitted to it all. Crazy, right?"

For a moment, she couldn't speak.

So...they go and talk to Drew, who had been vocal about the whole thing, but they didn't come talk to her? How freaking unfair was that?

"Oh, well...good for you," she said, even though it practically killed her.

"Okay, before you freak out–and I totally know you are–you should know that they talked about reaching out to you, but..."

"But...?"

"But, I kind of told them not to."

"What?! *Why?* Why would you do that?"

"Because it wasn't the most heartfelt get-together," he said.

"What do you mean?"

"It was like they were saying, 'Okay, we get what you're saying, but you were still a dick,' and honestly, it felt a little forced. Like they were expecting me to apologize."

"And did you?"

"Hell no! If they–or should I say, if *she*–apologized, I would have felt differently. But there was zero sincerity there, and I knew if she reached out to you, it was only going to be worse."

"Yeah, Bianca is the queen of the fauxpology."

"Um...what?"

"Fauxpology. You know, it's an apology, but not."

He didn't respond.

"You know, faux as in fake?"

"Ah. Gotcha. Yeah, that's exactly what it was like."

"So how'd you leave it with them?"

Another sigh. "They're going to go for premarital counseling, and they're having an engagement party next month."

Nodding, Chelsea fought the urge to be hurt.

And failed.

"Wow. So...good for them, I guess."

"I don't know how much it will help, but for now, they're trying."

"Sure."

"C'mon, Chels. Don't be like that."

"Like what?" she cried. "Hurt? Offended? Pissed off? Because it's not that easy! It pisses me off that I wasted so much time on a friendship that was a waste of damn time. Meanwhile, your bromance with Jimmy was barely affected!"

"We've been over this–it's not a bromance! That's not a thing!"

"Oh, please. It's totally a thing and the two of you are the model of it."

He groaned. "Okay, back to you and Bianca. I think it's just different for women. Guys get over things and don't hold grudges. You've said that yourself. You can't really be surprised by any of this."

"And I'm not surprised, but that doesn't mean I'm not hurt, Drew."

"Then go see them," he suggested. "I'll go with you."

She snorted with disbelief. "Great. So we have a repeat of the disaster we had in Bluffton. Awesome."

"It won't be like that..."

"Yeah, no. I'm not looking to get kicked in the face

again. And honestly, if I was going to go anywhere with you, it certainly wouldn't be to see Jimmy and Bianca."

If.

If I was going to go anywhere with you.

Shit.

This was getting him nowhere.

He knew it was risky to tell her about his meeting with their friends, but he believed in being honest with her.

And instantly regretted it.

"Look, I could have lied to you, Chelsea. I could have simply left off the fact that they came and talked to me, but I didn't want to do that. You deserve to know the truth."

"I get it, I do, and I appreciate it. That doesn't make it any less hurtful."

"Dammit, I thought I was doing a good thing, like I was protecting you."

"By telling me how they were willing to see you and not me?"

"But they *were* willing to see you!" he clarified. "I meant I thought I was protecting you by talking them out of it! I know I felt shitty when they left because it was all so anticlimactic. And after witnessing the way Bianca was toward you and the way she carried on after you left, I didn't think you'd want to deal with that. So...I'm sorry. It wasn't my call to make."

Then he held his breath and hoped she understood and wasn't going to be even angrier with him than she already was.

As if that was even possible...

"I'm really beginning to feel like this is all too much,

Drew. The hurt, the drama, the constant misunderstandings..." She paused and sighed. "The only way I'm going to be able to move on with my life and feel good about myself is to completely distance myself from all of it."

Uh-oh...

"And that kind of means that you and I probably shouldn't talk anymore."

"Chelsea, wait! Don't say that!"

"Not saying it won't make it any less true. You are always going to be friends with Jimmy, but I'm no longer friends with Bianca. How could anything possibly work? I would never ask you not to hang out with your friends, but I'm never going to want to do that with you. So..."

Okay, she completely had a point, but that didn't mean he had to like it.

"There's got to be a way," he argued, feeling more than a little desperate. "I don't want to lose you."

"Believe it or not, I really don't want to lose you either, but...there's no way this can work, so...I should probably go."

"Chelsea," he pled. "Please. We need to talk about this. You can't keep running away!"

"Excuse me?"

Probably not the smartest way to convince her...

"You ran from me in Bluffton, you've been running from me for weeks, and you're running now. We're both adults and we should be able to talk about this logically. Maturely."

"Are you calling me immature? Because if you ask me, you're the one who's immature."

"Okay, fine. I'm rubber, you're glue. Now we're both acting like children. Happy?"

She groaned before responding. "This is what I mean!

This isn't healthy! I swear, it still feels like we don't even like each other!"

In that moment, Drew knew he'd had enough. "Not like each other? Why? Because we don't get along 100% of the time or because we don't agree with everything the other says? I hate to break it to you, Chelsea, but that's the way things are in normal relationships! It's okay to disagree! It's okay to get mad! And I don't think this is a matter of not really liking each other; I think you're using it as an excuse to back off."

"That's not..."

But he didn't let her finish. "I'm not going to keep chasing after you," he said gruffly. "I can't. I feel like that's all I've been doing and there's only so many fiery hoops I'm willing to jump through before I need something in return."

"So...what are you saying?"

Swallowing hard, he said, "I'm saying that...you win. If this is too hard for you and it's not what you want, then... okay. I won't bother you again."

"Drew..."

"It's okay. I get it. Things just sort of spiraled out of control and there's too many people in this relationship for it to really work."

And it killed him to admit it–mainly because he didn't mean it. He just knew that pressuring Chelsea wasn't going to get him anywhere and he couldn't keep having this same argument for her. She was stubborn–more stubborn than he realized–and it wasn't fair for him to keep pushing her to change just to please him.

No matter how much he wanted to.

So he'd make the sacrifice.

"You have no idea how much I wish things were different," she said, and he heard the slight tremble in her voice.

"It can be," he replied miserably. "But I'm not going to push."

She sighed again. "If I asked you to stop being friends with Jimmy, would you?"

Damn. "I honestly don't know. I don't think it has to come to that."

"Really? So you're saying when this ridiculous wedding actually does go down, and you're asked to be a best man or something, you'd turn him down because I won't go?"

"I think we're getting a little ahead of ourselves here..."

"Drew, I've spent a lot of years not feeling good about myself and I realized that was largely because of the people I surrounded myself with. These last few weeks really opened my eyes to that. I may not be out socializing much, but my mental state is so much better. I actually like myself for the first time in years!"

And that was really it.

That was why he couldn't push on this.

No matter how much he maneuvered them so she didn't have to be around any of their–well, *his*–friends, they were still going to be there on some level. How could he ask her to sacrifice her mental health for him?

Bottom line, he couldn't.

She deserved to be happy.

Even if it wasn't with him.

"You're right."

"What?"

"You're right, Chels. You deserve to be happy and it's time for you to realize just how amazing you are. You don't need to keep walking on eggshells because of the people we know so...take care of yourself."

She was quiet for several moments and he heard her

soft sniffle and it just about gutted him. Finally, she said, "Yeah, you too."

And then she was gone.

Drew wanted to be pissed–knew he should be. If it weren't for their damn friends, who knows where he and Chelsea would be now? But other than going back to O'Dwyer's and punching Jimmy and yelling at Bianca, there wasn't a damn thing he could do.

He was getting pretty tired of feeling helpless where Chelsea was concerned.

But it looked like that's the way it was destined to be.

17

"Dammit." Muttering another more colorful curse, Chelsea looked at the manuscript again and offered a weak smile to her producer. "Sorry, Janelle. I feel like I can't get the words out today."

Or for the last two weeks.

Whatever.

"It's okay, Chelsea. You want to take a break and maybe have a cup of tea or something?"

"Yeah, that would be..." There was a loud ruckus coming from outside the studio and she and Janelle looked at each other with curiosity.

The door flew open just as someone yelled, "You can't go in there!" and Chelsea was sure her jaw hit the ground when Bianca breezed in.

Oh, for fuck's sake...

Luckily Chelsea and Janelle had worked together for years, and even though she had never met Bianca, Janelle knew about her.

And her theatrics.

Standing, she came over to Chelsea, looking mildly amused. "Want me to stay?"

Ugh...do I?

"It's okay but...don't go far."

"Gotcha." And with a small pat on the back, Janelle grabbed her coffee cup and walked out, leaving the door slightly ajar.

"It's a lot smaller in here than I thought it would be," Bianca said, her nose slightly wrinkled.

"It's normally only a person or two reading so we don't need more space." Rubbing her temples, she asked, "What are you doing here, Bee?"

Rather than answer right away, Bianca circled the room until she stopped in front of Chelsea's stool and manuscript stand. Leaning forward, she looked like she was reading it, but considering it was a history book about the Civil War, she doubted she'd read more than a few lines.

"Oh, my God is that boring! Ugh...how do you stand it!"

"Did you just decide to stop by to mock my job? Because if you did, you can leave now or I can have security come and escort you. Your choice."

Straightening, Bianca stared at her, completely dumbfounded.

Probably because other than their last conversation in Bluffton, Chelsea had never stood up to her.

Kind of loving my inner tough girl...Roar!

She expected a snarky comeback or–at the very least–a putdown. Instead, Bianca moved away from the script and looked a little...regretful.

Well, this is new...

With her hands in front of her, clutching her Coach purse, she said, "I'm sorry. That was disrespectful of me. You know I'm not a history buff or...you know...whatever you want to call it, but that doesn't mean that you or other people don't find it interesting." She met Chelsea's gaze solemnly. "You're very good at what you do and obviously you're in demand so, what do I know, right?"

It was like being in an alternate universe and she had no idea how to respond.

"I'm here because...well...I owe you more than that apology. I probably owe you dozens."

Or thousands...

Letting out a long breath, Bianca continued. "What happened in Bluffton really opened my eyes, and honestly, I didn't like what I saw."

Join the club.

"I didn't realize just how out of control I had gotten and when Jimmy said he didn't want to marry me, I fell apart." She started to walk around the room, but Chelsea stayed where she was, curious to see where all this was going.

"I blamed you, I blamed Drew, I blamed everyone, and Jimmy told me the only one to blame was me," she explained. "When I got home and told my parents about what happened, they weren't sympathetic like I expected them to be. They were totally on your side and boy, did I get an earful from them."

Chelsea had to smile because she knew that had to be a wild conversation.

"We're in counseling now," she went on. "It was supposed to be like a group thing, but the counselor listened to us talk that first night for all of five minutes before he suggested doing it one-on-one." She sighed. "I was mortified. All of a sudden, it wasn't just my friends and family seeing how crazy I was, but total strangers." She shuddered.

"And is it helping?" Chelsea couldn't help but ask.

"It is. I've learned how I...well...how much I mistreat

people. Especially you," she said sadly. "And not just recently, but for years. You were the one person who made me feel good about myself mainly because...um...because you made me look good."

Don't punch her...don't punch her...

"Next to you, I always felt like the pretty one and you were the smart one. And then I used you to help me with school. I don't know how you put up with me!"

There was no way to answer that right now, so Chelsea simply crossed her arms over her chest and waited for whatever verbal assault was coming next.

"Here's the thing, Chels. I know I've been horrible to you and you have every right to hate me. I don't blame you for it. I can apologize until I'm blue in the face, but it can never make up for all the things I've said and done."

All she could do was nod.

"But don't take this out on Drew."

Say what now?

"He's been miserable ever since you took off. He's not himself. Whenever he comes out, you can tell his heart's not into it and then he ends up leaving early. Jimmy says he's never seen him like this."

"Maybe he's just busy with work or he's sick," she said with a shrug. "It probably doesn't have anything to do with me."

"Oh, please. He talks about you all the time. He finds a way to mention your name in every conversation we have with him." Her shoulders sagged. "You really need to give him another chance."

"Why do you even care?" And yes, she couldn't help the slightly sardonic tone. "Do you miss having someone standing around to make you look good? Or do you need someone to constantly put down to make you *feel* good? Well, forget it! I'm done with that!"

"Chels..."

Dropping her arms, she took a step toward her former friend. "No, I'm serious! I've had enough of your attitude and all your demands! You're exhausting! It's like you never grew up and I need to be around people who make *me* feel good, who make *me* happy, and that's not you! Or Kendall. Or Shauna. Or Jimmy. Or..."

"Drew?"

"We'll never know, will we?" she asked with disgust. "You made sure you poisoned both our opinions of each other for the last year and...and thanks to you, everything's awkward and ruined!"

"I'm really sorry, Chelsea!"

"Oh, shut up! Save your phony apologies! I'm not buying them."

Gasping, Bianca's eyes went wide. "How dare you accuse me of making a fauxpology! I am being totally sincere!"

Chelsea almost laughed at the reference–remembered how she explained it to Drew not so long ago.

"Can't help it. I know you too well. You never mean your apologies. Ever. Why would I believe you now?"

Stomping her foot, Bianca growled with frustration. "What is it you want me to do here, Chels? Like I said, I get it, you hate me! I'm not asking you not to. But I am asking you to give Drew another chance! Please!"

It would be pointless to try to explain how *she* was the problem because Bianca–being Bianca–simply wouldn't get it.

"Drew and I have already talked about this and decided it was for the best for whatever we had to just...end."

And maybe someday her heart wouldn't ache just thinking about it.

"You've ruined it," Chelsea added. "You and your selfish ways ruined what could have been a great relationship for me. Drew could have been the one, but thanks to you, it's over! So you don't have to worry about any competition. No other couple will beat you and Jimmy to the altar, and no other couple will be more sickeningly in love than the two of you. So just...just go. Go away and leave me alone."

Turning her back on Bianca, she walked over to her script and tried to calm down.

"I can't believe you're going to throw away a great guy just to be spiteful to me," Bianca said, and *that* was the straw that broke the camel's back.

Oh, it's on, bitch...

"Here's a newsflash, Bee. Everything isn't about you!"

"But you just said..."

"Yeah, I know what I said!" *Dammit. I did sort of imply...* "You're the reason things are awkward! You're the reason everything bad in my life happens! But I did not end things with Drew just to *spite* you, you self-centered twit!"

And cue the dramatic gasp...

Gasping, Bianca's eyes went wide again. "Self-centered..."

"Twit! Idiot! Bitch!"

Okay, slow your roll, potty mouth...

"One of the reasons I don't want to be with Drew is because I don't want to be around *you*! I don't want to hear any more of your boring stories about your hair or your nails or your shopping! Most of the time, you look like a drag queen, not a supermodel!"

"Hey!"

"You're plastic and phony and you know what? Drew was right! You are like Malibu Barbie!"

"What?!"

"And you know that duck face you make when you take selfies? We all make fun of them! No one makes that face anymore! Especially at this age! You're not twenty-one anymore! We're almost thirty! Stop doing it!"

"I don't..."

"You do. All the time. And it's pathetic. Do you even know how to take a picture of somebody else? Even the Kardashians post pictures of scenery or their kids, for crying out loud! You should try it sometime."

"I posted a picture of Mrs. Fluffykins last week!"

"And you were holding her up and making that stupid duckface. I think the cat was even embarrassed for you." Her heart was racing, her throat was dry, and yet she felt invigorated. "Does Jimmy even know what you look like without makeup? Does he know those aren't your real boobs?"

Bianca's hands immediately covered her breasts.

"Or your real nose!"

"Chelsea!" One hand flew to her nose. "You know that was because of my deviated septum!"

"Was it?" she asked sarcastically. "Because I remember you telling that to people so they wouldn't know it was plastic surgery."

"Okay, you've made your point!" Bianca cried tearfully. "Did it make you feel better to put me down?"

Chelsea walked across the room until they were practically toe to toe. "No, because I'm not like you. Putting you down doesn't lift me up." Then she paused. "But it did help to finally get all those things off my chest."

"So, you *do* feel better."

With a careless shrug, she nodded. "I guess I do. The difference here is that I said it all in the heat of the moment while we were fighting, not just because it's a day ending in -y. What's your excuse for years of being a bitch?"

They stood there staring at each other for several minutes before Janelle walked back in. "Everything okay?"

Chelsea arched a brow at Bianca before responding. "Yeah. Everything's fine. We're done." She looked toward Janelle. "You ready to start up again?"

Bianca took a step back. And then another. She was practically out the door before she turned around one last time. "Drew misses you. He's a good guy and he genuinely cares about you. Just...think about it."

Refusing to let that thought take hold, she walked over and closed the studio door, and with a smile on her face, she said, "Okay, let's take it from the top again."

The paper in his hand was now damp and wrinkled from his holding it for so damn long, but Drew felt like maybe holding on to it was the answer to all his problems.

Or maybe he was just kidding himself and had become completely delusional.

Probably a little from column A and a little from column B.

Bianca had shown up at his office earlier and handed him a paper with the address of the studio Chelsea was currently recording at. She had urged him–in a very reasonable and very un-Bianca-like way–to go after Chelsea and convince her to give them a chance. When he had asked her why, she very meekly said, "Because Chelsea deserves to be happy. And I know you're the man who can make that happen."

Which had left him speechless.

He had almost called Jimmy to see if his fiancée had fallen and hit her head or something, but for some reason, he believed her. The problem wasn't finding Chelsea. The problem was convincing her without being too pushy. He swore he'd back off and he had, but...it wasn't getting any easier. He still missed her and he still believed they deserved a chance.

Still...would she appreciate him just showing up at the studio and interrupting her recording? She was there to work–to read and narrate and whatnot. Showing up there would probably not go over well with her author or producer or whoever it was she was working with.

How the hell does that whole process work anyway?

Putting the paper down and telling himself it was hopeless, Drew leaned back in his chair and let out a long breath. He stared at the walls for several minutes when the idea came to him.

It was perfect.

It was brilliant.

Booting up his laptop, Drew spent the better part of an hour clearing his schedule and doing everything he could to implement all aspects of his plan. By the time he was done and striding out of his office, he felt energized.

Out in his car, he contemplated his options. Driving would enable him to have his car, but taking the train was definitely faster. So he drove to the station in St. James and parked. He'd be in Manhattan in a little less than two hours, and with any luck, it would only take him fifteen minutes to get to Chelsea.

Okay, that last part was completely unrealistic. It was

Manhattan, after all. If a city could have a middle name, Manhattan's would be traffic jam.

During the entire train ride, he did the best he could to distract himself–he checked emails, read a couple of news stories on his phone, played some solitaire–but as soon as the train pulled into Penn Station, he was full of nerves.

Was this really the right thing to do?

Was he pushing too hard?

But rather than staying in his head too long, he joined the throngs of commuters and did his best to get up to the street while using his Uber app on his phone. It took close to seven minutes for a car to arrive, but once it did, Drew knew he had to do this–had to make things right. And if this didn't work, then...well...then he'd have no choice but to let things go and move on.

He'd hate it, but he'd do it.

The ride took almost fifteen minutes and he probably could have walked in it five, but again, he didn't focus on it and instead hopped out and sprinted into the building. It took a minute to get his bearings, but he hopped on the elevator and rode it to the fourth floor where the studio was. When he stepped out, he was met with a wall of total silence. The lobby area was empty and when he walked through the glass doors and over to the receptionist, he realized the only sound was his breathing.

Okay, this is awkward.

"Hey," he said, still a little breathless from the sprint. "I'm Drew Russo and I'm wondering if you could help me."

"Do you have an appointment?"

Something in her stiff tone alerted him.

Clearing his throat, he said, "Um...no. Like I said, I'm..."

"I know who you are. Chelsea mentioned you." Then she made a face like she was smelling some bad fish.

"Uh...yeah, so...I'd really like to..."

"You know, Chelsea is one of the sweetest people I've ever met!" she said, sounding a bit fierce–and considering she was around the same age as his mother, it made him stand a little straighter and listen. "And the fact that you played such an awful trick on her!" She huffed with disdain. "You need to leave."

He could argue that he wasn't playing, but...his mother taught him not to disrespect his elders. That left only one option.

Drew poured on all the charm he had while he explained why he was here and what he wanted to do.

It seemed to take forever–which turned out to only be ten minutes–but at this rate it was ten minutes longer that he was away from Chelsea.

"Will you help me? Please?" he softly pleaded.

She studied him hard, and any minute he expected her to tell him he was grounded and call him "young man."

Luckily, she didn't. He saw her features soften as her shoulders dropped a little. "Don't make me regret this."

He was behind her desk and hugging her before he could even stop himself. "Thank you! You have no idea how much I appreciate this."

After a brief hug in return, she held up her hand and picked up the phone with the other. "Hey, Janelle, it's Robyn. Listen, I need your help with something..."

Drew stood back and listened as she gave the Reader's Digest version of what was going on and then held his breath.

And prayed that whoever this Janelle person was, that she would help.

"Okay, thanks," Robyn said before hanging up. Smiling up at him, she said, "Chelsea will be out in five minutes.

Why don't you have a seat?" She motioned to the small sitting area, which consisted of a small love seat and two uncomfortable-looking chairs.

"But..."

"Five minutes," she repeated, a bit more firmly this time.

"Yes, ma'am," he murmured and walked over to the love seat.

And now we wait...

18

"*DREW?*" Chelsea asked incredulously. What on earth would he be doing here? Why would he come here?

He stood and she could immediately tell he was nervous. He had a folder in his hands that she could see he had a white-knuckled grip on. In all the time they'd known each other, she'd never seen him like this. For the first time ever, he didn't seem quite so cocky and confident and...it kind of intrigued her.

"Hey," he said, his voice low. "Can we...can we go someplace and talk?"

Looking around, she knew she didn't want to do this in front of anyone. Not that she had any idea of what exactly *this* was–she just knew talking in private was probably for the best.

"Um...we can use the studio. My producer had to take a call so..." Turning, she made her way back to the room with Drew right behind her. Once they were inside, she left the door slightly ajar–much like Janelle did when Bianca was here.

And that's when it hit her...

"Oh, my God...did you send Bianca here? Is that why she came?"

"What? No!" he cried. "I had no idea she was coming here!"

Crossing her arms over her chest, she stared at him.

His shoulders sagged. "She came to my office after she left here and told me about it, and that prompted me to come for myself."

"Well, you could have saved yourself the trip. It's the end of the day and I was just finishing up a few things before it was quitting time so...sorry you wasted your afternoon. If you'll excuse me..." She went to move past him, but his hand on her arm stopped her.

"Just a few minutes, Chelsea. Please. I came all the way here and your producer is on a call...please."

She let herself truly look at him and her heart ached. He looked sad and tired and so very different from the man she was used to. Maybe she was a glutton for punishment, but she felt like she had to know what else he could possibly have to say to her.

"Fine." She sat down on her stool and motioned to the other one that was in the corner, but he declined.

"Thanks," he said before letting out a long breath. "Okay, here it is...no, wait...that's not how I should start this."

It was a bit adorable to watch him try to find his words.

He gave her a lopsided grin before he spoke again. "Never in my entire life has a woman left me speechless. But you, Chelsea Cooper, do that to me. At first, it was with your intellect, and then your snark, but then your witty banter drew me in." He let out a soft laugh. "God, I used to look forward to Friday nights just to see what kind of ridiculous conversation we'd find ourselves in."

She couldn't help but laugh too. "Some of them were kind of crazy."

"And just for the record, I know togas were Roman and not Egyptian."

The memory of that conversation made her smile.

"Although, you'd still look hot in any ancient attire. And not because the togas hide anything like Bianca said, but because you'd be naked underneath." He waggled his eyebrows comically.

"Drew..."

"Here's the thing, Chels, all those things that came before the trip were light and fun, but your honesty is what leaves me speechless the most. And not in a bad way." Pausing, he took a small step closer to her. "I hang out with a lot of people who talk a lot about themselves, but none of it's serious and brutally honest, like the way you are. I think of all the conversations Jimmy and I have and they're mostly stupid and childish."

Now wasn't the time to point out how she completely agreed with that.

"I didn't realize how I needed to grow up or how much I needed someone who didn't talk to me like I'm an idiot."

"Well, since you think I'm so honest," she began quietly, "then I should apologize to you. Because in the beginning, I *did* talk to you like you were an idiot."

"In the beginning, I *was* an idiot. I'd like to think I changed–that during our road trip, I changed."

She nodded. "You did."

"I'm so sorry about how that all started. I wasn't being fair to you and I hurt you."

"Drew, we've been over it. I don't regret anything about how we ended up in the car together. I hate the way the trip ended, but..." She shrugged. "You've explained it all to me and I'm good with letting it go."

"Okay," he said, visibly relaxing. "Then..."

"But all the other issues are still there," she explained. "Bianca came here and apologized and I got a lot of things off my chest but...I'm still not going to want to go and hang out with her. That's a part of my life that I want to put behind me." Tears stung her eyes. "*You're* part of what I need to put behind me."

Now he stepped in close, cupping her cheek with his hand. "I love you, Chelsea. I am so freaking in love with you that I can't function." Resting his forehead against hers, he closed his eyes. "I don't want you to put us behind you. Please."

It was crazy for her to even be considering this. It was complicated and had the potential to get messy, and she hated messes.

"I...I don't know, Drew. I can't make that kind of decision right now. It's too hard."

She expected him to argue or plead his case a little more, but he surprised her by taking a step back and gripping the folder tightly again with both hands.

"What's in the folder?" she asked softly, amazed her voice didn't crack.

He sighed and stared down at it. "I was thinking of getting into some different kinds of media advertising and doing an audio manual for the company. You know, since most people prefer to listen to books rather than reading them."

"I never said most people prefer it, but a large number do."

"I didn't mean to imply that you had said it, but I've

been doing a little research and thought it might be something to look into to give employees the option."

"And the folder?"

Lifting it up, he explained, "Oh, I was also hoping you'd consider being the narrator for it."

Chelsea knew her jaw was practically on the floor. "Excuse me?"

Nodding, he said, "Yeah, I really love the way you read, and your voice is very pleasant to listen to–even when the subject matter is less than thrilling."

"Gee, thanks."

Jerk.

"So...I guess this is a little awkward considering our... personal situation, but...would you consider reading it?"

"You can't be serious right now." Crossing her arms again, she glared at him. "Why would I want to narrate your business manual? And besides that, there are channels for you to go through first. You can't just walk in here and ask me to read it!"

"Oh, well..."

"Read what?" Janelle asked as she walked back into the studio. She introduced herself to Drew and he explained his stupid plan to her. Chelsea knew her producer would back her up and then she'd toss him out and solve this problem for her.

Feeling a little smug, she sat back and waited.

"Sure!" Janelle said, smiling. "Let's give it a test run!"

"*What?!*" Chelsea cried. "Why? We're in the middle of our script! You know, the one from a *paying* client?"

Janelle simply waved her off. "Please, we both know you're bored silly with it for today and we're at a good stopping point. Go ahead and give this one a test and then we'll call it a day."

"Janelle..."

But clearly, no one was listening. Janelle walked back into her booth and Drew took a seat on the stool in the corner. With no other choice, Chelsea placed the folder on her stand and glared at the two of them.

"Whenever you're ready," Janelle said sweetly, causing Chelsea to glare at her harder.

"Fine, whatever. Let's get this over with." Opening the folder, she scanned the first few sentences and froze.

It wasn't a manual.

It wasn't anything business-related.

It was a letter from Drew to her.

For the life of him, Drew had no idea how he wasn't throwing up right now.

He finally understood every ridiculous rom-com he'd ever seen–the ones where the hero looks like he's going to either be sick or cry at the end.

Only those guys were just pretending–he was actually living it!

Those lucky bastards. They had no idea what kind of hell this feeling really was.

"We're recording, Chelsea," Janelle said from the booth.

"I...I don't think I can read this out loud," Chelsea said, her voice shaking, but when she turned and looked at him, he saw the uncertainty there.

"Read it," he said quietly. "Please."

Facing the microphone, she gently cleared her throat and began to read.

"Chelsea, do you remember the night we met? You talked to me about how you had just finished narrating a book about the Pilgrims. I made jokes about the first Thanksgiving and you walked away without a laugh. I swore to myself that night that I would do my best to make you laugh at least once. I accomplished it the following week with my Marco Polo impression, remember? I know you thought I was a complete doofus, but it was worth it to hear you laugh.

We spent every Friday night together for the better part of a year, and I know we didn't always like each other, but I've never been so happy to realize how wrong I was. I hate how we wasted all that time with animosity when there was so much more there.

You're everything to me. In a matter of a few days, you made me realize all that was missing from my life. I had become so jaded with everything and had little connection to anything or anyone, and after an hour in the car with you, I began to actually feel again. Granted, some of that feeling was annoyance, but again, I came to realize I was wrong.

The first time we kissed, my fate was sealed. You were it for me.

I look at you and see my future. You're what I want. Everything else–everyone else–is my past. I don't want to keep looking back–not at them and not at my mistakes. I want a chance at the life I know we can have together."

Pausing, Chelsea reached up and wiped tears from her face–something Drew wanted to do for her–but he knew she was going to finish reading first.

"I want to listen to you read. I want to start my day to the sound of your voice and end it with you beside me saying 'goodnight.' There's something I never told you, and maybe I should have, but...I've listened to every book you narrated. Granted, that was after our trip, but I did read all the books first–and that was all before. Whenever you mentioned what you were narrating, I would read it. I didn't think I'd enjoy listening to books, but when it's your voice, I find that I do.

I'm rambling and I'm sorry about that but...please tell me we can try. I miss you so much and I just want a chance. Let me prove that you are my only priority. You're the one I love, the one I want to come home to and spend time with.

I love you.

Love, Drew"

The room was painfully quiet for all of three seconds. In the distance, he could hear Janelle sniffling and then Chelsea, but he was paralyzed and too afraid to move.

Was she crying because she was going to turn him down, or was she crying because he won her over?

Why was this so hard?

His eyes never left Chelsea as he watched her close the folder and wipe at her face again. He saw Janelle leave the booth and give him a small wave before she walked out of the studio and then they were alone.

Just him and his girl.

Well, hopefully his girl.

She stood and straightened and looked at him and looked completely miserable.

Oh, shit. That's not a good sign.

Resigned to being rejected, Drew stood and slowly walked over to her. "Chelsea, I..." But he never got to finish. She closed the distance between them and cupped his face in her soft hands and kissed him.

Thank. God.

Her kiss was everything he could want and more. It was sweet and soft and then turned a little frantic and needy. If they were anywhere else, he'd be maneuvering them to the nearest flat surface so he could have his way with her, but... this was clearly not the time or the place.

When they finally breathlessly broke apart, he waited for her to speak.

"Drew Russo, how dare you make me read that out loud in front of Janelle!"

Okay, not exactly the words he was expecting...

"How am I supposed to show my face around here knowing she heard all that? And worse, it's all on tape!"

"I'm sure she could erase it...or give us the recording..."

"Ugh...you don't get it," she said with a small snort. "Now what am I supposed to do?"

"Um..."

"Did you take the train here?"

All he could do was stare at her like she was crazy because–let's face it–she sounded like it at the moment.

"Uh, yeah. Why?"

"Well, I guess that's something."

She stepped away and walked to the corner of the room where she picked up her purse and a sweater before walking to the door.

"What the hell's going on?" he demanded.

"We're leaving for the day. Why?"

Pinching the bridge of his nose, he silently counted to ten. "Why? Because I thought we were in the middle of something here!"

Her smile was patient and just so...Chelsea. She walked over and patted him on the cheek. "Yes, but the something we were in the middle of was going to require something big and very private to finish." Then she pressed in close and whispered in his ear, "Like us being naked and in a bed."

Pulling back, she winked at him and turned toward the door again.

"Wait, so...where are we going? Do you have your car with you?" he asked, trailing after her.

"I do, but traffic will be a beast." Then she gave him another saucy wink. "I tend to get lost a lot when I try to drive home from here. Lots of wrong turns. Just think of all the foreplay the ride home will give us."

Once they were inside the elevator, she kissed him again.

And it was even hotter than the one from minutes ago.

There was no way he was going to survive the long drive–which is what he told her.

Out on the sidewalk, she paused and looked at him. "Sweetheart, there is one very important thing I've learned about getting lost while driving."

"And what's that?"

"That sometimes a wrong turn can lead you in the right direction," she said, smiling. "Everything about our meeting and early relationship was wrong. We let other people direct us in what we should do and say. But look where it brought us."

And damn if that wasn't the most perfect description of their relationship.

EPILOGUE

SIX MONTHS LATER...

"I CAN'T BELIEVE I let you talk me into this."

"It's going to be fine."

"Says you."

"I also said you were free to change your mind–no questions asked."

"Okay, I've changed my mind."

"We're halfway to the airport!"

Sighing dramatically, Chelsea leaned her head back against the passenger seat. "I know! I thought I was going to be okay with it, but...now I'm just not sure."

"Say the word and I'll turn the car around and make the call."

Is that what she wanted? Really?

They'd overcome so many things in the last six months; they could get through this too, right?

"Chels?"

"I'm thinking!" Staring out the window, she watched the unremarkable scenery of the Northern State Parkway pass her by.

This won't be so bad, she thought. They were in a good

place right now. They'd moved in together just last month and were already talking about getting married. And the thought of marrying Drew simply made her giddy with excitement. She couldn't wait to be his wife and for them to start a family.

But that didn't mean this trip was the best thing for them.

Jimmy and Bianca were getting married.

For real this time.

And yes, in Bluffton.

It had taken *months* for Chelsea to even *begin* to entertain the thought of hanging out with the two of them, but once she agreed and the four of them went out for dinner, she was glad she did. Her friend changed–for the better–and it was like they were all meeting for the first time. It gave her a little peace to know Bianca had a real chance at a happy marriage.

It was the only reason she had finally agreed to go.

Even though she was having second thoughts now.

Going back to the place where so many things had gone wrong brought back a lot of negative feelings, but Drew assured her it was all going to be okay. And she wanted to believe him–she truly did. After all, he'd been right about just about everything.

It was painful, but she could admit that now.

They took the exit ramp and it took her several minutes for her to get out of her own thoughts and get her bearings.

"Where are we going?"

"We're crossing over to the Southern State Parkway," he said, smiling at her.

"The Southern State? But..."

That's when it hit her.

"I thought you said we were flying out of LaGuardia," she said playfully.

"That I did," he replied, winking at her.

"But this is the wrong way." And she couldn't help the small giggle that escaped.

"Sweetheart, have you ever driven to LaGuardia? No, right? Trust me. I know where I'm going."

"Oh, I believe you," she said smoothly as she leaned over and kissed him on the cheek. "I just hope you don't make any wrong turns and get us lost."

"You know, someone once told me how sometimes a wrong turn can take you in the right direction."

"Did they?"

Nodding, he said, "Sure did."

"And is that what we're doing? Heading in the right direction?"

"Anywhere we go together is the right direction; don't you know that?"

She wanted to tell him how corny that sounded, but...it was kind of sweet.

Taking one of her hands in his, Drew squeezed it. "Chels, we can go anywhere you want. Just say the word and we'll head anywhere in the country and blow off this wedding. I'd follow you wherever you want to go."

"Wow, that's a lot of pressure on me and my sense of direction."

"No pressure. Just love. And trust. Program the GPS and leave the driving to me."

A slow smiled played at her lips as she did just that.

"You sure about this?"

"Only if I get to drive over the Chesapeake Bay Bridge again."

It was both a challenge and a sign that she was strong enough to do this. All of it. The trip, the wedding, all of it.

"Let's make all new memories this time around."

"That was my plan all along," he said, kissing her hand. "Trust me, by the time we get back home, you'll remember this trip for all the right reasons. Possibly for the rest of our lives."

And she could only hope it meant there was a proposal coming.

If it did, she would act completely surprised.

WANT A SNEAK PEEK AT WHAT'S COMING NEXT IN THE ROADTRIPPING SERIES??

HERE'S A PREVIEW OF

TEST DRIVE

"DAMN. THAT'S A GOOD WORD."

Staring down at her phone, Willow Andrews sighed. It looked like her grandmother was going to win yet another game of *Words With Friends,* and she wasn't sure which was sadder – the fact that she was going to lose again or the fact that this was what she was doing on a Friday night.

"I clearly have a problem." She was about to put her phone down when it rang. Looking at her grandmother's sweet and smiling face, she knew it would be rude – and pointless – to ignore the call. Swiping the screen, she said, "So now you're calling to brag?"

The soft chuckle greeted her first. "Oh, now don't be like that, my little Willow bell. I can't help it if I'm good with words. I did spend forty years as an English teacher, you know."

"You could just let me win once in a while," she said miserably. "You know, something to boost my confidence a little."

"Still no luck with the job search, hmm?"

"Nope. I swear, it's like there must be some sort of

poster with my face on it with a big circle with a slash going through it. No one will hire me, and if I don't find something soon, I don't know what I'll do. I'm babysitting my neighbor's little boy in the morning and then take care of the dogs in the afternoon."

"How many are there now?"

"Um...I'm up to twelve. I added a French Bulldog last week."

"Gracious! Twelve dogs? You're not taking them all out at the same time, are you?"

"I tried that once. It didn't go well, as you can probably imagine. The leashes all got tangled, I nearly had an asthma attack because they pulled me along, so I had to run instead of walk, I skinned my knee and twisted my ankle so...lesson learned."

"Well, it sounds like you're not doing too bad, Willow. You have two jobs, and obviously, you're getting out and meeting people."

"Yeah, not so much. These are all people in my apartment complex that I knew already. However, the dog-walking gig gets me out of the house. Getting my Vitamin D and all that." She sighed. "But...I'm never going to get ahead at this rate and my savings isn't going to take me much further. I need something with more stability and that pays better."

"Sweetie, you know you really should talk to your parents. I'm sure they would help you out..."

"Gammy, we've been over this," she explained. "I got my degree in psychology because that's what *they* wanted. It was never something I was interested in and I graduated by the skin of my teeth. And look where it got me? If I ask them for help, they'll lecture me on all the ways I'm self-sabotaging myself and how if I would just focus, I'd be able to find a real job." Groaning, her head fell back against the cushions.

"You know they'd love for you to join their practice, right?"

It was a topic that came up often, but it was never going to happen. "I know, but that would mean re-locating to Seattle, and that isn't something I'm willing to do. I'm a New York girl. All my friends are here."

"But not your family."

Unable to help herself, she chuckled. "All the more reason to stay here."

Luckily, Gammy laughed too. "Okay, sassy pants, let's get serious. If you could do whatever you wanted to do for a career, what would you do?"

"Gam..."

"No, I'm serious, Willow. This is a judgment-free zone. You know you can tell me anything."

"Well...I always wanted to be a Rockette..."

There was a soft tsking sound before her grandmother said, "Willow, I'm being serious. And remember your ballet recital?"

"I was seven!" she cried. "I'm sure given enough time, I would have learned to balance better."

"And gotten over your stage fright?"

"Not sure I want to risk throwing up in front of a crowd again."

"I know, dear. So let's cross Rockette – or dancer of any kind – off the list. Okay?"

"Fine."

"What about a chef? You were always good in the kitchen!"

"I hate the feel of raw chicken. It freaks me out."

"What about a baker? You always make the most decadent desserts!"

"You have to get up at like...three a.m. to go to work, and you know I'm not a morning person."

"Hmm...okay, what about a nurse? You could always go back to school. I'm sure your parents couldn't possibly find fault with you wanting a career in the medical field."

"Gammy, I pass out at the sight of blood. I fainted the last time I got my flu shot."

"Oh my goodness! How much were you bleeding?" she asked, sounding horrified.

"I wasn't. I was just afraid that I might and..." Willow paused and put a hand to her forehead. "Can we change the subject? I'm feeling woozy."

"From just talking about blood?"

"Gammy!"

"Okay, okay, okay...what if you found a full-time job to tide you over? There's waitressing?" But before Willow could answer, her grandmother said, "No. You're a bit accident-prone."

"Gee, thanks."

"Need I remind you about the Japanese tea set incident?"

Groaning, Willow closed her eyes. "No. But in my defense, your cat tripped me."

"Mr. Marshmallow would never do such a thing, and he doesn't appreciate you pointing the finger at him."

"He's a cat, Gammy. He has no idea about any of this."

Gasping dramatically, she replied. "Nonsense. Mr. Marshmallow understands everything I say to him!"

"Right."

"He's also an excellent judge of character. Why, just the other day, we were talking about the Romeos and..."

"The what?"

"Not what, who."

"What?"

"Willow, focus!"

"On what?"

"The Romeos aren't a what, they're a who. Actually, they're a group of whos."

"You're literally making no sense right now."

"Romeos – retired old men who eat out," Gammy explained.

"That doesn't spell Romeo, that spells Rom-we-o. You'd think for an English teacher..."

"And you'd think at your age you'd learn not to sass your grandmother," she huffed.

"Sorry."

"It's alright, dear. I know you're stressed."

"You have no idea."

"Well, when you come to visit at the end of the month, we'll carve out some time just for the two of us. You know I prefer talking about things like this in person. Oh, and are you bringing that boyfriend of yours with you?"

Oh. Crap.

"Um..."

"I'm very excited to meet him, Willow. He sounds wonderful. Plus, I'd love to get his input on what career path you should be taking. You're far too smart to be wandering like this, and I hate hearing you sound so sad." She paused. "Why isn't this young man perking you up more?"

"Perking me...?"

"Back in my day, a man knew how to keep a smile on a girls face." Then she giggled.

Seriously. Giggled.

"Then again, the Romeos are pretty good at that too."

Oh, dear Lord...

"Now I'm not going to be a prude while you're here and insist that the two of you sleep in separate rooms or anything," she went on. "Your folks are staying at that little boutique hotel down by the town square that they love so much because I told them I promised you the room here."

"Gammy, you didn't need to do that."

"Well, you know how they prefer their privacy and how much I enjoy sitting and talking with you. I'm getting up there in years and there's only so much time left for me to impart my wisdom onto you."

Here it comes...

"I see so much of myself in you, and talking on the phone is all fine and well for casual stuff – you know, basic blah-blah stuff – but I want to see the look on your face when we talk and laugh. I hope your young man won't mind giving us some girl time."

"Yeah, about that..."

"Oh! We can send him out with the Romeos! I bet he'd have a fabulous time!"

"No, Gammy, you don't understand..."

Off in the distance, she heard a doorbell ring and knew their conversation was about to end.

"Willow dear, I need to go. That will be Donald. He's a Romeo. Sweet man, really. He has the eyes of a wolf and the hair of a silver fox!"

"There's an image for you," she muttered.

"What?"

"Nothing! Go and enjoy your date! We'll talk soon!"

"Yes, we will! Now don't quit our game! Let's finish it up! And who knows, maybe you will beat me! Love you!"

"Love you, too!"

This time she did toss the phone aside with a groan of disgust. Willow knew she was many things, but she wasn't normally a liar. Unfortunately, sometimes desperate times called for desperate measures.

And listening to her grandmother go on and on about her romantic social life definitely qualified.

It had seemed like a harmless thing to do – make up a boyfriend! And with Willow living eleven-hundred miles away, she really didn't think it would ever be an issue.

Like now.

Gammy was turning 75 and wanted her whole family to come down to celebrate with her. That meant her fake boyfriend was either going to have to break up with her or become miraculously real.

Well, crap.

Her phone chimed with a reminder that she was due to meet up with the girls at McGee's Pub for their end of the workweek roundup.

Seriously, she felt like a fraud going since she was the only one not really working. Well, she babysat and walked the dogs, but that really didn't count. The babysitting was so much fun – Josh was the cutest little boy, and they shared a love of trains and Mickey Mouse. And the dogs were...well, that was fun too. While her friends were out working real jobs, Willow felt like she was just sort of hanging out and doing enjoyable tasks that she happened to get paid for. There was no workweek to end, so why go out to celebrate it?

The other thing that made her hesitant about going?

Her fake boyfriend was based on a real guy.

The bartender at McGee's – Levi.

Unable to help herself, she sighed dreamily.

"I am so screwed."

Of course, Levi had no idea she was using him in her make-believe relationship, and if he ever found out, she'd be mortified.

And that was saying something since the only reason they ever met was because she had fallen flat on her face on the sidewalk right outside McGee's and he had witnessed the whole thing. He had run out of the pub and helped her up and then carried her inside.

Was it any wonder she was crushing on him? He was practically a knight in shining armor for crying out loud!

He'd cleaned her up and made her call her friends to come and hang out with her at the pub until she felt better. After that, it had become a weekly thing for them.

Not her falling on her face, but the hanging out part.

Although she had been known to trip a time or two...

Her phone chimed again and she picked it up and swiped the screen to shut it up. Sighing, Willow considered her options. She could bail and text the girls that she wasn't feeling well, but, like she said, she hated lying. Another option was she could go for just a little while and then fake a headache...

"Pretty soon I'm going to be smelling smoke because my pants will be on fire! Why is this so difficult?"

Knowing she'd feel too guilty with either of those choices, she got up and went to freshen up her makeup and put on something other than yoga pants.

"Why haven't yoga pants become acceptable sociable attire yet?" she wondered. But once she walked by the full-length mirror in her bedroom, she knew it wouldn't matter even if they were. There was no way she was going to parade around the pub in front of Levi – or any male for that matter – looking like this. Willow knew and accepted the fact that she wasn't one of those girls who looked super-cute in yoga pants.

She just looked schleppy.

"So not the look I want to be remembered for."

Fifteen minutes later, she grabbed her purse and headed out the door like she was heading to her own execution.

And secretly hoped she could get from her car to the pub without hurting herself.

"Hey, Boss, can you add a case of beer glasses to the next order?"

"Why?"

"Because Dex just dropped a rack of them when he was unloading the dishwasher."

Groaning, Levi walked into his office and turned on his computer. With a frown, he pulled up the program he used for orders and quickly made the notation. "That's the third rack this month. From now on, he mops floors and takes out the trash. That's it."

"You got it."

He waited until the office door closed before relaxing in his chair. It was a Friday night, and McGee's was busy as usual, and yet not so busy that he didn't notice that Willow and her friends hadn't shown up yet. Besides the fact that he'd just walked around the pub looking for her, no one had mentioned it to him either.

Friday nights had become fun again since meeting Willow and he couldn't help that he looked forward to seeing her and hanging out with her. Ever since the day he saw her face-plant on the sidewalk and ran out to help her, they'd bonded. Granted, he was friendly with everyone who came into McGee's, but...some more than others.

Willow was sweet and shy and funny, and he found himself stepping away from the bar more and more on Friday nights so he could hang out with her.

And her friends.

Okay, he seriously wouldn't mind if her friends opted to skip a Friday or two – or seven – but they were a package deal and it was fine.

Sort of.

Mildly annoying but...whatever.

Normally he would have considered flirting with Willow or simply asking her out, but she was different. Not only because she seemed incredibly shy, but he was enjoying getting to know her without the pressure of it turning into something more. And again, she was never alone – seriously, her friends were *always* with her – no matter how many times he casually dropped hints that she should come in any other night. Alone.

And he'd dropped a lot of them.

He thought he saw a hint of interest on Willow's part, but it had been so long since he'd gone out on a date he might have been imagining it.

The real problem was that McGee's was his life. Two years ago, he had officially taken over the pub and ever since, he'd been consumed with making it a success.

Okay, the pub had been his grandfather on his mother's side, and Levi had been working here since he was sixteen.

Well, *formally* working there. He'd been going there for years and hanging out with his grandfather and learning all about the business.

When his grandfather passed away two years ago, Levi had been shocked to find out he had willed the pub to him.

There was a stipulation that if he didn't want the responsibility of taking on the business that he could sell it and split the profits with his sisters. But it had been a no-brainer. McGee's had always been a part of his life, and he loved it, and everyone in the family knew it. His sisters had been adamant that he take it on – even if it meant less of an inheritance for them.

Not that it was the only thing their grandfather willed to them. They also received some money and some sentimental items he knew they would love. But ever since the papers were signed and the pub officially became his, Levi had spent all his time making sure he was doing everything that would make his grandfather proud and make the pub even more successful than it had ever been.

It was, but that didn't mean he should slack off and get too comfortable. There were always improvements he could make, new things he wanted to try, and even though he had a great staff – with the exception of the accident-prone Dex – he never felt right about taking any time off for himself.

But if he ever got up the nerve to point-blank ask Willow – or anyone – out, he'd take the night off.

Probably one of the slower nights, but...still. He'd do it.

Maybe tonight he should test the waters. Maybe he could flirt a little bit and see how she responded, or maybe he should just ask her point-blank and see what she said. Or...maybe he was just crazy and shouldn't rock the boat. He would hate losing her as a friend because...well...he genuinely liked her.

Raking a hand through his closely cropped hair, he let out a long breath as he started to think about some possible ways to broach the subject.

And his mind went completely blank.

"How is that possible?" he muttered. "I've dated dozens

of women over the years. How the hell can I have no idea how to do this?" It was a bit mind-boggling how nervous he was and how badly he wanted her to say yes.

But seriously, what the hell was he going to do if she said no?

How would he face her? Would she even want to talk to him afterward or would she even come back to McGee's ever again? Would her friends all glare at him or mock him?

"Great, that's just perfect. Psych yourself out with every worst-case scenario. Awesome."

And yet...that's exactly what happened. It seemed his brain was in rejection mode and all Levi could envision was getting his face slapped, Willow running from the pub, her friends kicking him in the nuts, and everyone in the pub looking at him with a mixture of pity and disgust.

"Okay, so maybe tonight isn't the night..."

There was a knock on his office door and his assistant Anthony came in. "Hey, I just wanted to let you know your girlfriend just came in," he said with a knowing smirk.

Closing his eyes, he grimaced. Had he been that obvious all this time?

Opening his eyes, he forced a smile. "Thanks. I'll be out in a minute."

"Want me to tell her that?"

"What? No!" he cried. "I mean, not unless she asks for me. Which, let's be real, she won't. She doesn't, right? She never asks for me when she gets here with her friends. Are her friends with her? Is she alone?" With a snort of derision, he went on, "Of course her friends are with her. Why the hell would she come here by herself?" Slapping himself in the head, Levi let out a string of curses. When he noticed Anthony's wide-eyed stare, he snapped, "What?!"

Hands up defensively, Anthony said, "Nothing.

Nothing at all. I'll just leave you and your multiple personalities to work it all out."

"Shut up." Standing, he kicked the chair away from him. "And I don't have multiple personalities."

"That dialogue you just had would say differently."

"You're crazy. I was talking to you."

"Were you? Because you asked questions and then answered them yourself. I had very little to do with any of it."

Walking around his desk and toward the door, Levi muttered, "You're a dick."

Chuckling, Anthony replied, "Tell me something I don't know." Together they walked down the hall that led out to the pub. "You ever going to ask this girl out or what?"

"None of your damn business."

Another low chuckle was Anthony's response before adding, "You really should make your move or someone else will."

Levi immediately glanced around the pub to see if anyone was looking in Willow's direction – other patrons or anyone on his staff – but luckily, they weren't. Clearly they were all blind because his eyes were always immediately drawn to her.

Because we're friends and I'm just looking out for her.

No big deal.

"If you're looking to worry about something, go make sure Dex isn't breaking anything. At the rate he's going, we're going to have to restock all of our glass inventory." Luckily Anthony took the hint and walked away. Meanwhile, Levi felt like his feet were glued to the floor. Willow and her friends were sitting at one of the high tables near the front corner of the room. In a minute, one of them –

whoever drew the short straw – would go up to the pub and buy the first round of drinks.

And that meant he needed to get behind the pub pronto and play bartender.

Okay, he wasn't really *playing*. He *was* the bartender.

Groaning, he walked over to the bar and nodded to Maxi and Eric – the other bartenders. Friday nights were always busy and it wasn't unusual for him to step up and make drinks, but he'd taken a renewed interest in it lately.

No sooner was he in place and wiping down the bar than Willow was approaching.

Perfect. Timing.

He looked up and smiled at her and noticed the slight flush in her cheeks. Her lips were pink and glossy, her dark hair fell past her shoulders, and her curvy body was wrapped in faded blue jeans and pastel pink top. She looked way too soft and feminine to be hanging out in a pub and she wasn't a big drinker – neither were her friends – so he had to wonder why they kept coming back.

Part of him was hopeful that maybe *he* was the reason, but...he was also a realist. Willow didn't flirt with him or show any interest beyond their friendly conversations over the bar. That couldn't possibly be enough to keep her coming back week after week, was it? Did she feel obligated because he had helped her up when she had fallen?

God, I hope that's not the reason...

She smiled at him as she stepped up to the bar. She had a great smile.

"Hey, Levi," she said softly. He could barely hear her over the noise and wanted to shout out for everyone to shut up.

That wasn't an option so he just made sure he leaned in

close to hear her when she spoke again. "Hey, Willow," he replied. "Did you have a good week?"

Resting her arms on the bar top, she shrugged. "It was okay, I guess."

"Uh-oh. That doesn't sound good. The big dogs giving you trouble again?"

"Scout had a bit of a run-in with a squirrel that I got dragged into – literally – and Matthias ate one of my hats, but other than that..." She shrugged again.

"That sounds like a bit of a nightmare for his owners."

"Nah, he didn't eat it whole. Definitely got some big pieces of it, though. But they're used to it. Apparently he's famous for eating socks."

"Those poor people."

"Yeah, but they love him." She let out a soft sigh as she looked down at her hands.

"You sure that's it? You look like you've got something on your mind." To busy himself, he began making her drinks – their order was always the same: draft beer for friend number one, a Cosmopolitan for friend number two, and a Malibu and pineapple for Willow.

I should probably learn her friend's names...

Whoever was the designated driver only had one drink and they tended to stay for several hours so they were clear to drive. Plus, they normally ordered food. So he had to wonder...

"Who's the DD tonight?"

She slowly raised her hand. "I drew the short straw again."

He put the beer on the bar. "That's three weeks in a row, isn't it?"

Nodding, she sighed. "It's okay. I'm not much of a

drinker anyway. Besides, Donna and Jen both had rough weeks so they deserve to kick back and unwind."

"A minute ago it sounded like *your* week wasn't so great either. Don't you deserve to kick back and unwind?" He placed the Cosmo on the bar.

"Well, my week wasn't really bad, just today."

"How come?"

"Just family stuff."

Bracing his hands on the pub, he stared at her until she explained further.

"I lied to my grandmother and now I can't go and see her for her birthday," she said sadly. "This will be the first one I'm missing in like...ever."

"Damn, Willow. Whatever you lied about, I'm sure she'd forgive you."

But she shook her head. "It's complicated. And on top of that, I can't afford to fly down and sec her. I'm still not working steadily so..."

"No leads on anything, huh?"

"Nothing I'm good at."

"Any chance you're good at waitressing?" For the life of him, he had no idea why he was offering. It wasn't like they were hiring.

With a small laugh, she shook her head again. "I can barely walk and chew gum at the same time without hurting myself. I have a feeling I'd end up owing you money at the end of my shift."

"Good to know," he replied with a wink. "What kind of job are you looking for?"

"That's the problem, I don't know." She sighed. "I graduated back in the spring with a degree in psychology, but it's not what I want to do."

"Then why get your degree in it?"

"It wasn't my idea, trust me."

"Ah. Gotcha. Parental pressure, huh?"

"Bingo."

Placing her drink on the bar, he offered a small smile. "Want me to help you carry these over?"

"That would be great. Thanks."

He used to think she accepted so they could keep talking, but now he realized it was because she was afraid of dropping the beverages.

Well, damn.

Stepping around the bar, he picked up the beer and Cosmo and followed her over to her table.

While admiring the soft sway of her hips and how perfect her ass looked in her jeans.

"Good evening, ladies," he said smoothly, placing their drinks down. "Having a good night?"

"Absolutely," Jen said.

At least, he thought that was Jen.

"We're just trying to cheer Willow up," Donna chimed in.

"Oh, uh...really?" he asked, unsure of how interested he should sound.

Jen nodded. "We're trying to convince her to go and see her grandmother and to stand up to her parents."

"Jen!" Willow cried, her cheeks turning a furious shade of red.

"It's true," Donna stated. "We just need to find a way for her to get down to Florida and get everyone off her back."

"Um..."

"You guys know why I can't do that!" Willow argued, although really, there wasn't a lot of heat behind her words. "I'm not going to argue with my parents and ruin Gammy's birthday. That wouldn't be fair."

Gammy?

"Oh, please! You know they're not going to care about making a scene. They're completely okay with poking at you and picking at you in front of everyone, so why do you care about doing it to them?" Donna asked before taking a sip of her beer.

Willow glanced nervously in his direction and Levi thought that maybe that was his cue to leave.

"Um...you ladies have a good night," he said, taking a step back. "If you need anything, you know where I'll be."

"Levi, wait!" Jen cried, reaching out a hand toward him. "Can we ask you something?"

"Jen..." Willow warned.

"Oh, shush." She grinned at Levi. "Let me ask you a question – do you think it's wrong to lie about being in a relationship?"

"Uh...what?"

This time Donna spoke. "Yeah, like if it meant getting your family off your back, would you be opposed to making up a fake girlfriend – or boyfriend – just so they'd stop worrying about you?"

He glanced at Willow as some of this was starting to make sense.

"You told your grandmother that you had a boyfriend and that's why you can't go visit her," he stated, waiting for her to make eye contact with him.

All she did was nod.

"It's not a terrible lie, right?" Jen asked.

Shrugging, Levi said, "No, it's not terrible. And it's not hurting anyone either. If you go down and visit her, all you have to do is say your boyfriend couldn't get the time off or say the two of you broke up. I don't see it as a big deal."

"That's what we said," Donna commented. "Hell, we even suggested she ask a friend – a guy friend – to go with her to play the part if she didn't want to go with the breakup thing."

Suddenly, Levi felt like he had the perfect solution.

For both of them.

And he was either completely crazy or absolutely brilliant.

"I'll go with you," he said simply.

"*What?!*" All three women cried.

Nodding, his eyes never left Willow. "If you don't want to go alone and you don't want to admit there never was a boyfriend, I'll go with you. I'll be your boyfriend."

COMING 6/23/20!!

https://www.chasing-romance.com/the-roadtripping-series

ALSO BY SAMANTHA CHASE

The Enchanted Bridal Series:

The Wedding Season

Friday Night Brides

The Bridal Squad

Glam Squad & Groomsmen

The Magnolia Sound Series

Sunkissed Days

Remind Me

A Girl Like You

In Case You Didn't Know

All the Befores

And Then One Day

The RoadTripping Series:

Drive Me Crazy

Wrong Turn

Test Drive

Head Over Wheels

The Montgomery Brothers Series:

Wait for Me

Trust in Me

Stay with Me

More of Me

Return to You

Meant for You

I'll Be There

Until There Was Us

Suddenly Mine

A Dash of Christmas

The Shaughnessy Brothers Series:

Made for Us

Love Walks In

Always My Girl

This is Our Song

Sky Full of Stars

Holiday Spice

Tangled Up in You

Band on the Run Series:

One More Kiss

One More Promise

One More Moment

The Christmas Cottage Series:

The Christmas Cottage

Ever After

Silver Bell Falls Series:

Christmas in Silver Bell Falls

Christmas On Pointe

A Very Married Christmas

A Christmas Rescue

Christmas Inn Love

Life, Love & Babies Series:

The Baby Arrangement

Baby, Be Mine

Baby, I'm Yours

Preston's Mill Series:

Roommating

Speed Dating

Complicating

The Protectors Series:

Protecting His Best Friend's Sister

Protecting the Enemy

Protecting the Girl Next Door

Protecting the Movie Star

7 Brides for 7 Soldiers

Ford

7 Brides for 7 Blackthornes

Logan

Standalone Novels

Jordan's Return

Catering to the CEO

In the Eye of the Storm

A Touch of Heaven

Moonlight in Winter Park

Waiting for Midnight

Mistletoe Between Friends

Snowflake Inn

Wildest Dreams (currently unavailable)

Going My Way (currently unavailable)

Going to Be Yours (currently unavailable)

Seeking Forever (currently unavailable)